Her warrior heart admired his skill; her woman's body admired him on a whole different level. . . .

Lusahn dropped the bundle of clothing on the ground. "Put these on. The shirt and pants should fit. You'll have to wear your own . . ."

She lost the word she was looking for at the sight of Cullen stripping off his shirt. His skin was smooth and golden, his muscles flexing as he moved. She forced her eyes down to the ground and away from all of that skin that her fingers itched to touch. As soon as they reached his feet, the word came back to her. "Shoes. You must wear your shoes."

When he reached for the fastening on his pants, she felt her face go hot and turned away, pretending to be standing watch. As a Guardian, she had served alongside men for years. It was nothing for her and her Blade to strip in front of each other, but that was different. They were her kind and of her world.

This Cullen Finley disturbed her in ways she did not understand. She kept her eyes firmly focused away from him and all of that warm golden skin. The only normal thing about him was his dark hair, although he wore it cut too short for her taste. And those dark eyes looked at her with too much curiosity and far too much heat. His gaze had a weight to it that she'd never felt before, as if he could caress her with merely a glance.

DARK PROTECTOR

"An innovative storyline, passionate protective champions, and lots of surprising twists. . . . Don't be left out—pick up a copy, settle in, and enjoy the journey."

—Romance Reviews Today

"A complex paranormal fantasy that pulls readers in from the first page and doesn't let them go."

—Paranormal Romance Writers

"Alexis Morgan enchants the reader immediately. . . . *Dark Protector* is an exciting new book in the paranormal genre and one readers definitely should not miss."

—Kwips and Kritiques

DARK DEFENDER

"An intense plot with twists and turns and wonderful surprises."

—Paranormal Romance Writers

"Tons of suspense and drama. With her latest, Morgan proves that she's . . . here to stay!"

—Romantic Times

Redeemed in Darkness

Alexis Morgan

Pocket Star Books
New York   London   Toronto   Sydney

Pocket Star Books
A Division of Simon & Schuster, Inc.
1230 Avenue of the Americas
New York, NY 10020

This book is a work of fiction. Names, characters, places, and incidents either are products of the author's imagination or are used fictitiously. Any resemblance to actual events or locales or persons, living or dead, is entirely coincidental.

First Pocket Star Books paperback edition December 2007

POCKET STAR BOOKS and colophon are registered trademarks of Simon & Schuster, Inc.

For information about special discounts for bulk purchases, please contact Simon & Schuster Special Sales at 1-800-456-6798 or business@simonandschuster.com.

Cover illustration by Craig White

Manufactured in the United States of America

10 9 8 7 6 5 4 3 2 1

ISBN-13: 978-1-4165-4713-6
ISBN-10:   1-4165-4713-4

Acknowledgments

I'd like to acknowledge all those fans who take the time out of their busy days to let me know how much my Paladins have meant to them. Thank you for making my work such a joy!

I would like to dedicate this book to my big brother and his wonderful wife—John and Diana Rodgers. Thanks for always being there.

Chapter 1

*T*he barrier shimmered and stretched thin, its beautiful cascade of color giving way to streaks of sickly light. Lusahn shared her brother Barak's ability to read the barrier's moods and knew it would fail soon. Very soon.

She drew her sword, its familiar weight grounding her against the emotions threatening to shatter her control: anger, grief, and a deep sense of betrayal that made her blood boil.

Barak was alive.

Alive, but living and thriving among the enemy. The evidence of his treason was a note he'd written and tossed across from the enemy world into hers. By the laws of her people, he was condemned, only awaiting the swing of a sword to carry out the execution. Her sword, her duty. Her brother.

She closed her eyes.

She had grieved over him when he'd sought out

the light of the other world, knowing that it meant certain death at the hands of Earth's warrior clan. Yet as she'd mourned his passing, she'd at least understood it.

Glaring at the note in her hand, she once again read Barak's angular scrawl, asking for a brief meeting at an appointed time, asking that she cooperate with the enemy for the sake of both of their worlds.

He had to know that she would be waiting for him, sword in hand. Her first duty as a Sworn Guardian was to protect their people, even from themselves. And with their parents both gone, defending the family honor was her duty. At least they'd been spared knowing of their son's treason. No matter what pressures had driven him into the light, she would not, *could* not, forgive a betrayal of this magnitude.

Barak had been considered truly blessed in their world because of his affinity with not just the blue jewels that gave them light, but with stones of all kinds. A gift as strong as his came along perhaps once in a generation.

How could he live among the enemy, when his own world needed him so badly? When *she* needed him? What had he found in that strange place of light that had ensnared him?

In her mind, she saw the warrior whom she'd fought on her single crossing into the light. She and the three members of her Blade had followed the trail of stolen blue jewels across the barrier with the intent of dragging the thieves back to stand trial for their crimes. Unfortunately, the Paladin warriors had already executed the traitors.

She and her Blade had hoped to return to their world without incident, but they'd run into two of the enemy at the edge of the barrier. She'd signaled her Blade to occupy the green-eyed devil while she took on his companion.

Even now she could remember the power with which her opponent had fought. With his dark eyes blazing, he'd dazzled her with his sleek moves. His bigger friend fought her Blade with brute strength and muscle, but this one had danced with lethal grace and beauty.

Her warrior heart had admired his skill; her woman's body had admired him on a whole different level. More often than she cared to admit, the human had revisited her in dreams. She shook her head. Now was not the time for such thoughts.

The barrier flickered again, almost but not quite failing. She moved closer, ready to face her brother one last time. Her soul ached with the pain, but she would do her duty. It was all she had left.

Cullen Finley had a decision to make. Among his fellow Paladins, he was nicknamed "the Professor" because of his calm, thoughtful demeanor. If he did what he was contemplating, though, his image would change forever. As would his life.

He studied the envelope in his hand for the umpteenth time, unable to read more than one word: Lusahn. The rest was written in an alien language. But he knew the woman the name belonged to—enough to whet his appetite for more.

He had to be out of his freakin' mind.

Sure, someone had to deliver Barak's message to his sister, asking if she'd be willing to call a truce long enough to solve the mystery of who was smuggling the blue stones from her world into his. Ever since someone had told the Others that they could buy their way into this world with blue garnets, they'd been pouring across the barrier in ever-increasing numbers.

Far too many Others had died, learning too late that the Paladins' swords were all that awaited them here. He'd killed his fair share; they all had. And the constant fighting had taken its toll on the Paladins. Even though their genetic makeup allowed them to come back from the dead, it did so at a terrible cost.

If things continued so, there wouldn't be enough Paladins left to mount a defense against the crazed Others. Someone had to stem the tide of invasion, or swarms of the bloodthirsty bastards would run free in the streets, out of their minds and killing anything that moved.

Barak had planned to meet with his sister himself, but he'd been faced with a nightmare of a choice: save the human woman he so obviously loved, or wait at the barrier to confront his sister. It had taken Barak less than a heartbeat to choose. After scribbling a note to Lusahn, he'd asked Cullen to throw it across the barrier, the same way they'd delivered the first letter asking for a meeting. Then he'd charged off to rescue Lacey Sebastian.

Which brought Cullen back to his own situation. Lusahn—he'd never forgotten their encounter. She'd left him with a small scar on his face, a much bigger one on his ribs, and her image burned into his brain.

The barrier was weakening again, the vibrant colors fading away. He had hoped that it would hold long enough to give the rest of the Seattle Paladins a chance to rest. After restoring the barrier when it had failed, they'd spent the entire night digging Barak out from under tons of rock. From what Lonzo had told him, the Other had sacrificed himself to give Lacey's brother time to get her out of danger.

Barak's injuries had been serious and someone should let Barak's sister know why he couldn't come. Just that quickly, Cullen made his decision. He would hand-deliver Barak's message to tell Lusahn why her brother wasn't there. The only question was whether she would let Cullen live long enough to explain.

He hoped so. She would doubtless carve him into little pieces for even thinking such a thing, but he very much wanted to taste her passion. The idea had him grinning as the barrier disappeared with a flash of light, bringing the shadow world beyond into view.

And then there she was, her pale angry eyes glancing around before finally focusing on Cullen. She wore her dark, silver-streaked hair in a waist-length braid. Her black tunic and close-fitting pants outlined her lithe figure in exquisite detail. The impact of her stark beauty slammed into his chest, making it difficult to breathe.

With a nod, he sheathed his weapon and stepped forward. Her blade came up to rest against his throat just as the barrier flickered back to life, cutting off his avenue of retreat. Cullen smiled and wondered if he was about to meet his fate or his future. Holding out the envelope, he waited to find out which it would be.

Her chin came up a notch and her eyes narrowed. "Where is he?"

Her words were heavily accented, but intelligible.

"Last night, he was injured badly enough that he couldn't be here. Before that happened, he wrote you a message." Cullen slowly raised his hand with the envelope in it.

Lusahn glanced at it long enough to read the message Barak had scrawled on it, her mouth set in a grim line. "Open it."

He did as she ordered, careful not to make any sudden moves. His close-up view of her sword told him that it had been honed by a master's hand. One slip this close to his carotid artery, and he'd bleed out before she could summon help—if she would even bother. More likely she'd wait until the barrier flickered again, and roll his dead body across for his friends to find.

He eased the letter out of the envelope and slowly brought it up for her to read. As her eyes moved swiftly down the page, he didn't need a translator to read her body language. The woman was seriously pissed, and getting more so by the moment—which didn't bode well for him, since he was stuck in this world until the next time the barrier went down.

Her silver eyes, so like her brother's, studied the paper for several seconds before turning back to Cullen.

He said, "I know I'm not who you expected, but that doesn't change anything. We need to stop the theft of the stones. Can we talk?" He held his hands out to the side, palms up, trying his best to look harmless.

She kept the sword firmly against his neck. "I didn't come here to talk. I came to execute a traitor."

He'd known she might be angry that her brother had chosen to live with the enemy, but hadn't thought she would come after Barak with deadly intent. He felt obligated to speak in Barak's defense.

"Barak has told us nothing of your world, nor has he aided us in any way that would bring your people harm. He wants to stop the theft of blue stones as much as we do."

Barak had guarded his secrets well—unless he'd let something slip to Lacey Sebastian or Laurel Young. He was as much a mystery today as he had been when he'd first crossed the barrier and risked his own life to save Laurel's.

"He has chosen the enemy over his own people." Bitterness and anger underscored every word.

"I can't argue about that. But I do know that your people are dying in bigger numbers, and so are my friends. You can kill me instead of your brother, but that will only add to the bloodshed."

She stared at him in silence, as if to measure his worth. Finally she eased the blade away from his neck far enough that he could swallow without fearing the motion would kill him.

"Paladins have always killed my people. Why do you care how many die?"

It was an honest question that deserved an honest answer. "It is my job to defend my world with my sword and my blood, just as you defend the people of this one with yours. That doesn't mean I enjoy killing."

In fact, he'd killed until his muscles and soul ached from the pain of it all. As resilient as Paladins were, eventually they did die, usually with a shitload of poison shoved in their veins by the very people they were born to protect. No one had ever questioned the constant cycle of fighting and death, because the Others crossed the barrier out of their minds and with weapons drawn.

Until Barak. The bastard could swing a sword with the best of them, but he was no crazed killer any more than Cullen was. Lusahn might not see it that way, though, having once faced him in battle.

"Do you remember me?" The words slipped out.

Her hand touched the side of her face where a small scar marred her otherwise-perfect skin. "Is that why you came? You thought I would show mercy because we once danced in battle."

No, he'd come because he wanted to dance with her in a way that involved the two of them getting naked. Now probably wasn't the best time to mention that.

"I thought if you recognized me, you'd let me live long enough to explain what we wanted."

"And if I don't care what you want?" The sword moved closer again, but clearly she did care. It was there in the pain showing in her beautiful eyes, and in the fact that she hadn't killed him.

Yet.

"We have to do something to fill the time until the barrier goes down again. We can talk, or . . ." He let his eyes journey down the length of her long, lean body, taking his time and enjoying the trip. When he got back to her face again, he smiled.

Her pale skin flushed pink, although that could be temper rather than interest in what he'd been offering. Then she frowned.

"We would have to talk a long time, Paladin. The barrier will be up for most of the next moon cycle."

How long was a moon cycle? On Earth, it was a little more than four weeks. Here, he had no way of knowing.

"How do you know it won't go right back down? It's been unstable for weeks."

"I was born with the same ability as my brother to know such things."

That sneaky bastard! Barak had never mentioned that little fact. And he'd been working with Lacey Sebastian, who was trying to find a way to predict the earthquakes and volcanic eruptions that usually preceded the barrier's failing. Devlin would find Barak's talent most interesting—if Cullen lived long enough to tell him.

He carefully turned his head to look back at the barrier. Its bright colors were back to full strength.

Son of a bitch, she was probably telling the truth. And here he was without his toothbrush, or even a clean change of underwear.

"So how long is a moon cycle? A month? A day? A week?"

She scrunched up her nose, looking adorable as she calculated the time. "Two of your weeks, maybe a little less or more."

He glanced around the shadowy passage they stood in. "Then I guess I'll make myself comfortable here and wait it out."

Lusahn rolled her eyes. "And live on what, Paladin? You would either starve to death or die at the hand of my Blade on their next patrol."

He crossed his arms over his chest and widened his stance. "I'm open to suggestions, Lusahn."

His use of her name startled her. She stepped back, letting her sword fall to her side, and stared at him as if really seeing him for the first time.

"Your name?"

"Cullen. Cullen Finley. It's nice to see you again, Lusahn." He held out his hand, wondering if she would respond to the overture.

She stared at his hand as if it were a snake ready to bite her. Finally, she shifted her sword to her left hand and reached out to let her fingers brush his. It was enough to send a flash of heat through to the core of him, and she felt it, too, judging by the way she instantly jerked her hand back.

Good.

She glanced around as if looking for something, then turned back to him.

"You cannot remain here, Cullen Finley, but I can't take you with me looking like that. Stay out of the light until I return." She looked at his tan cargoes and bright red T-shirt with disapproval. "I will bring you something else to put on."

"Where will you be taking me?" Not that it mattered. He'd live longer following her than he would wandering around by himself.

"Does it matter?" she asked with the first hint of a smile. She sheathed her sword and walked away into the shadows where the light of the barrier faded into darkness.

The energy that had been buzzing through him faded away as soon as she left, and the air around him felt colder. He looked around for an out-of-the-way spot where he wouldn't be an easy target if someone else happened by.

After studying the surrounding cavern, he decided it looked natural rather than hand-carved out of the surrounding rock. Most of the areas where Paladins fought were man-made, although the Missouri installation was located in a large limestone cave.

He finally found a well-shadowed place to sit where he could watch for Lusahn's return without being out in the open. After laying his sword within easy reach, he pulled out his deck of cards and started shuffling. It was too dark to play, but the repetitive motion was soothing.

Unfortunately, it left his mind free to drift. How long would it take for someone to notice that he'd disappeared? Would they guess where he'd gone? They'd worry, and he regretted that. The Paladins he fought and died with were like brothers to him, and Dr. Laurel Young, the Handler who took care of them when they were injured, worried too much about them as it was. Devlin Bane, her Paladin lover, would kick his ass from one end of Seattle to the other for adding to her burden.

Yet he couldn't regret his decision; his gut feeling was that he'd done the right thing by coming here. Maybe, just maybe, he could make a difference. Either way, he would have tried.

He let loose a huge yawn, a reminder of how long it had been since he'd last slept. As tired as he was, he wouldn't be fit to defend himself if he was discovered. Maybe it wouldn't hurt to close his eyes. For a few minutes he listened to the soothing buzz of the barrier, and then there was nothing.

The muted sound of footsteps startled Cullen awake. How long had he been asleep? He grabbed his sword and watched the shadows until Lusahn stepped out of the darkness, a bundle in one hand

and her weapon in the other. He moved just enough to catch her eye. Was that relief he saw flash across her face? She was too far away for him to tell.

He tucked his cards back in his pants pocket and stood up with renewed energy now that she was back. After sheathing his sword, he walked toward where Lusahn waited, drinking in her warrior's grace. Oh, yeah, he'd made the right decision. And he had a moon's cycle to convince her of that.

Lusahn dropped the bundle of clothing on the ground at the human's feet. "Put these on. The shirt and pants should fit. You'll have to wear your own . . ."

She lost the word she was looking for at the sight of Cullen stripping off his shirt. His skin was smooth and golden, his muscles flexing as he moved. Unlike the men of her world, he had a dusting of hair on his chest that trailed down to disappear into the waistband of those odd pants he wore.

She forced her gaze down to the floor, away from all of that skin that her fingers itched to touch. As soon as she reached his feet, the word came back to her. "Shoes. You must wear your shoes. At least they are the right color."

Something that she'd said made him laugh as

he picked up the trousers she'd brought. "I guess black is a color. I've never seen anyone from here wear anything but black or gray."

His comment stung. "You would insult our ways?"

His smile disappeared.

"I meant no insult, Lusahn. We've never known if all of your people wear black and gray, or if it's a uniform."

His dark eyes were difficult for her to read, but now was not the time for doubts. By letting him live this long, she'd already committed herself to keeping him that way until she could decide the right course of action.

"We can't stay here much longer. Finish changing so we can go."

When he reached for the fastening on his pants, she felt her face go hot and turned away, pretending to be standing watch. As a Guardian, she had served alongside men for years. It was nothing for her and her Blade to strip in front of each other, but they were her kind and of her world.

This Cullen Finley disturbed her in ways she didn't understand. She kept her eyes firmly focused away from all of that warm golden skin. The only normal thing about him was his dark hair, although he wore it cut too short for her taste. And those dark eyes looked at her with too much curiosity and far too much heat. His gaze had a weight to it that she'd never felt before, as if he could caress her with merely a glance.

"I'm decent."

She frowned, not quite understanding what he meant. Although all of the Guardians learned the rudiments of the human language, the subtleties were difficult. If he meant he was again dressed, why didn't he say so?

"Wrap your things in the bag and put on the cloak I brought."

When she heard him pick up the sack, she turned back to face him. The dark clothing suited him—maybe too well, from the way her body was reacting. Obviously she had been too long without a lover if she found this human so desirable. Lately her life had been too complicated to allow time for seeking out a partner. Maybe once she returned this Cullen to his world, she should make time.

"I am taking you to my home. Do not speak to anyone, or we both risk death."

He nodded.

She reached out to pull the hood of the cloak closer to his face. "Keep your eyes down. They are too dark, and your hair is too short."

He grinned at her. "Is there anything about me that you do like?"

She was not about to answer that. "If we walk unusually fast, we will only draw unwanted attention. The same if we walk slowly."

"How long will it take us to get there?"

"Long enough. I'm going to check to see if the patrol is coming. Come when I call."

"All right."

He had his hand on his sword. She didn't blame him. If they were attacked, it would take both of their weapons and a miracle to keep them both alive. She studied the man in front of her, wondering what about him made her want to take such risks. She had others who depended on her, whose welfare should come first.

But she'd always had a weakness for lost causes. And a human alone in her world definitely fell into that category.

"I won't be long."

Cullen fought down the surge of excitement that hovered inside him. Was he the first of his kind to see more than just this small stretch of rock in this world? If he'd been thinking straight, he would have brought along a digital camera. The Regents wouldn't allow the pictures to be seen outside of the organization, but he wasn't the only one who wondered what about the Others' home drove them to abandon it in such numbers.

He would keep his eyes and ears open and learn all that he could. It would help if he spoke the language, but he didn't, and two weeks wasn't

enough time to learn it. How had Lusahn and her
brother learned English? Another question he'd
never thought to ask Barak.

"Come, Cullen Finley." Lusahn motioned him
to follow her.

He hurried forward and fell into step beside
her, noticing he didn't have to shorten his stride in
order to walk comfortably with her. He was a
shade over six feet tall and guessed that she was
probably less than two inches shorter. Good. He
liked women with long legs.

"Just beyond that turn, we will be leaving the
caves. That is when we must be careful."

His hood had slipped back slightly, so he pulled
it forward. It restricted his peripheral vision, but
secrecy was more important.

"Thank you for taking me to your home."

She shot him a quick glance. "Wait to see if we
live long enough to get there."

Then they rounded the corner, and he abruptly
stopped at his first sight of Lusahn's world.

Chapter 2

*T*he scene had the feel of a cloudy winter day, giving the air a dank chill that cut clean through to the bone. Except this sky was devoid of clouds, with the dim circle of a pale yellow star perched just above the horizon. A stark white moon loomed overhead, reflecting only the barest hint of the star's warmth.

Vegetation was scant and scraggly, nothing at all like the lush green of the Pacific Northwest. In the valley below, buildings were laid out in a regular pattern, regimented in their position and style. None were more than three stories tall, which gave the city a strangely stunted look. He took a step forward to get a better look, but Lusahn caught his arm and pulled him back.

"You are acting like you've never seen this place before!" Her words came in an angry whisper.

"I haven't," he reminded her with a smile. "You're right, though. Sorry."

He turned his attention to the path in front of them. They'd stepped out of the cavern near the top of a barren hillside. A gravel trail sliced back and forth down the steep incline to the valley floor.

As they started downhill, he found himself breathing hard as his lungs struggled to capture enough oxygen from the thin atmosphere. The air smelled dusty and tasted stale, making his mouth dry and his teeth gritty.

The bottom of the trail crossed a narrow road, but there were no vehicles in sight as they continued on. So far they hadn't run across any of her people, but that was bound to change as they reached the edge of town.

"My home is only a short distance from here, but we will be passing by the Guild. It is there we face the most risk."

What was the Guild? He adjusted his hood as he fell in step beside her, their pace neither fast nor slow. She walked with the same arrogant swagger as the Paladins, that warrior's assurance that he was the toughest s.o.b. around.

On Devlin or Trahern, it looked tough. On Lusahn, it looked sexy as hell. Luckily, his cloak hid his resultant erection, which was hard enough to hurt. He resisted the urge to glance at Lusahn again. Those pretty, pale eyes of hers saw too much as it was. If she guessed that he had this irrational urge to bed her, she'd throw him to the wolves.

The set of her shoulders warned him that they were approaching the Guild that she was so worried about. A tall building loomed ahead on the right. There were no sidewalks, only a narrow road paved with rounded stone, which seemed too rough for vehicle traffic, if there was any. He couldn't imagine never knowing the sweet purr of a monster engine roaring up the highway. Did the Others walk everywhere? That would get old pretty damn quick, especially if his breathing didn't acclimate to the atmosphere soon.

They passed by several Others, all so intent on their own business that they didn't even make eye contact. If he wasn't mistaken, they all cut a wide path around Lusahn as if she was someone to be feared. Well, whatever kept them at arm's length made it less likely that they'd notice him.

The stone front of the Guild was a muddy tan covered with ugly black streaks. It looked about as welcoming as a mausoleum: cold, hard, and fetid. Lusahn paused, pretending to adjust her scabbard, then positioned herself between him and the Guild as if to shield him from threat. Damn it, he could take care of himself! He bit back the urge to yank her behind him, knowing that would only put them both at risk.

His mind knew she was neither weak nor innocent, but his instincts were too well honed to believe it. There had never been a female Paladin, and he wasn't used to sharing the burden of duty with any woman, much less one he found this compelling. Maybe their luck would hold long enough that they wouldn't have to find out which one of them was the better fighter.

As if his thought jinxed them, a male voice called out, "Lusahn!"

Her head whipped around to face a male standing near the top step of the Guild building. Under her breath, she whispered, "Keep walking. I will rejoin you shortly."

He didn't want to, but she left him no choice as she trotted up the steps. He risked one look back over his shoulder as she greeted the Other with far more warmth than she'd shown him. It pissed him off, but he gritted his teeth and kept walking.

Meanwhile, a pair of Others were headed straight for him. His bad mood almost made him forget to keep his eyes down. At the last minute, he bent his neck forward enough to shadow his face inside the cowl as they silently passed by. Once he was in the clear, he paused briefly to listen for the telltale sound of Lusahn's footsteps. When he heard her coming, he slowly continued on his way until she caught up.

"Everything all right?" He wanted to demand that she tell him who the bastard was, even though he had no claim on this woman that gave him the right.

"Yes. A question about tomorrow's patrol. Nothing more." She sounded a bit breathless, a sign she wasn't quite as calm as she would like him to believe.

"Is he a *close* friend?"

That brought her up short. "How do you mean close? He's of my Blade."

Now that was a puzzler. "He's part of your sword?"

A small smile tugged at her mouth as she finally understood what he really wanted to know. "I am a Sworn Guardian of my people. Each Guardian has a Blade that patrols and fights together. He is of my Blade, not my sword."

Okay, so they were like a squad who worked together regularly. "Did he ask about me?"

"I told him I was showing an old acquaintance around. He wouldn't question that. Many pass through the city."

They reached an intersection where another small street branched off to the right. "We turn here."

She seemed less tense now that they were past the Guild, and she picked up the pace a bit. "My home is at the end of the next turn."

The pale star had disappeared beyond the horizon, leaving deep shadows in its wake. Streetlights were few and far between, shrouding most of the city in darkness, with only the Guild remaining brightly lit.

Now that they were off the main road, the buildings were smaller, most likely private residences. With flat roofs and narrow windows, they were built out of some kind of clay or adobe. Come to think of it, he hadn't seen wood of any kind since entering the city.

He had so many questions, but didn't know if Lusahn would answer them. She might keep her world secret, fearing that knowledge could be used as a weapon against her people.

"There." She pointed just ahead to a small house on the right.

All that distinguished it from the other houses around it were the two young faces pressed against the front window, watching for Lusahn's approach. He hadn't thought to ask if she lived with anyone—like a husband. Wouldn't that be a kick in the pants? He sure as hell hoped she didn't. No matter how attractive she was, he wouldn't poach on another man's territory.

Before they reached the small path that led toward her home, Lusahn stopped. "You must stay out of sight for now. There is a door around back that leads to a room underneath the house. Once I'm inside, go there and stay until I come for you." Then she walked away, leaving him stranded in the darkness.

"But—"

Before he could argue, the front door flew

open, and the two kids came flying out. They charged right for Lusahn, laughing and jabbering all at once. He could see the flash of her teeth as she smiled and bent down to hoist the smaller one up in her arms.

He backed farther into the shadows, fighting a sick case of jealousy. If she had children, there must be a man in her life. He may not have known her long, but he knew in his gut that this woman took the idea of family very seriously.

He should be heading for shelter, but he watched the house for a few minutes more for some sign of the male who had given Lusahn children. He had an intense desire to use his fists to get some questions answered. Like, why had he let Lusahn place herself in danger? And where had the bastard been while she waited alone for the barrier to go down?

What if Cullen had charged across, sword drawn and ready to kill? She could have died right there, leaving those children without a mother.

For her sake, he'd go hide. But if he met up with her husband, he planned on having a talk with the male about how a man should treat his woman. Especially a man lucky enough to have one like Lusahn.

He waited until she and the children had been inside for a few minutes before moving. After rounding the corner of the house, he slipped from shadow to shadow. When he reached the side of the house, he ducked down under the window, resisting the urge to take a quick peek inside. He wanted Lusahn's trust more than he wanted to indulge his curiosity. There would be time for answers later, when he'd had some rest and could think beyond the effort it took to put one foot in front of the other. Right now, he was so tired that he was a danger not just to himself, but to Lusahn as well.

He forced himself to keep moving as he felt his way along the house in the thickening darkness. Then the solid ground disappeared, and he stepped out over emptiness. At the last second, he managed to grab onto a railing to keep from tumbling ass over end down the stone steps. He wrenched his shoulder, but that was better than bashing his head in. At the bottom of the stairs, he felt for the door and found a rope handle.

The door creaked open to reveal a small room dimly lit by a flickering candle. The scant furniture consisted of a futon-like bed with a low table next to it. Two narrow windows flanked the top of the door. The rest of the room was apparently underground.

The opposite corner was curtained off. He pushed the curtain to one side with the tip of his sword, revealing a small, primitive bathroom. On the far wall, a staircase led up to another door.

Cullen's stomach growled as he sat down, a reminder that it had been too many hours since he last ate. Nothing he could do about that. Damn, he wished he'd brought his backpack stuffed full of life's necessities. But when he'd left home to give Barak a ride, he hadn't been planning on taking a trip—especially this one.

After kicking off his shoes and setting his sword within easy reach, he dropped down on the bed and stretched out, his hands linked together under his head.

There was no way of knowing how long the nights were in this world, or even where this world really was. Some of his buddies who liked science fiction thought maybe it existed in an adjoining dimension. Others thought the barrier was some kind of portal that transported the Others much farther than the few steps it took them to cross it.

Frankly, he didn't give a damn. He'd been born to protect the barrier with his sword and his life, same as all the other Paladins. The job paid well, although he couldn't say much for the retirement plan. Someday he'd run out of lives to give, and he'd be given a one-way ticket to hell at the business end of a long needle.

His eyes grew scratchy and heavy, so he turned over to blow out the candle before giving in to the need to sleep. But before he mustered up the breath, the flame flickered as a slight breeze set it to dancing. He reached for his sword and waited to see what happened next, dividing his attention between the door to the outside and the one at the top of the stairs.

"Human?"

Even at a whisper, he recognized Lusahn's voice. He pushed himself up off the bed and crossed to the bottom of the steps.

"I'm here."

"Good." She slipped down the stairs, carrying a tray. "I brought you something to eat."

He set down his sword and took the tray from her, setting it on the table. A bowl contained a thick soup and a hunk of rustic bread. The spices were foreign to his nose, but not unappealing. "Thank you. It smells great."

She shrugged. "It's nothing special, but it's filling." Then she handed him a small pack that she'd had slung over her shoulder. "I brought you a few things so you can bathe and brush your teeth."

Her thoughtfulness touched him. "I appreciate it. Will the noise disturb your family?"

She shook her head. "The children are sound sleepers. If you wait until after you eat, it should be safe."

"Is there anyone else I should worry about?"

The question clearly puzzled her. "There is only me and the children."

Then where was their father? He knew for a fact that Others were physically very similar to humans,

their differences detectable only at the cellular
level. Since Lusahn had children, there had to have
been a male in her life at some point. Had he
crossed the barrier only to die at the end of a
Paladin sword?

He had to know. "What about their father?"

She tipped her head to one side and studied
him before answering, perhaps trying to decide
how much to tell him. "The children have only recently come to live with me. Their parents were
driven to cross into the light, leaving Bavi and his
sister behind. My Blade and I caught him stealing
food for the girl. Rather than turn them in, I convinced them to come home with me. We are learning to be a family."

Damn it all to hell. Their parents probably
hadn't come back because they'd died crossing the
barrier. Worse yet, he could have been the one to
end their maddened rush into his world. In all the
years they'd fought, had no one ever considered
that in protecting their own world, they were leaving children orphaned and alone in this one?

As if sensing where his thoughts were taking
him, Lusahn's expression hardened. "We don't
need your pity, Paladin. It is not your problem.
Now eat before the soup grows cold. I'm not much
of a cook; it will taste better hot."

More to keep his hands busy than out of any
real desire for food, he picked up the bowl and

began shoveling the spicy mixture into his mouth. A few minutes later, he sopped up the last of the broth with the bread and set the dishes back on the tray. "Thank you, Lusahn. That was good."

She arched an eyebrow, clearly questioning his sincerity. "I will check on you in the morning. Once I've had a chance to talk to Bavi, I will see about allowing you upstairs."

"I'm fine down here. I wouldn't want to scare the children."

"We will see. Now I need to get some rest. You should be able to sleep undisturbed down here."

He doubted that; his dreams had been disturbed by her image for weeks already. Now that he knew her name and the sound of her voice and the scent of her skin, his dreams would be even more vivid.

"Good night, Lusahn. And I promise you, we will get to the bottom of the theft of the blue stones."

Her pale eyes studied him for several seconds before she nodded. "We will see what we can do."

He enjoyed watching the graceful sway of her backside as she went up the steps, but cursed the effect the view had on his body. When the door closed, he picked up the supplies she'd brought him and headed for the bathroom. The sooner he was asleep, the sooner he would see her again.

• • •

Lusahn decided to make double their usual break-fast the next morning. If Cullen's appetite was any-thing like Barak's, he'd need a fair amount of the hot cereal to satisfy his hunger.

As she considered what to do next, Bavi walked into the kitchen looking more asleep than awake. When he stretched and flopped down in his chair, she poured him some juice and set the glass in front of him. After downing it in quick order, he held it out for more.

As she refilled his glass, she told him, "I need to talk to you about something important before your sister comes in."

He sat upright, going from drowsy to fully alert in the space of a heartbeat. "What's wrong?"

Sometimes she forgot how grown-up he could be; the burden of keeping his sister alive had aged Bavi far beyond his real age. They had recently cel-ebrated his thirteenth birthday, five years short of adulthood by the calendar. By life's experience, though, he was ancient.

"Nothing is wrong—not exactly, anyway." She put the cereal on to cook before sitting down be-side him. "It's important that you keep what I'm about to tell you to yourself."

She added honey to her tea and stirred. She dreaded telling him that her brother had survived his crossing into the human world, for fear of giv-ing the boy false hope that his parents had survived as well. But maybe he wouldn't care if they had: after all, they'd abandoned him and his sister for the light. He was bitter, and had every right to be.

"I received news that my brother Barak is not dead." She ignored the pain of his betrayal. "I was supposed to meet him at the barrier yesterday on Guild business."

The boy knew not to ask about the work she and her Blade did for the Guild, but the questions were there in his eyes. This time, she would make an exception and explain what she could.

"He was unable to come, so a human male came in his place. His name is Cullen Finley."

She had to choose her words carefully. Paladins were reviled and feared; if people knew that she had one hidden in her home, she would be ostracized or even executed.

"Did you show him the edge of your sword?" Bavi's expression was fierce, as if he wished he'd been the one to wield a weapon against the intruder.

"Yes, I did."

"Did he bleed for all of ours who've been lost?"

She shook her head. "He came with an honorable purpose and sheathed his weapon. As a Sworn Guardian, I respected that."

"So if he did not fight, what is the problem?"

Now for the tricky part. If Bavi thought she'd brought danger near his sister, he was likely to bolt, taking her with him. She couldn't bear the thought of them back out in the darkness, cold and starving.

"For a short time, less than a moon cycle, this human will remain with us. Once our business is finished, he will return to his world and leave us in peace."

Except for her dreams of his dark eyes and heart-stopping smile.

Bavi lunged up from his chair, his hands clenched in fists. "You brought a human home with you? Where is he?"

She reached out to rest her hand on Bavi's arm, hoping that he'd trust her to keep him and his sister safe, but he jumped back out of reach.

Maybe words would work. "He's downstairs. I locked the door against him last night to make sure he couldn't bother us in our sleep. But I want you to meet him, so you can decide for yourself that he can be trusted."

At least, she hoped he could. And if she was still having doubts, maybe she should turn Cullen in to the Guild and surrender herself for judgment.

No, she'd survived this long relying on her instincts, and she would trust them now. Unless Cullen made a false move; then he would die.

"Bavi, I know we are new to being a family, but I would ask you to trust me enough to give this man a chance."

The boy was clearly not happy. "And if I see that he cannot be trusted? What then? Will you choose this human over us?"

His furious words lashed at her, but she couldn't blame him. Bavi had little faith left in most adults, but she'd hoped that he thought better of her. Still, he had the right to know where he and the girl stood.

"If he cannot be trusted, I will cut out his heart while you watch. I make this vow with a Guardian's honor."

Bavi's chin came up as he met her gaze head-on, judging and weighing her vow. Then he nodded, accepting the pact between them.

In the middle of a hot dream, Cullen went from deep sleep to full alert in a heartbeat. Someone was close by and watching him.

He gripped the knife he'd stashed under the pillow last night, the last intelligent thought he'd had before crashing. Slowly raising his head, he turned to face a possible attack. As soon as he spotted the intruder, he released his weapon and rolled over to greet his guest.

"Good morning."

A little girl sat on the bottom step, watching him. As soon as she saw that he was awake, she popped her thumb out of her mouth long enough to whisper something. Then she came across the room to tug at his hand, trying to get him out of bed.

"Do you want me to follow you, ladybug?" He hoped she understood that he meant well.

She tugged again, so he sat up, careful to keep the sheet across his lap since he'd been dreaming about Lusahn, with the predictable effect on his anatomy. Having accomplished her mission, the little girl nodded again and scampered up the stairs, leaving him smiling. What was it about these Other females that tugged at his heart?

He quickly ducked into the bathroom before any more surprise visitors arrived. Lusahn had returned his cargoes and T-shirt to him in the pack she'd left the night before, and it felt good to have his own things back, a touch of normalcy in this strange world.

There was no razor among the few toiletries she'd provided, so he hoped she didn't mind men with whiskery faces. He used water to get his hair to lay reasonably flat, then went in search of his hostess and some breakfast.

The little minx who had gotten him up was evidently on lookout duty. As soon as he set foot on the steps, she was off again. She looked so cute, running through the house with her bare feet peeking out from under a long nightgown.

She skidded to a stop long enough to make sure

he was still following before she turned the corner. Her brother immediately popped out of the kitchen, frowning and obviously not at all happy to see him. Cullen didn't take offense at the boy's protective instincts. He clearly thought that Cullen was up to no good—and regarding Lusahn, the boy was right on the money. Besides, Cullen had been born with the need to fight and protect hardwired into his DNA; he couldn't fault the boy for being the same way.

Lusahn was busy at the stove. The little girl was already seated at the table when her brother joined them.

"Good morning, everybody." He smiled as he took a seat at the far end of the table, figuring the boy would find Cullen less of a threat sitting down. The small girl watched him with curiosity but none of the hostility of her sibling.

"Good morning. I was just going to come get you." Lusahn handed him a bowl of hot cereal that looked similar to oatmeal.

"Your friend there beat you to it." He nodded at the little girl.

Lusahn turned away to finish serving the children. "Cullen Finley, this is Bavi and his sister, Shiri."

Bavi glared at Cullen, while the girl offered him a shy smile.

He let the children look their fill, guessing he

was the first human they'd seen. When Lusahn noticed they were staring, she said something in their language. They immediately picked up their spoons and dug into their breakfast, although the boy kept a wary eye on Cullen.

He noticed both children ate with intensity, as if they weren't sure where their next meal was coming from. Damn their parents! These kids deserved better. When he set down his spoon, Lusahn immediately reached for the pot from the stove to refill his bowl.

He shook his head. "Make sure the kids have as much as they want first."

His response clearly surprised her, but she did as he suggested and gave each of the children a little more before splitting what was left between the two adults. He yearned for a cup of coffee, but he couldn't expect her to magically produce something that didn't exist in this world.

A few more minutes passed without comment until the little girl said something to Lusahn, then left the table. Bavi made sure Cullen was staying put, then followed his sister out of the room.

"He does a good job watching her." It was too damn bad that the boy had had to grow up so quickly.

"He tries." Lusahn began clearing the table. "We're trying to adjust to being a family. I'm a better Guardian than a mother."

"You seem to be doing a great job."

Her young charges seemed healthy enough, but then what did he know? He wasn't a monk by any means, but he'd been damn careful not to leave any little surprises behind. He knew living with a Paladin as a husband or father could be a bitch, his mother had told him that often enough—not that she'd really known what his old man did for a living.

When Lusahn started washing the dishes, Cullen got up and tugged the towel from her hands. "You wash; I'll dry."

Since she didn't seem to be in any hurry to discuss business, he didn't push it. He wasn't going anywhere. Besides, the more time they spent together, the more comfortable she would be with him. And he wanted to get damned comfortable with her as soon and as often as possible. He grinned.

Lusahn gave him a suspicious look and put a little more room between them. *Nothing wrong with the woman's instincts.* Then she got a curious look on her face and ran her soapy fingers down his cheek.

"You didn't have that last night."

Had she never seen a man's beard before? He let her explore.

"I couldn't shave this morning."

"Few of our men have . . ." She paused, searching for the right word. "Whiskers. Few of our men have whiskers."

He covered her hand with his. "We vary a lot, too. I have to shave in the morning, and again in the evening if I have plans."

"What kind of plans?"

"This kind." Then he kissed her.

Chapter 3

Shock robbed Lusahn of all rational thought. That was the only explanation for how her hands, dripping soap bubbles and dishwater, came to be wrapped around Cullen Finley's neck. The press of his warrior's body against hers as he plundered her mouth made her skin ache and her heart race.

She tried to protest. Really, she did. But when her lips parted, he misinterpreted it as an invitation to deepen the kiss, his tongue swirling in and out, saying without words how much more he wanted from her. He tasted of temptation and danger, his kiss so much more than anything she'd ever experienced.

She should stop him, shove him away, run from him—but her body argued that she'd be a fool if she did. It had been far too long since any male had held her, reminding her that she was a female, even if a Sworn Guardian.

And she'd known this moment was coming, from the second the barrier had failed and Cullen had looked her in the eye and smiled. She moaned with the sweetness of his kiss and leaned closer, finding their bodies fit together perfectly. Enemies or not, they'd found common ground in at least this.

Then the sound of childish giggles in the next room hit her like a pan of cold water. Gods above, what was she thinking? Here they were on the verge of sinking to the kitchen floor to take this heat to its fullest, right where the children could walk in and see them! She shoved her way free from Cullen's arms.

"Stop."

His smile was too knowing. "That's not what your hands were saying a minute ago."

"I know, but the children!"

Cullen's head whipped toward the door, and his relief at not seeing the two kids watching them was obvious. He turned back to her with a rueful smile.

"We'll have to be more careful in the future." He ran a strand of her hair through his fingers.

"We can't . . ." She couldn't finish her thought; it hurt too much.

"We can and we will, Lusahn. We both want it too much."

"And then what, human? You'll go back to your world and tell all your friends about the silly Other who let you into her bed." She knew she wasn't being fair, but she couldn't betray her people like her brother had. Someone had to uphold the q'Arc name.

Cullen went from sexy and playful to furious male in the blink of an eye. "I don't deserve that, Lusahn. Whatever this is between us, it isn't some locker-room joke."

She didn't understand the reference, but she did understand that her panicky words had hurt him. For that, she was sorry, but it didn't change anything.

Turning her back to him, she said, "I believe you mean that, Cullen Finley. But we are enemies who live in different worlds."

His arms slipped back around her waist as he closed the small distance between them, cradling her against the strength of his chest. He laid his cheek against hers, offering the quiet comfort of his touch.

"Please don't slam the door on me yet, Lusahn. We've got almost two weeks together, if everything goes right. At least let us have that much."

His face with those dark whiskers felt prickly against her skin. She liked the strange sensation, but then, she liked most everything about this male. If she gave in to the temptation of Cullen Finley, it would very likely kill her when—and if— she was able to send him safely back across the barrier.

She was already risking her life by keeping him in her home. How much worse could it be to risk her heart?

"I . . . we must slam the door."

She felt his frown against her cheek right before he stepped away from her and shoved his hands in his pockets. "I will give you some time to get used to the idea of us, Lusahn. But don't believe for an instant that this is over."

Even with the space between them, he was crowding her, making her feel edgy and angry. She changed the subject, hoping that would give her room to breathe. "We must make plans. I have duty today and can't risk being late."

"Okay, we can talk." But his brown eyes burned dark with a heated promise that later they'd be picking up where they'd left off.

She simply nodded. He might not be ready to accept that they had no future together, not even this handful of nights, but she knew better. Still, something deep inside her whispered that a few stolen hours in Cullen's bed would never be enough.

Cullen sat back down at the table and nudged the chair next to his toward her with his foot. She ignored the invitation and chose the seat across from him.

He frowned, but then let his mouth quirk up in a small smile. "Chicken."

Another reference she didn't get. She gave him a suspicious look, but didn't pursue it. They needed to get on with their plans.

"What did you want from me?"

Cullen arched an eyebrow and let the laughter in his eyes answer that question, obviously the wrong one to ask. Her cheeks flushed hot as he finally answered.

"Barak said you might be able to help us trace the source of the blue stones. Or at least find out how people from my world are contacting yours."

"My brother . . ." Her voice stumbled over the reminder that Barak was alive, but choosing to live in the human world. She closed her eyes and centered herself before speaking again. "Barak's note said to cooperate with you. What do you already know?"

He ran his fingers through his hair as he leaned forward, elbows on the table. "We don't even know what you use the blue stones for, or of what use they would be in my world. We have red stones called garnets that have a similar crystalline structure to your blue ones, but nothing exactly like them."

So Barak had kept her world's secrets. Good. At least he hadn't shamed their family name completely.

She sat back and considered how to answer Cullen. If Barak had not shared much about the nature of the blue stones, he must have had his reasons. Why did he want her to be the one to explain what they were dealing with?

She had loved and admired her brother even when he'd taken controversial stands on the problems their world faced, but maybe she could no longer trust her brother's motivations. Yet Cullen Finley was sitting right here in her kitchen, at great risk to himself. That kind of bravery she understood and believed in.

Looking out of the small kitchen window at the early-morning sky, she told him, "Our world grows darker."

Cullen followed her line of sight. "Your sun is failing?"

She frowned as she considered his choice of words. "Yes, failing. It's been going on for centuries, and most of us have adapted to living in the increasing cold and shadows. The gods have gifted us with a few like my brother, who have an affinity with the blue stones and who can call forth their light and warmth—a gift much prized by my people. Barak can also read the moods of the mountains and knows when the barrier will fail."

Cullen heard the underlying pain and hated how much Barak's desertion hurt her. From what he'd seen of the Other male, though, Barak was a man of dignity and honor, so something powerful must have driven him from this world. Barak wouldn't have left his sister behind easily.

"So stealing the stones takes more than just their beauty from this world. They aren't just jewels for decoration."

"No—if handled by the right person, they provide a great deal of light and heat. Even a small one"—she held up her fingers in a circle about the diameter of a golf ball—"can heat a house or provide enough energy to raise a crop."

It didn't take a physicist to understand the stones' possibilites on the other side of the barrier; a new energy source would be worth billions. But the greedy bastards were stealing the light from a world where it was already in short supply.

A loud knock suddenly sounded at the door, and judging by the startled expression on Lusahn's face, she wasn't expecting company.

"Get below!" she ordered. "Quickly, before one of the children answers the door."

It went against his grain to be ordered out of the line of fire like a child, but he wouldn't endanger Lusahn and the children. "I'll have my sword in hand if you need me."

Her gray eyes met his as she stood up. "It is most likely one of my Blade. They would come if the Guild needs me earlier than planned."

"Fine. But if you need me, just yell."

She nodded. "Go now. I will return when I can."

When he started past her, she surprised him by grabbing the front of his shirt and pulling him down for a quick kiss. If she wanted him to hurry, she'd picked the wrong way to do it. Only the knowledge that he would further endanger her kept him from finishing what she'd started.

He went two steps down the stairs and pulled the door almost closed, hearing Lusahn whisper a warning to the children. Though he wouldn't be able to understand the conversation with her guest, their tone would give him warning if something went wrong.

However, Lusahn sounded relaxed and friendly. Whoever was at the door may not have been expected, but he was certainly welcome. She laughed at something the male said, which should have reassured Cullen. Instead, it pissed him off. He was feeling less and less like the Professor his friends knew, and more like the Terminator, about to go kick some Other butt. This powerful need to hit somebody brought him up short. If he didn't know better, he'd think he was actually jealous of the Other male.

The front door opened again and then closed loudly. Was Lusahn letting him know the coast was clear? Being cautious, he counted to twenty; then he stepped out in the hallway with his sword drawn, pausing to listen. Nothing. Not even the sound of the children talking among themselves, which alarmed him even more. He turned the last corner to confront a scene that would have made him laugh if it hadn't been so very sad.

Bavi and his sister were staring right at him, the boy's pale complexion washed out with fear. He had shoved Shiri behind him and stood bravely ready to defend her, should Cullen decide to attack. The weight of the heavy carving knife made Bavi's hand shake, but there was no doubt that the boy would use it.

Cullen did what warriors did when confronted with a superior force: he surrendered. He immediately laid down his sword and held up his hands as he moved away from the blade to sit on the closest bench. They'd probably been raised from birth hearing horror stories about the Paladins.

"I won't hurt you." He doubted they understood his words, so he kept his voice soft and even, hoping to reassure them that he meant them no harm.

Bavi wasn't buying it. Keeping his eyes carefully on Cullen, he motioned for the girl to escape to the kitchen. When Shiri stopped and smiled at Cullen, her brother barked an order at her. She gave him a stubborn look and took her own sweet time sashaying out of the room.

Once she was out of sight Bavi backed toward the kitchen, leaving Cullen alone. He shivered, feeling colder than the temperature warranted.

Was this how Barak felt all the time? How had he stood it so long?

He closed his eyes and sank back against the wall. The long hours until Lusahn would return stretched out before him. Back home, his duties as a Paladin kept him busy. He wasn't used to being a complication rather than an asset.

Feeling frustrated, he reached into his pocket for his deck of cards and cleared a spot on a nearby table. After shuffling the deck several times, he quickly dealt a game of solitaire and began playing the black cards on the red. Whether he won or lost didn't matter; he found relaxation in the familiar routine.

After about five minutes he got that itchy feeling on the back of his neck, the one that warned him he was no longer alone. Was his little friend back?

He gathered the cards back into a pile and picked them up. Careful to keep his eyes on the table, he started shuffling the cards again, fanning them out and using every showy trick he knew.

The soft whisper of cloth over the tiled floor stilled his hands briefly as his lips twitched. Flashy moves were the right bait for this particular trap. He risked a quick look up, which sent Shiri skittering back a step or two. He went back to shuffling, listening for signs that his audience was drawing nearer.

When he saw a pair of small feet at the edge of

his peripheral vision, he stopped shuffling and began building a house out of the worn cards. At four stories tall, it collapsed. The little girl giggled around the thumb in her mouth.

He winked at her and started over, this time with more success. When he'd reached about as high as she would be able to reach, he held out a card and motioned for her to try. Naturally, the cards collapsed. Her eyes were huge as she held out the card to him.

"That's all right, sweet pea. I knock them down all the time myself." Once again he regretted that he didn't speak her language.

"Let's try it again."

He built the base and then gestured for her to give it another try. This time the cards held as she carefully placed the one he'd given her. Her bright smile over her success warmed places inside him that he hadn't realized were cold. Together they alternated placing cards until her brother stormed into the room, grabbed Shiri by the arm, and began dragging her away.

"Stop pulling on her!" Cullen forced himself to stay seated, knowing any aggressive moves would only worsen the situation.

Bavi glared at him, although he did ease up on Shiri's arm. He gave his sister her marching orders in their language before rounding on Cullen again. "My sister. Not yours. Stay away, human."

His accent was so strong that it took a second or two for Cullen to realize that the boy was speaking English. Even if the pronunciation was off, the meaning was clear.

He looked Bavi straight in the eyes. "I mean her no harm."

Bavi stubbornly shook his head and repeated himself. "My sister. Not yours. Stay away, or Lusahn will kill your heart." He pantomimed stabbing himself in the chest before walking away.

So Lusahn would kill Cullen's heart if he bothered the children. That sounded like a promise she would have made to Bavi. Cullen wasn't sure how he felt about that. It was only logical that she would choose to protect her newfound family from an outsider. Trouble was, despite their brief acquaintance, he didn't feel like an outsider.

Rather than torment Bavi anymore, he picked up his cards and went back downstairs. The light from the two narrow windows did little to dispel the gloom in the room, but he didn't want to risk attracting the neighbors' attention by opening the door or burning the candle while Lusahn wasn't at home.

He began pacing the floor, wishing he'd brought something to read or even his laptop with him. He could have at least done some work on the security program updates that he and D.J. were working on.

Inactivity didn't set well with any of the Paladins, and Cullen was no exception.

For lack of anything else to do, he removed his scabbard and began going through his usual exercise regimen. It would help him keep in shape, but also take the edge off his mood. If he worked hard, he might get tired enough to take a long nap to pass the time until Lusahn returned.

It was better than doing nothing at all, but not by much.

"Where were you yesterday?"

Lusahn ignored the sinking feeling in her stomach as she considered how to answer her Blademate's question. She settled on part of the truth. "I was home with the children yesterday evening."

The ploy failed miserably.

Larem shook his head. "No, earlier. Didn't Bavi tell you that I stopped by?"

"No, he must have forgotten. I regret that I wasn't there if you had need of me."

She concentrated on finishing the paperwork that the Guild thought was crucial, but she and her Blademates thought was a waste of their time. What did the Guild do with all of the paperwork anyway? Once it was turned in, no one ever saw it again. Maybe the Guildmaster heated his home with piles of worthless reports. She wouldn't put it past the greedy fool.

"I was more worried that you might need me, Lusahn."

Her hand froze as she slowly looked up at her friend, hoping the panic she was fighting didn't show. "Why do you say that, Larem? Do you think that I can't handle two children?"

"It's not them I'm worried about." Larem wasn't smiling. "We've been friends since we were their age, Lusahn. I know when something is bothering you. I haven't seen you look this sad since Barak embraced the light."

She flinched at the mention of her brother's name. "I have been thinking of him lately."

Larem reached across the table to place his hand over hers. "He's been gone for a long time, Lusahn. I understand that you miss him, but I thought you were getting past the grieving. What has happened to make it all come back again?"

She had chosen Larem as part of her Blade because he knew her so well. Until now, she'd never had reason to regret that decision. Pursing her lips, she forced the pen to continue its journey across the page.

"I'm sorry if I've been worrisome, but truly I am fine." She managed a smile. "It's just, sometimes it all hits me again, and I hurt for a few days. It will pass."

"Yes, it will. I know it was harder because no one expected Barak to be among those driven to cross the barrier. We all thought his gift for the stones should have protected him from that madness."

"The strength of Barak's gift was rare enough that we have no way of knowing how it worked. My own gift has never been as strong as his was, so maybe weaker is somehow better." She pretended to check over the form for mistakes, but at that moment she couldn't have recognized her own name.

Larem started to say something else, but then the other two members of the Blade entered the small room that the four of them shared with two other Guardians and their Blades. The high-ranking members of the Guild were stingy with the Guild's resources. Since Guardians and Blades did most of their work out in the world, it was considered a waste of space to grant them much room in the luxurious offices enjoyed by the management.

Larem ceased his questioning, for which Lusahn was grateful. It had started to have the feel of an inquisition, which bothered her a great deal. Maybe she was suffering from a guilty conscience that made her react too strongly to a friend's well-meant concern.

Or did Larem have some reason to suspect that she was hiding something? It was a struggle to act normal when so much of her life was reeling out of control. She fought the urge to run home just to make sure that Cullen Finley was still safely tucked away in her house.

Instead, she had hours of patrol to get through before she could go home. The strain was giving her a headache, but she could ignore that. What troubled her more was how much of her energy was focused on a human male whom she'd known less than a day. Cullen's dark brown eyes had been haunting her since she'd left the house that morning.

How was Bavi handling the human's presence?

And what could she do to help Cullen solve the problem of the stolen stones? Who among her friends could she trust with such a dangerous mission? Did she have the right to involve them, after she'd already made the decision to allow the human to live?

If the two younger members of her Blade hadn't walked in, maybe she could have talked to Larem about her predicament. It wasn't that she didn't trust Kit and his brother Glyn, but the more people who knew a secret, the less likely it was to remain one. Besides, as their leader, she wouldn't risk ruining their careers.

She straightened the pile of papers and shoved them into a file. That's when she noticed the unusual silence in the room. The worried look was back in Larem's eyes, but the others were grinning at her.

She leaned back in her chair and glared at the three of them. "All right, what did I miss?"

Kit laughed. "I asked you twice if we were about to leave. That paperwork must be enthralling. Maybe we should mention to the Guildmaster that you have a newly discovered talent for it. I'm sure he could find you enough forms to fill out to satisfy you."

His younger brother snickered and elbowed him in the ribs. "Maybe that is why she never invites a male to her bed—she requires everything to be done in triplicate."

Now all three of her Blade were laughing at her. Normally she tolerated a bit of rough humor, but right now, she was in no mood to think about her empty bed and a certain human male.

If she reacted badly to their teasing, though, it would only alarm Larem even more. "Next time I have paperwork that needs doing, gentlemen, maybe I'll see if any of you are up to the job." She wiggled her eyebrows at them in a parody of flirtation. When they laughed, she reached for her sword. "Gentlemen, our patrol awaits us."

The three males fell into their usual formation, with the younger two flanking her while Larem covered her back. As they walked in formation through the heart of their city, any civilians on the road stepped aside and bowed their heads as Lusahn and her Blade passed by. She hated that they were feared rather than respected, but the nature of their job kept their fellow citizens at arm's length.

As they reached the outskirts of town, Kit spoke up. "Shall we check the tunnels today?"

"The barrier is stable."

He didn't need to ask how she knew; all Sworn Guardians had a strong affinity for the barrier and its moods. Only a few also carried the traits that her brother had been blessed with in such quantity.

The four of them slowed to a stop as they passed the last few houses. "Shall we turn back toward the Guild?"

That was the last place she wanted to be. She considered their options. "I would like to speak with my former mentor."

Her Blade knew better than to question her reasons, although Larem shot her a concerned look. If she felt the need to consult with one of the retired Guardians, they would follow her. That was their job, and they did it well.

Besides, all of them enjoyed the occasional long walk out past the trappings of civilization. Before she'd been promoted to Guardian, she'd served as a member of Joq's Blade. He'd taught her almost everything she knew about swords, the barrier, and the duties of a Sworn Guardian, not to mention the inside workings of the Guild. After a lifetime of dealing with Guild politics, Joq had abruptly retired and moved far enough out of town that he was rarely bothered by anyone. He claimed to like it that way, but he always seemed happy to see Lusahn whenever she dropped in on him.

Today was no exception. He actually walked out to meet them a short distance from his small farmstead.

"Lusahn! You bring joy to this old warrior's eyes." He nodded at her Blade, but didn't greet any of them with the warmth he always showed to her.

"Your Blade can rest in the shade of the hillside and help themselves to water at my well." He held his arm out to Lusahn and patted her hand when she placed it in the crook of his elbow. "You, my lady, may come inside and try out my newest batch of ale and tell me what you think."

She cast an apologetic look back over her shoulder to her men, but they waved her on. They all knew and accepted that Joq had become a recluse since his retirement, although he was willing to offer his advice on any matter that Lusahn felt the need to bring to him.

Inside Joq's kitchen, Lusahn sloughed off some of the tension she'd been carrying on her shoulders for two days. She didn't know when she'd decided to share her burden with her old friend rather than her Blademates, but it felt right.

"Here, drink this. You look like you could use it." Joq thrust a tankard into her hand.

She took a cautious sip; Joq's enthusiasm for brewing didn't mean he had a talent for it. But this time he'd managed to come up with something drinkable.

"Well?" He perched on a nearby chair and motioned her to sit down beside him.

"It's the best you've made so far," she answered truthfully. "You may yet master the art of brewing."

He laughed. "You have a talent for a compliment laced with an insult, my dear. Maybe you should run for Guildmaster one of these days."

She shuddered, having as much love for Guild politics as her mentor did. "I thought you liked me, Joq."

"I do, but the Guild could use some new blood. Especially someone who has eyes and a mind that understands what she sees." He sat back in his chair and crossed his arms over his chest. "So tell me, what has put such dark shadows in those pretty eyes of yours?"

She hesitated, trying to decide where to start.

He knew her too well. "Just begin at the beginning and leave nothing out."

"I have several things that seem separate, but are all connected." She traced a pattern in the condensation on the tankard before meeting Joq's gaze. "You are always good to listen to me, but promise that you will let me finish before you ask questions."

"You have my word." His eyes gleamed with knife-edge sharpness. Despite his years, there was nothing wrong with Joq's mind. He settled back into his chair and propped his feet up on the edge of the kitchen table.

"You know that sometime ago my brother Barak sought the light."

"The fool!" Her old friend never missed an opportunity to berate what he saw as her brother's many failures.

Lusahn staved off the familiar tirade. "Joq, you promised you'd be patient and listen."

"As I did, but that makes him no less of a fool."

Ignoring his jibe, she continued on, the words starting to tumble out. "But you see, Barak is not dead. He's very much alive and living among the humans. He has asked me to cooperate with the enemy long enough to stop the flow of our blue stones across into their world. It would seem that some of their Paladins have had enough spilling of blood—both ours and theirs."

Her friend's eyebrows shot almost to his hairline. "And how do you know all of this?"

She drew a deep breath, well aware that she was about to confess her own treason to a man sworn to protect their world. Once a Sworn Guardian, always a Sworn Guardian. By Guild rules, Joq would be obligated to report her, but she owed him the truth. "One of his new friends, a Paladin warrior, crossed the barrier yesterday to deliver the message, because Barak was injured and unable to come himself."

"And did you slice this Paladin to pieces for his trouble?"

"No, I didn't." She set the tankard down, prepared to surrender to her friend's custody if he deemed it necessary.

Joq tilted his head to one side, studying her reactions with a frown. "You're one of the best with a blade I've ever seen. Don't tell me that you let a Paladin scare you."

"No, he didn't scare me." At least, not in the way Joq meant.

"Did you run him back across the barrier?"

"No, not that either."

"Then what did you do with him?" Joq's eyes narrowed, as if he already suspected the answer to his question, and he leaned in close as if to better hear her words.

She braced herself for an explosion. "I took one look at this man and knew I couldn't kill him. And the barrier went back up and feels like it will stay that way for days to come. For lack of a better choice, I took him home with me."

Chapter 4

Of all the reactions Lusahn could have foreseen, Joq's loud bark of laughter would have been the last on the list. She didn't know whether to be relieved that he didn't instantly put her in custody or insulted that he thought her crisis was funny.

She settled on exasperation. "Joq, I fail to see what's funny. If the wrong person finds out about Cullen Finley, he and I both will be dead."

Joq tried to sober up, but wasn't particularly successful at it. He swiped at his eyes with the back of his hand and bit his lip until he could quit grinning.

"I'm sorry, Lusahn, I really am. I always knew you had it in you to do something extraordinary if pushed far enough, but I thought you'd settle for challenging the Guildmaster for his job." He hoisted his own tankard in salute. "You have surpassed any ambitions I've had for you."

She blinked and shook her head. "You're not shocked that I've committed treason? And what am I going to do about the stones? We've all known that those seeking the light were taking them with them, but I had no idea that someone on our side of the barrier was working with the enemy. Our people think they are bribing their way into the other world, but they are only dying in larger numbers."

She held her hands up in frustration. "But am I any better, letting a Paladin live?"

Joq's expression turned serious. "Tell me about this Paladin."

Cullen's image filled her head, momentarily stealing her breath. "I first met him a short time ago, when my Blade and I tracked some of our people into his world. While Larem and the others fought against an enormous Paladin devil with black hair and green eyes, I faced Cullen Finley. It was an honor to cross swords with such a worthy opponent."

Her hand strayed to the small scar on her cheek, but she jerked it back down to her lap. "When the barrier fell, we retreated back home."

"So this human was no stranger to you when he crossed into our world."

"Not exactly." She wasn't about to admit how he'd haunted her thoughts since that first meeting. "A short time ago, Barak had several letters to me thrown across the barrier, proposing that we work together from opposite sides of the barrier to stop the thefts. But evidently he was injured badly enough that he couldn't meet me at the appointed time. He gave Cullen Finley another note to toss across, telling me that we would have to reschedule our meeting. Just so you know, I had planned to execute my brother for his treason when he crossed over." Her voice cracked.

"And why would you hurt yourself like that, young woman? No matter what Barak has done, he is your brother, and you love him."

"Barak's refusal to share his gift with them has always rankled the Guildmaster, and he would have made an example of my brother. Even if Barak had to die for his actions, he didn't deserve that. So I'd have made his death clean and fast." Even if it had killed her soul.

Joq shrugged. "None of that matters now, because Barak didn't come. Put that aside and concentrate on the situation as it is now."

Good advice. "Cullen decided to deliver the message so I would know why my brother couldn't come. He was afraid I wouldn't cooperate if Barak missed the appointment."

Joq arched an eyebrow. "I doubt that was his only motivation, Lusahn."

Her heart gave a nervous flutter. "Why do you say that?"

"Don't you think he could have yelled a message across the barrier without risking his life? I suspect he remembers the day you two faced each other at sword point as clearly as you do."

Her face flushed hot. Was her fascination with Cullen Finley so obvious? "Regardless of his reasons, I am stuck with the problem of what to do with him until I can shove him back across the barrier."

"Let me think about this." Joq fell silent for several long seconds.

Feeling restless, Lusahn left her seat to stare out of the window at her Blade. Kit and his brother were stretched out in the shade, taking advantage of the opportunity to doze. Larem was staring right at the house, clearly not happy to be left out of her conversation with Joq.

Too bad. If she was going down, she wasn't going to drag her friends with her. Joq's career was over, and he had already separated himself completely from the Guild. But Larem and the others deserved better than to lose everything because she couldn't resist a pair of laughing brown eyes.

Joq joined her at the window and nodded in Larem's direction. "Does he suspect something?"

"He knows I've been distracted lately, but not why. Since he knows me so well, it is difficult to hide things from him. I wanted to deal with Barak on my own, but Larem would have insisted on coming with me."

"Will he make trouble if he finds out about your guest?"

"Yes. Maybe." Frustration had her mind whirling in circles. "By the stones, I don't know. Larem's loyalty to me has been without question, but the threat of high treason could change that. I'm the last of the q'Arcs, so my honor is my own to keep or lose, but Larem has family to consider. It's hard, because I'm not used to hiding anything from him."

She stepped away from the window. "I should be going. We need to make one last patrol before I can go home, and I don't want to leave Bavi and his sister alone for too long."

"I think I will come with you." Joq reached for his cloak and strapped on his sword. "If Larem needs an explanation, I will tell him that I need to visit the market in town."

"He's no fool, Joq. Won't your coming with us only make him more certain something is wrong?"

"It can't be helped. I need to meet this Paladin who has captured my star apprentice's eye—or perhaps her heart." He grinned when she glared at him.

"That isn't funny."

"No, but I was beginning to worry that you'd forgotten that you're an attractive female. I want to see what there is about this Paladin that has shaken your world." His expression turned serious. "A lot is at risk, Lusahn. More than you know. I must know the quality of this man's steel before we go any further down this road. If he cannot be trusted, he must die—immediately, with no hesitation. But if he is an honorable man, perhaps we *can* work together to help both sides."

"All right, Joq. But what shall we tell my Blade?"

He took her arm. "That I'm an old man and appreciate your assistance in walking a long distance. Once we reach the edge of the city, we'll separate. I will make a point of being seen leaving town by myself. Once the star has disappeared into the west, I will meet you at your home. Leave the back door unlocked."

"I will," she said, glad of her friend's help. "Would you like to join us for dinner?"

He grimaced, reminding her what he thought of her cooking. "I suppose I must."

She punched him on the arm to protest. "I haven't made anyone sick in a long time."

"That's not as comforting as you may think." He gave her a wry smile as they walked outside, pulling the door shut behind them.

Since he was the one she had made sick, she let his remark slide. Her Blade immediately jumped to their feet, ready to resume their duties.

"Guardian Joq asked if he could accompany us back to town to the market, and I agreed." She didn't allow time for discussion, especially since they were obligated to accept her decisions as law.

The three men arranged themselves around the two Guardians and began the trek back to town. Joq kept up a steady stream of conversation with her Blade, relieving her of any need to talk. Although she appreciated his intent, it left her alone with her own thoughts for too long.

How were the children doing without her? Had Bavi and Cullen come to blows? What did Joq know that he wasn't telling her? She shivered in the gray light of the late-afternoon sun. Her life felt as if it was careening out of control. All she could do was hold on for all she was worth and hope that the decisions she made were the right ones.

But despite her worries, she was glad to be heading back to where Cullen Finley waited for her. Once again his crooked smile and warm eyes filled her mind, bringing with them the memory of their kiss. Her body remembered every detail and wanted more of his dark, spicy taste.

Joq chose that moment to squeeze her arm, jerking her awareness back to the dusty path they were on. She shot him an apologetic glance. Her Blade had grown silent, making her wonder if she'd missed something important, but Joq gave no indication that anything was wrong. Just in case, though, she resumed conversation.

"So tell me, Guardian Joq, what did you do differently with this batch of ale?"

Her friend took the hint and launched into a discussion about the art of home brewing. He was still explaining when they reached town, keeping her Blade from noticing that she wasn't really with them.

For the first time in her career she felt a wide chasm opening between her and her friends, and she hated the feeling. The sooner she could finish this business with the stones and send Cullen Finley back to where he came from, the better.

Cullen cocked his head to one side and studied the ceiling. The sound of footsteps up there had changed in the past few minutes. Unless he was mistaken, Bavi and Shiri had both suddenly gone to the front door. Hopefully that meant Lusahn was back.

A few seconds later, the door at the top of the stairs opened, and she appeared. He immediately stood up, far happier about seeing her than he should have been. Though he was here on Paladin business, one glimpse of those long legs of hers and all sense of duty went flying out the window.

Well, not completely, but enough that he knew he was in serious trouble. She paused halfway down the stairs and nodded in greeting. "Did the day pass easily for you?"

He noted the lines of strain around her mouth and eyes. "I'm fine. How about you? Was your patrol uneventful?"

She joined him at the bottom of the steps before answering. "The patrol was quiet. However, there is someone . . . my old . . . a friend, that's what he is. Anyway, he wants to meet you." Her words came out in a nervous rush.

"Should I be worried?" Because she clearly was.

Her eyes slid past his face to stare at a spot somewhere over his shoulder. "I don't know. I trust him implicitly. The question will be if he feels he can trust you."

"And if he doesn't?" His hand strayed to the pommel of his sword, her tension heightening his.

"He will."

"Why? Because you do?" He stepped closer to her, deliberately crowding her.

She stood her ground, bringing her chin up. "I don't know you well enough to make that decision."

Liar. If she hadn't trusted him on a pretty deep level, she would have never left him home with Bavi and his sister. But rather than continue to provoke her temper, he dropped his hand back down to his side.

"Would it be possible to get something to eat? Breakfast was a long time ago." He gave her a hopeful look.

"Bavi didn't feed you?"

He hadn't meant to get the boy in trouble. "He may have tried, but I slept most of the day. I'm still getting used to your atmosphere, and I was pretty tired after my workout."

"Come upstairs, and I'll fix you something now. The friend I mentioned will be here after darkness falls, so we'll be eating dinner later than usual."

Interesting. Was her so-called friend's late arrival deliberate? It seemed likely, and it would be interesting to know why they wanted to keep the visit a secret. When they had time to talk, he would try to pry some details about the relationship between the Guild and the Guardians from her.

He sat down at the table while Lusahn quickly fixed him a plate. While he was waiting, little Shiri came into the room. As soon as she saw him, her face lit up with a happy smile. She climbed up in the chair next to him and gave him a hopeful look. He immediately pulled out his cards and handed them to her.

The little girl immediately began building a house of cards, following the same pattern they'd used earlier. Lusahn turned around to watch.

"When did you teach her that?"

He reached over to better align one of the cards before answering. "I was going to talk to you about that. This morning, after you left. When I came upstairs, Bavi was waiting for me with a knife. I don't blame the boy for not trusting me, and I admire that he's so protective of his sister."

He looked up. "This little one, though, seems to think I'm okay. She helped me build with the cards until Bavi made her go in the other room. I realize that it wouldn't do for her to get attached, since I'll be leaving soon."

He couldn't resist reaching over to ruffle Shiri's soft dark hair. "She's a heartbreaker, though."

"They both are." Lusahn set a plate heaped with cheese and vegetables in front of him. "Bavi is slow to trust, but that's not surprising. Shiri is more open."

"I was interested to learn that Bavi speaks a little English." Though he was more interested in what the boy had said.

"Why? What did he say?"

Rather than rat the boy out, Cullen shrugged. "Something about Shiri being his sister. He was harder to understand than you are."

"If he's a problem, let me know."

"Don't sweat it." He nibbled a piece of cheese, which reminded him of goat cheese. "What kind of animal does this come from?"

"No animal. It's made from the juice of a plant that grows high in the hills."

"So you don't eat meat?"

Barak was vegetarian, so it wouldn't surprise him if Lusahn was as well.

"We keep few animals, mostly only pets. Meat

is too expensive to produce when energy is in short supply."

Another reason to stop the energy thefts. He almost shoved the plate away, feeling as if he were stealing food from people who had little to spare.

"How soon until dark?" When his judge and jury would arrive. Did the man also plan on being his executioner?

Lusahn was filling a large pot with water. "Not long. I need to start dinner cooking, but afterward maybe we could practice with blades."

"I'd like that, if you promise to go easy on me. The last time we crossed swords you left me bleeding on the tunnel floor."

That was clearly news to her. "I marked your face as you marked mine."

"And on that last lunge before you crossed back over the barrier, you sliced my ribs up pretty good." He stood up to yank up his shirt to show her where her blade had caught him.

Her horrified look was gratifying as she reached out to trace the faint scar. "Is it true that you can die from a wound and yet live?"

"The wound wasn't that serious. We Paladins are tough to kill." He wasn't about to confirm or deny any rumors she'd heard about the Paladins, even if it felt a little like lying to her. He hated this dance of avoidance between them, but feeding information to an Other, no matter how he felt about her personally, skated too close to treason.

The concern in Lusahn's face immediately disappeared. "I would say I'm sorry, but that would be a lie."

"I wasn't asking for an apology, just a rematch." He laced his words with enough temper to match hers.

"Fine." She dropped a double handful of vegetables into the water and adjusted the heat on the stove. "Let's see if you've learned anything since the last time we fought."

He let her lead the way downstairs. Perhaps sensing the tension in the air, Shiri followed them down and perched on the steps, where she had a clear view of both Lusahn and Cullen.

Lusahn kicked off her boots before going through a series of movements that reminded him of the routine Barak used to warm up for sparring. He'd referred to it as a dance of some kind. Several of the other Paladins had tried to mimic the movements without much success, perhaps because they were more heavily built than Barak was.

Cullen had picked up a few steps of the routine from watching, and Barak had shown him some more as time permitted. Without saying anything, he kicked off his own shoes and socks and fell into step beside Lusahn. Lusahn faltered a bit when he twirled and kicked in unison with her, but then her movements smoothed out again.

She had a few flourishes that he hadn't seen Barak do, but he did his best to keep up. After about fifteen minutes the two of them had worked up a sweat, their muscles thoroughly stretched and ready for action.

"I see my brother has been teaching our ways to your people." She didn't sound happy about that.

"No, we saw him in action and tried to copy him. He's a helluva swordsman."

"Yes, he is."

Lusahn pulled a long, narrow chest out from under the bed and opened it. Inside was a pair of matched weapons with wide, curved blades. "These were Barak's practice blades. Let's see how you handle one."

He accepted the weapon. Even with a dulled edge, it had the feel of a quality blade. It was heavier than the sword he fought with but lighter than the battle-ax he used, so the weight shouldn't make much of a difference. What would, though, was fighting with a single-edged weapon.

He gave the sword several wide swings through the air. "Your brother has good taste in weapons."

She clearly didn't want to talk about Barak. Instead, she paced off a short distance and turned to face him. With a wicked grin, she offered him a quick salute with her blade, and then the game was on.

• • •

Lusahn had to admit that other than Joq and her brother, Cullen was the worthiest adversary she'd ever faced. Even with a weapon strange to him, he quickly adjusted both his style and his response to her attacks. Both of them were soon grinning like fools as the advantage quickly switched from her to him and back again.

She was about to lunge forward with the intent of scoring a telling point when a loud shout startled her. Only quick action on Cullen's part kept them both from getting hurt. Once she had her feet under her, she turned her temper on the culprit responsible for the near accident.

"Bavi! What were you thinking? You could have caused one of us to be badly hurt!"

The boy glared down at her from the steps, clearly not about to back down. "He deserves to bleed. Ask him how many of our people he has killed to become that good with a sword."

"I will do no such thing. I do not believe he is our enemy, Bavi. Can't you accept that?"

Cullen stepped between them. He hadn't understood anything they'd said, but he seemed intent on intervening. Maybe the two males needed to fight it out between themselves.

The Paladin spoke slowly, choosing his words carefully. "Bavi, have you ever fought with a sword?" He held the blade out, as if offering it to the boy.

For a minute she thought Bavi would pretend

not to understand, but then he shook his head. "I am not a Blademate nor a Guardian."

Cullen shot her a questioning look, asking for an explanation, which brought back a little of her temper. He'd avoided answering her questions about Paladins, but he expected her to tell him about their culture.

"As a member of my family, I was born into the warrior class. I served in a Blade until I became a Guardian. Bavi is neither. Without his parents to sponsor him, he has not received training by the Guild."

"So he can't defend himself or his sister in a world where people routinely wear swords?" Cullen's dark eyes snapped with anger. "How in the hell does that make any sense? If he's your family now, doesn't that make him a warrior, too?"

Bavi was doing his best to follow the heated exchange, his head swiveling back and forth. Finally, he charged down the remaining steps and thrust himself between Cullen and Lusahn.

"What saying?" he demanded in English.

Lusahn shot Cullen a look that should have fried him on the spot before gentling her voice to speak to her adopted son. She answered him in their language, deliberately shutting Cullen out of the conversation.

"He is trying to push himself into Guild business. I can't allow that."

"What does he want?"

They were treading on dangerous ground. On one level, she agreed with Cullen: Bavi would be better able to protect himself and his sister with some solid weapons training. But no one outside of the warrior families could be taught self-defense without Guild approval. She hadn't thought to submit Bavi's name, something she'd rectify as soon as she had control over her life back.

"He wants me to submit your name for training. No, that's not what he said." She made it a habit never to lie to Bavi; the trust between them was too new to test. "He said if you are now my family, then you should be a warrior, too."

Bavi looked past her to where Cullen stood glaring at them both. The son of her heart stared at the human as if seeing him for the first time.

"Why care if I fight?" he asked Cullen.

"You took on a man's responsibilities with your sister. You should have a man's skills to protect her with." Once again, Cullen held out the practice blade. "If Lusahn won't teach you, I will."

That did it. "Bavi, go upstairs and take your sister with you."

"But I want—"

"Not now, Bavi." She used the same voice she used to show new recruits who was in command, then softened her expression. "I'm not saying no, and I promise we will discuss this later."

The boy reluctantly retreated, shooing Shiri up the stairs ahead of him. When Lusahn heard the click of the door closing, she rounded on Cullen.

"Don't you dare question my decisions in front of the children." She got right up in his face. "How much do you think you can teach him in a single moon cycle? I will tell you: enough to get him killed. Right now, if threatened, he runs. That works for both him and his sister."

She poked Cullen in the chest with her finger. "But if you convince him that he knows enough to stand and fight the wrong person, he *will* die. Maybe you can live with that on your conscience, if you have one, but I can't.

"Furthermore"—she poked him again—"this is *my* world, not yours. You don't understand it and you never will, so stay out of my business."

Cullen caught her finger and brought it up to his mouth for a soft kiss. "Let me start again. Would you like me to teach the boy some of the basics, just to get him started? I've nothing better to do with my time, and I'd like to feel useful."

How dare he be reasonable when she wanted to fight! But the way he gently massaged her finger was turning her temper into something else completely. When he released her hand and slid his arms around her waist, she forced herself to step back. Then back again. But Cullen followed her step-for-step until he'd backed her into the wall, leaving her no room to move or even breathe.

Warmth, rich and potent, surrounded her as Cullen eased closer, gradually leaning his muscular body into hers. When he kneed her legs apart to settle himself against her, she sighed and surrendered, the last bit of her temper banished by his gentle touch.

"This won't solve anything, Cullen Finley," she warned, feeling better for having made that clear.

He nibbled kisses down the side of her neck. "No, it won't. In fact, things are only going to get more complicated."

Her fingers felt the muscles in his arms, loving the hard feel of his warrior's body against hers. When he settled his mouth—finally!—over hers, she went on the attack, demanding he allow her to deepen the kiss. She felt him smile against her lips just before they parted in invitation.

As their tongues dove and stroked, his hands slid down the curve of her back to cup her bottom. He squeezed; she moaned as he lifted her more solidly against his erection. She rocked against him in approval. She'd never felt this needy, this close to falling over the edge from only touch and taste.

She wanted to strip them both down to the skin so he could plunge inside of her to ease this awful, lovely ache between her legs. As if sensing her thoughts, Cullen's hand eased between them, centering right over her core, and squeezed slightly.

Her lungs emptied of air, leaving her panting.

"Come for me, Lusahn. Give it to me now." His voice was rough even as his touch was gentle. One by one, he released the buttons on her trousers until his hand found its way between her clothes and her skin. Instinctively she spread her feet farther apart, giving him easier access to work his wicked magic on her. His fingers teased her slick heat with just enough pressure, making her moan. She buried her face against his chest, trying to hold back the need to shout her approval.

"That's it, honey, just let it fly. I'll catch you."

He eased two fingers deep inside of her, at the same time teasing her sensitive nub until she shattered into tiny little shards of light and energy.

Afterward, as she tried to gather up all of the pieces, Cullen held her sweetly, murmuring gentle nonsense near her ear.

When she could once again string a sentence together, she cupped the side of his face, letting his whiskers tickle her hand. "That wasn't a fair way to end an argument."

He grinned unrepentantly. "No, but it worked."

When he planted a kiss on her nose, she gave him a gentle shove back. "I will talk to Bavi about training, but he is my responsibility, not yours."

"I know."

Was that hurt she heard in his voice? Surely not. Why would a Paladin warrior care so much about a boy who had been nothing but rude to him from the first?

The upstairs door opened, and Bavi called down, "Lusahn, that pot on the stove smells funny."

Not again! If she burned dinner, Joq would never let her live it down. "I'll be right there." She told Cullen, "My friend will be here soon, now that it is dark. Speak to him carefully."

"I will." Gone was her gentle would-be lover; in his place was the hard-faced warrior whom she'd faced in combat. "But if he attacks, Lusahn, I will fight back."

That would be her worst nightmare—her mentor and this man fighting to the death. They were warriors both; it would go against their natures to surrender.

"We will have dinner and then talk afterward. He knows something that will help us investigate the thefts; I'm sure of it."

"Then you did the right thing in talking to him."

"I hope so, Cullen Finley." She wished she could feel more confident about that, but only time would tell whether Joq would offer her advice or Cullen's head.

Figuring Lusahn needed a little time alone with her kids, Cullen decided to wait in the basement until her mysterious friend arrived. He found it interesting that the man felt it necessary to cloak his arrival in darkness.

Who did he think would be watching the comings and goings at Lusahn's house? Whoever was coming clearly needed to preserve secrecy as much as Cullen did.

If he hadn't been expecting someone, he would have missed the soft brush of a boot sole on the stone steps outside. He drew his sword, stepped to the far side of the door, and waited to see who had come in and what kind of mood the man was in.

The door opened no more than a hand's width. "Human, I can hear your heartbeat. Stand back and I will enter, sword sheathed."

Just because Lusahn trusted this guy didn't mean Cullen did. Hell, the man might have brought reinforcements. He considered his options and finally decided to see what the man had to say. "I'm backing away."

When he'd gone a handful of steps the door swung open completely, revealing an Other male dressed in the usual black and gray. He stepped across the threshold, meeting Cullen's gaze directly, his eyes narrowed and suspicious.

"So we meet, human." He stared for several long seconds in silence. Then he grinned, the sudden change in demeanor startling Cullen into stumbling back a step.

Just that quickly, he had a knife blade at Cullen's throat. "You aren't bad looking for your kind. I can see why she wants you. By the gods, it's been long enough since she unwound enough to let a male so close. But what I want to know, human, is what do you want from my apprentice besides the chance to share her bed?"

Cullen ignored the blade and the question, answering with his fists and temper. "Show her respect, or I'll beat you senseless!"

The older man took the punch and then held up his hands. "You've answered my question well enough, human."

"My name is Cullen Finley. Not 'human.' "

"And mine is Joq." The older man calmly sheathed his knife. "Now, shall we find Lusahn and see if her cooking is as bad as I remember it?"

He started up the stairs, leaving Cullen to follow.

Chapter 5

*D*inner was . . . interesting, Lusahn decided. Both children sat with their eyes flitting from one adult to the next, no doubt picking up on the tension that simmered below the surface of everyone's good manners. She drew comfort from the fact that while they eyed the two males with suspicion, they looked to her for reassurance.

She wished she was as calm as she led them to believe. Both Joq and Cullen ate the meal she'd set in front of them, but she seriously doubted either of them could have told her what they'd eaten. They were too busy exchanging dark looks to take note of anything else going on around them.

Would Cullen even notice if she stripped off her clothes and danced naked around the room? The idea made her smile, which did catch his attention. His spoon paused halfway to his mouth.

"Did I miss something important?" he asked, setting his spoon down.

"No, my mind was just drifting." Back down the stairs, and right back to where the two of them had left off earlier.

He gave her a knowing smile. "Mine, too." Then he went back to eating the soup. Joq watched the brief exchange with great interest, his pale eyes revealing nothing of what he was thinking, unlike Cullen's expressive dark ones.

"More soup for anyone?" She reached for the ladle, ready to dish it out.

To a man, everyone quickly shook their heads and pushed their bowls toward the center of the table. Rolling her eyes, she set the pot back down.

"It wasn't that bad, Lusahn." Joq's eyes crinkled as he crossed his arms over his chest and leaned back in his chair. "It's just that I have a long walk home and don't want to do it on a full stomach."

As excuses went it was a poor one, but it was Joq's way of saying they needed to get down to business. Her stomach did a slow somersault. With some effort, she managed not to look at Cullen but began collecting the dirty dishes and setting them near the sink.

"Bavi, Shiri, I would appreciate it if you would go to your rooms for a while. These gentlemen and I have much to discuss."

When Bavi didn't immediately leave, Lusahn

gave him a pointed look that said remaining behind wasn't an option. She wasn't about to involve
innocent children in Guild business, even one far
too mature for his age.

He protested, "But the dishes—"

"It's my turn to do them," Cullen said.

Bavi conceded defeat and led Shiri down the
hall.

When she was sure they were gone, Lusahn
turned to Joq. "Since you need to leave soon, I suggest we leave the dishes for later and deal with more
important things."

Her mentor nodded and studied Cullen's face
for several seconds before speaking. "So, human,
you are here because of the blue stones. Lusahn
says they are being stolen in our world and carried
into yours."

She didn't like Cullen staring at her, but when
he shifted his gaze back to Joq, she found she
missed it.

"They are, although the only stone currently in
the Paladins' possession was found in Missouri.
That's a long way from where I crossed the barrier.
I assume that means the problem is widespread in
your world, if your people are crossing from multiple sites with the stones in hand."

Joq remained impassive. "Why do your people
want the stones in the first place? Even in the
hands of a major talent like Barak q'Arc, the power

they generate doesn't compare to the light and power in your world."

Cullen sat sprawled in his chair, but she could sense his rising tension when he spoke.

"Even in our world, energy comes at a price. If the people behind this could harness the energy in your stones, or figure out how to make the jewels found naturally in our world emit the same energy, they would gain both money and power. I don't know much about your world, but I would guess those two things have value here, as well."

Lusahn said, "Of course. It is why the Guild and the Guildmaster work hard to regulate the use of the stones, so that no one person profits too much. It would seem that someone has gotten greedy."

Joq gave an eloquent shrug. "Anytime our people come in contact with humans, there is corruption. What they don't steal at sword point, they steal with lies. Our people lose while his people grow rich."

"Like hell!" Cullen sat up taller and snarled, "I'm not denying we've got our own fair share of greedy fools, but we wouldn't even *know* about those damn blue stones if someone over here hadn't decided to make a profit off of them."

Joq's pales eyes flashed with growing anger. "So how *did* they find out about them, if someone on your side of the barrier hadn't been sneaking over here?"

"Listen, Other, the real problem is that your people have been led to believe they can buy their way into my world with the stones by someone from here. Yet all it gets them is a sword in their gut." Cullen held the pommel of his sword in a white-knuckled grip.

"That's all your kind understands—violence and death. And despite what you've told Lusahn, I'm not convinced that you came here to stop the thefts at all."

Joq shifted in his chair. Cullen might not realize that the older male was on the verge of drawing his own weapon, but Lusahn recognized the signs.

"Joq! Cullen Finley is a guest in my home, just as you are. If you two cannot have a civil conversation without resorting to swords, then perhaps it is time for you to leave."

Joq relaxed enough to let her know that the crisis had passed, at least for the moment.

Cullen gradually sat back, although his hand never left his sword.

"So, can we agree that the flow of stones must be stopped for the sake of both worlds?" She glared at each man.

Joq nodded, then Cullen did the same.

Her mentor shot Cullen a nasty look. "Even if we stop the theft of stones, our two people will still be at war; it is the way it has always been. How many of my people have you killed with that blade you keep caressing as if it were a woman's body?"

Lusahn had never known Joq to be so antagonistic. What had gotten into him?

"I've killed enough, Other—but I've always got time for one more." Cullen's voice sounded reasonable, but something deadly shifted in the glitter of his eyes. As gentle as he'd been with her, this Paladin would fight to kill if Joq kept prodding him.

She had no taste for seeing blood spilled at her kitchen table.

Before she could respond, Joq changed directions. "So why does her traitor brother Barak still live, if you enjoy killing us so much? I would have thought a prime male like him would have drawn Paladins as soon as he crossed the barrier."

"I won't discuss Barak with you."

"Why not? He has chosen your people over his own—even over his only sister. In your world is such behavior condoned, or have you no honor? He would have been executed had he returned. Come to think of it, since you chose to take his place, perhaps you should die in his place."

Lusahn gasped in outrage. "What game are you playing, Joq? I brought you here to help, not to cause a private war."

She'd left her sword in her bedroom, not liking to wear it around the children. But the real question was, if this discussion continued to deteriorate, whose side would she be fighting on?

Cullen's—because he was either her guest or her prisoner. He was in her home and therefore deserving of her protection. He might not think he needed it, but he'd never seen Joq fight. On a good day, Barak could have beaten Joq. She had no idea if Cullen could, and didn't want to find out.

The Paladin's smile was cold and unfriendly. "I don't know what Barak's problems were in this world, Joq, but he has proven himself to be an honorable man in my world. That is good enough for me."

"So you don't hate all of us, just most of us."

It wasn't a question, but Cullen answered anyway. "I wouldn't hate any of you at all, if you'd stay on your side of the line. But as long as your people insist on invading my world, with swords drawn and murder in their eyes, we'll be there to stop them."

Lusahn leapt up and slapped her hands down on the table. "Enough! If you two can do nothing but bicker, then shut up. Joq, go home. Cullen, go to the basement."

Cullen wasn't about to be banished like some child being sent to his room, but she was right. This old friend of hers was deliberately trying to get a reaction out of Cullen. The question was, why?

"I'm willing to be civil if he will be, Lusahn."

"Joq?" Her tone made it clear that no more trouble would be accepted from either of them.

Joq changed tactics again. "I would take you

both to see something tomorrow before midday. Can you bring him to my place about that time?"

Lusahn studied him, probably as confused by the abrupt about-face as Cullen was. "I can if I can avoid my Blade. We aren't on duty until just before the star sets tomorrow. If we're careful, I should be able to get him there safely enough."

Cullen wasn't going anywhere until he knew for certain they weren't walking right into a trap. "Why should we trust you?"

"I don't care if you die, human, but I do care about Lusahn. She has endured enough pain without me adding to her burden by killing you."

Okay, that was an explanation he could accept and believe. Joq seemed to treat Lusahn like a star pupil, or even a favorite younger sister. But there was something about the way the man looked at her when she wasn't aware of it that made Cullen think that Joq's true feelings for her were far different.

"If she thinks we should come, then we'll be there."

"Good." Joq reached for his cloak. "I'll slip out through the back door again. Human, I want you to watch from the window downstairs to see if any of the shadows out there have more substance than they should have."

Lusahn followed the two men to the basement door. "Who would be following you, Joq? I know how invisible you are when you want to be."

He stared out into the darkness. "I've lived by the sword, Lusahn, and I've never had your talent for getting along with everyone. I've made enemies along the way."

"But the Guild protects its own." It was a promise made to every Sworn Guardian and every member of the Blades.

Joq looked back over his shoulder at her. "I'm not Guild anymore, remember? That means I am a target for anyone with a grudge over how I handled my job."

When he started to step through the door, she caught his arm. "You were the best, Joq. We all look up to you. I hold with my vow to protect."

He covered her hand with his. "That means a lot coming from you, Lusahn. If the rest of the Guild members were like you, I'd still belong." Then he threw his shoulders back and forced a smile. "Now, unless you want me snoring on your floor, I'd better get going. I need my sleep."

Cullen read the very real regret in the man's eyes when he looked back at Lusahn one last time, and a shiver of premonition ran up Cullen's spine. Something in the man's demeanor made Cullen think there was an undercurrent of farewell in Joq's words.

But maybe that was just petty jealousy that the Other had spent years in Lusahn's company, while Cullen had at best a double handful of days left with her. He watched her continue to study the shadows outside.

"He's gone."

She wrapped her arms across her chest and shivered. "I know, but I worry about him." She closed the door and threw the bolt to lock it. "I know he deliberately provoked you, Cullen, but he's been a good friend to me."

"I can see that." He reached out to tuck a strand of her hair back behind her ear. "He obviously cares very much for you and doesn't like me being here."

"He has good reasons not to like Paladins. We all do." A smile softened her comment.

"Do you think that for a few hours you can forget that I'm a Paladin and see me as a worthy male?" He ached with the need to carry her to his bed, to lose himself in her arms and her body.

Her eyes strayed past him to look in that direction, clearly understanding the real question he was asking. He wouldn't push, and he wouldn't crowd her, but damn, he burned to taste her passion.

"I have to see to the children."

He turned away to keep his disappointment to himself. He couldn't really blame her. A few days—or nights—wasn't much to offer a woman, especially one like Lusahn. She had enough on her plate without him adding to her problems.

Then her arms slipped around his waist as she

laid her cheek against his back. "I'm sorry, but I promised to read to Shiri. It's important that I don't disappoint her unless I have to."

"I understand."

"But once she and Bavi are both asleep, I will return to see how worthy you are."

By the time he realized what she'd just said, she was already halfway up the stairs, giggling. He fought the urge to drag her right back down, since that would only delay her returning to him for the night.

He looked around for something to do, something quiet that wouldn't disturb the children. A shower, maybe. Yeah, he decided, stripping off his clothes. Nothing like a nice long shower to while away the minutes until his soon-to-be lover returned.

Shiri frowned and pulled her thumb out of her mouth long enough to complain. "You missed a word."

"Sorry, little one. I'll try to do better." It wasn't as if she hadn't read the book dozens of times before, but it was her first time with an impatient male waiting downstairs.

One more book, and then she'd see if she really had the courage to walk back down those stairs. She concentrated on the words, careful to repeat the familiar words in the usual way. Already Shiri's eyes were drifting shut.

She could hear the sound of the shower running down below. Cullen, wet and naked, only a few steps away. The image had her stirring restlessly on the edge of the bed, which caused Shiri to wake up again.

Lusahn started reading the book from the beginning again, forcing her attention to follow the words on the page, ignoring the fact that a handsome man was waiting for her, wanting her.

Finally, she eased off the side of the bed and tugged the covers up over the sleeping Shiri's shoulders. How the gods had blessed her when they'd led her and her Blade down the road to Bavi and his sister. How had she lived without them to fill up her hours and her heart?

She stopped by Bavi's room to peek in, even though he was too old to tuck in like she did Shiri. That didn't keep her from brushing his hair back off his face or picking up the book he'd dropped on the floor. He needed to be fussed over every bit as much as his sister did, even if he'd deny it.

Back out in the hall, she leaned against the door frame and prayed for guidance at this crossroad in her life. There had been so many changes in the past few months: the disappearance of her brother, the addition of the children to her household, the discovery that Barak still lived, and now the biggest change of all: Cullen Finley.

She'd come to terms with her brother's death; somehow she would deal with his new life. The children were a constant challenge and a constant joy, enriching her soul. But Cullen Finley was a puzzle, one she had no idea how to solve.

Many of the Sworn Guardians and the Blade-mates indulged in the pleasures of the body, changing partners as often as the mood struck. While far from innocent, she'd never wanted to indulge herself with her Blademates, although all three of them had made it clear they were willing. That sort of intimacy felt wrong when she was responsible for their honor and their lives. When she'd been part of Joq's Blade, he had followed the same unspoken rule.

She drew a shuddering breath, recognizing that all this thinking was just a delaying tactic. Her body was demanding that she rush down those stairs into Cullen's waiting arms, while an increasingly faint voice in the back of her mind screamed out warnings of danger ahead.

She closed her eyes and reached out to listen. The shower was still running. Just think: Cullen Finley with that fine warrior's body, all soap-slick and waiting just for her. What was she doing lurking in the hallway when she could be joining him?

She flew down the steps, not sure if her feet even touched down as she peeled off her shirt and tossed it to the side. At the bottom, she hopped on each foot in turn to pull off her boots and socks. It took her longer than she liked to unbutton the front of her pants, and she almost tripped in her haste to shed them.

When she touched the curtain that sheltered the bathing area from the rest of the room, she hesitated. This wasn't like her at all, but it felt right. Their time was limited; playing coy games would only waste precious moments they would never be able to reclaim.

She straightened her shoulders, took a deep breath, and stepped around the curtain.

Cullen was waiting for her, the spray of the shower doing nothing to disguise how his body reacted to her arrival. He was well built from head to toe, and her reaction caused his mouth to quirk up in a half smile.

"I wondered if you were ever going to come in." He held out his hand, inviting her to come closer.

She walked right into his arms and pulled his head down for a kiss, her blood rushing through her veins, her heart racing with the need to taste him.

His tongue plunged into her mouth, then retreated until hers darted out to join in the dance. His powerful arms cradled her against his body, his erection hard against her belly. She eased a hand between them to caress its length as he murmured encouraging sounds.

Suddenly the sensations were too much, too soon, yet not nearly enough. She was already poised at the precipice, once again ready to shatter and let the pieces tumble to the tile below their feet.

Cullen obviously felt the same way, because he pulled back, his breathing shallow, his hands unsteady. "Let's slow down and savor this." He picked up the washcloth and soap and worked up a thick lather. Starting at her shoulders, he traced each curve of her body, using long, slow strokes that had every nerve in her body begging for more.

She caught his hand and stole the washcloth, thinking a little retribution was in order. "My turn."

Her plan backfired. Running her hands over all that sleek muscle and strength only heightened her own awareness. Finally, she tossed the washcloth aside and turned off the water. Cullen immediately reached for a towel, the promise that gleamed in his dark eyes keeping her warm.

Who knew that a towel could be used as a tool of seduction? He brushed the soft cloth across her back before planting a soft kiss on the top of her shoulder.

"I love the feel of your skin, Lusahn."

Leaning against him, she arched back to offer him better access to her neck. When he lapped up a few drops of water at the base of her throat, she moaned her encouragement and reached back to wrap her arm around his neck, holding him close.

The sharp spice of Cullen's scent filled her senses, rendering her aware of nothing except where their bodies touched with almost painful intensity. She captured one of his wandering hands and urged it up to capture her breast. It was impossible to tell which one of them enjoyed it more.

"Take me to your bed, Cullen."

"Yes, ma'am."

He surprised her with a quick move, sweeping her up in his arms. She was not a small woman, but his careful embrace made her feel feminine and ever so safe in his arms.

The curtain surrounding the bathing area caught on her damp skin, making it difficult for them to get free of it. Their brief battle with the fabric had her giggling as Cullen cursed and managed to break them free. Had she ever been with a lover who made her laugh before? Not that she could remember.

The laughter died away as he lowered her, oh so slowly, to his bed. He knelt over her, his eyes drinking her in as if he'd been in the desert, only to stumble upon an oasis.

"Like what you see?" She tried to sound nonchalant, but she desperately needed to know that she pleased him as much as he did her.

"You are perfect."

Cullen forgot how to breathe as Lusahn looked up at him, her damp hair spread upon his pillow, her soft mouth swollen from his kisses. He was so hard, he hurt. The urge to tumble down on the bed and just take her was driving him crazy, but she deserved better.

"It's been a long time for me, Lusahn. I'll try to go slow, but I don't know that I can." He stretched out beside her, leaving enough space between them to keep him sane for a few seconds more.

Her silver gray eyes and siren's smile were enough to tempt a saint. And he sure as hell was no saint. Her long legs tangled with his, and her fingertips traced his jaw, carefully brushing his day-old beard.

"I'm sorry I couldn't shave." He kissed her finger.

"Don't be." She smiled. "I find I like whiskers."

"You won't when you get whisker burns on your face." He glanced down the lean length of her body. "And other places."

She gave him a puzzled look, then blushed when she realized what he meant. But his woman was a warrior, made of tough stuff.

"I'm willing to risk it." Then she cupped her breasts and offered them up to his mouth.

She tasted so damned sweet, her breasts the perfect size for his hands and mouth. He suckled one and then the other gently. When he grazed her nipple with his teeth and then soothed the small hurt with his tongue, she moaned and eased her leg up over his, pulling him farther into the cradle of her body.

But they had all night, and he didn't want their first time to be rushed. He slowly kissed his way down her body, lingering at the curve of her waist, again at her navel, and then at the juncture of her legs. She clenched her thighs, but he would have none of that.

"Let me in, Lusahn." He used his hands to gently spread her legs apart, sliding his arm underneath to lift them up slightly. "Watch me, lover."

Her eyes were wide open as she held her breath, waiting for what was coming next. He smiled to reassure her before slowly lowering his mouth to brush a kiss across the very center of her need. She immediately threw her head back and whimpered. Oh, yeah, she liked that, and was going to like what came next even more.

Using his tongue and teeth and lips, he drove her higher and higher until finally she dug her hands into the sheets, tossing her head from side to side. He eased a finger deep inside of her and then kissed her deeply one last time, sending her flying.

He climbed back up her body, stopping to admire all his favorite spots until he was poised at her entrance. Bracing himself on his elbows, he slowly thrust forward, burying himself deep inside her welcoming heat. It felt like coming home—as if he'd been waiting for this one perfect moment his entire life.

When her legs stirred restlessly underneath him, Cullen guided them up around his hips as he gave her time to adjust to the fit of their bodies. But he didn't know how much longer he could last before his restraint shattered.

Her hands fluttered near his shoulders before finally coming to rest on his back. She moved them in soft circles, gradually down to rest on his hips. Gifting him with a smile that melted his bones, she kneaded his backside and thrust upward where their bodies were joined, whispering, "You feel so right. Let me know your strength."

That did it. His control snapped as his muscles flexed, pounding his body against hers, striving to get closer, deeper, farther, in this race they were running. His hips swung with powerful strokes, plunging and retreating, fueled by the urgent little noises Lusahn made with each stroke.

The friction between their bodies generated a maelstrom of breathtaking heat, driving him onward, harder, faster, deeper. He wanted, *needed*, to mark this woman, to claim her, and to surrender himself to her. Their breaths met and mingled; the sweat on their skin scented the air as they met in a pulsating rush that made them one.

Afterward, Lusahn softly moaned as her legs eased back down onto the bed. Her hand brushed the back of Cullen's head as he waited for his heart to start again and his lungs to rejoin the party. Finally he mustered the strength to roll to the side, taking Lusahn with him, cradling her head against his shoulder.

He had no words to describe what had just happened between them, even if he'd been able to catch his breath enough to talk. Maybe the silence could speak for him, letting her feel the slow slide of his hand up and down her back, and the way his pulse still pounded in his veins.

After a bit, as their skin cooled, he reached down to retrieve the blankets that they'd kicked out of their way and covered them both.

"Thank you," she said softly.

"I thought you might be getting cold."

Lusahn lifted her head and grinned. "I wasn't talking about the blanket."

"Oh. Well, in that case, it was very much my pleasure, and will be again if you give me time to recuperate." He planted a quick kiss on her mouth. Maybe it wouldn't take as long as he thought before they could pick up where they'd left off.

Then sleep claimed them both.

Lusahn stared at their intertwined hands as they lay dozing spoon-style on Cullen's bed. His fingers were broad and strong, making hers look more slender and female than usual. As different as they were, though, both of their hands bore the same calluses and small scars from handling swords for a living.

"Does the difference in our skin tones bother you?" Cullen's voice was a deep rumble from behind her right shoulder.

"Not at all. I'm just not used to waking up with a man in my bed." Even when she had indulged in passion, she'd never slept in a lover's arms afterward. That required a degree of trust that she didn't often feel.

"I could tell." His mouth brushed her shoulder with a soft kiss.

As the meaning of his words sunk in, she stiffened, embarrassed. "I'm sorry."

"Don't be. I wasn't complaining." He raised himself up and met her gaze with a slow, sexy smile. "When a choosy woman chooses me, I should feel honored." He kissed her shoulder. "And believe me, I do."

The appreciative heat in his eyes and smile warmed her heart . . . and a few other places. She pushed back against his body, pressing her bottom directly against his manhood, which swelled at her touch.

"Are you trying to tell me something?" His hands were already on the move, tracing her ribs on their way to capture the sensitive swell of her breast.

"I choose you again, human."

"Yes, ma'am."

As he kissed her thoroughly, his hand splayed low on her belly, making its way down to tangle in the curls between her legs.

She could feel his blunt length already poised to take her. He stroked her, his fingers growing damp with her body's readiness for him. She nudged backward, gasping with the thick intrusion, yet loving the overwhelming sensations he created within her with each touch.

"Oh, yes, Cullen Finley. I choose you." Then she gave herself up to the moment.

Chapter 6

*S*eattle had a well-deserved reputation for long stretches of cloudy, rainy weather, but Cullen found the early-morning gloom of Lusahn's world far more dreary. The sky was an unrelenting dusty gray that blended into the distant hills. Low and tired looking, they were barren and brown, an occasional clump of scraggly shrubs the only splash of color.

Cullen kept his borrowed cloak pulled close to his face to disguise his alien nature, but also to ward off the bone-chilling cold. Lusahn looked as miserable as he did.

"Does your weather change with the seasons?" He knew she didn't like answering questions about the differences in their worlds, but climate seemed an innocuous enough subject.

She gave him a puzzled look. "What do you mean, seasons?"

"Back home we have four seasons of the year: spring, summer, fall, and winter. Each has different weather, which controls the growth cycle of plants and affects most animals, as well."

She shook her head. "Our history speaks of such things. But as the star fades, it is always more of the same. Sometimes colder, sometimes warmer, but always gray."

He hated the sadness in her expression, and changed the subject. "What do you think Joq wants to show us?"

"I don't know." At the mention of her friend's name, fleeting worry crossed her face. "Joq is a law unto himself. Even when he was a Sworn Guardian, he ignored the rules of the Guild if he felt the situation merited it. The only reason the Guildmaster put up with him was that Joq got results. People respected him, and that kept the peace."

"I'm familiar with the type."

After all, he fought alongside a whole cadre of the toughest sons of bitches around. Paladins played hard, fought even harder, and lived their lives on the wild and raw edge of violence. Most viewed operating outside of the rules imposed by the Regents as a game. But to a man, they took their duty to protect damned seriously.

"He doesn't seem all that old. Why did he retire?"

Lusahn sighed. "Partly because of me. The

Guild only allows so many Sworn Guardians at any one time. Joq kept pushing them to give me my own Blade, but they wouldn't make an exception. In a fit of temper, he offered to resign if that's what it took to get me my own command. The Guild-master was only too glad to accept."

She stopped talking long enough to pass by a group of young Others, her hand resting on the pommel of her sword. They automatically stepped to the side of the road, giving Lusahn and Cullen plenty of room. Once they were well beyond hearing, she picked up where she'd left off.

"I tried to talk Joq out of his foolishness, but he says he has no regrets."

"He wouldn't have wanted you to have your own Blade if you didn't deserve it, Lusahn. There's no reason for you to feel guilty."

She gave a soft laugh. "You sound just like him. I know I'm good at my job, but I wish I hadn't had to climb over a friend to get it."

They'd finally reached the far edge of town. The terrain grew rockier, and their feet stirred up small clouds of dust as they walked.

The thinner air kept Cullen silent as he struggled to catch his breath and maintain the brisk pace Lusahn had set once they'd left the town behind. If his pride had allowed him to ask her to slow down, she probably would have. Although he kept thinking his body would adjust, maybe there was some other component in the air that affected his breathing.

When they reached the top of a small rise, Lusahn paused for several seconds. Maybe she wasn't as unaware of his struggles as he'd hoped. She smiled at him. "We're almost there."

"Good." As they started downhill, he moved out at a faster pace. He knew his ego was pushing him along, but he also needed to know how much his body could handle if the need to fight arose. He hadn't survived this long without knowing his weaknesses as well as his strengths.

When they circled around a cluster of large boulders, he had a clear view of a small house nestled against a rocky incline. Joq was sitting on a bench against his house. His eyes were closed, his arms crossed on his chest, but he wasn't asleep. There was too much tension in the set of his shoulders, nor had Cullen missed seeing the sword lying by Joq's right hand. He'd bet it wasn't the only weapon Joq had within easy reach.

The Other male stirred and sat up. "I was beginning to wonder if you'd changed your mind about coming."

"If I had, I would've sent word, Joq. I know you too well to leave you waiting." Lusahn gave her mentor an impudent grin. "I'd have been looking over my shoulder until you got even."

"See, human, I taught her well." Joq rose to his

feet. "Come inside for a cool drink and to catch your breath. We still have some distance to cover today, and I'd just as soon not end up carrying you."

Cullen ignored the jibe, figuring any reaction would only encourage Joq to keep poking and prodding at his temper until he got the response he was after. As Cullen ducked his head to walk through the low doorway into the house, Joq's nostrils flared, his eyes narrowing. Whatever he sensed didn't improve his mood.

Regardless, Joq poured them each a tall glass of the juice Lusahn served with meals. Its sharp citrus flavor washed the dust out of Cullen's throat. He leaned against a nearby counter and waited for their host to reveal his plans.

Lusahn drank about half of hers before setting down her glass. "Where are you taking us, Joq?"

"To the eastern tunnels."

She frowned. "Why there? We haven't heard about any activity along that stretch of the barrier recently."

"Just because you haven't been told about it doesn't mean there hasn't been any, Lusahn. You know the Guildmaster doesn't tell the Guardians any more than he absolutely has to."

"But if he knows something is going on, why hasn't he been sending in the Blades to deal with it?" She stood up, hands on her hips.

Cullen quickly finished the last of his juice before pushing away from the counter. He was getting a bad feeling about Joq's plans for them. He put his hand on the pommel of his sword, an action that Joq didn't fail to notice.

Widening his stance, Cullen spoke to Lusahn, but kept his eyes solely on Joq. "I think what he's hinting at, Lusahn, is that your Guildmaster either doesn't know that something is going on in your eastern tunnels, which makes him incompetent, or he *does* know and doesn't want the Guardians involved—which means he's involved up to his eyeballs."

Lusahn frowned. "I don't like the Guildmaster any more than you do, Joq, but we can't accuse him of something like this without proof. He could have us both up on charges of treason for spreading such a rumor."

"Do you want to find out what's going on with the blue stones or not?" Already reaching for his cloak, Joq didn't wait for her answer.

Cullen blocked the doorway. "If the evidence is so clear, why haven't you reported it yourself? Why involve Lusahn at all?"

"Because I'm no longer a Guardian. It's not my job; it's hers." Joq clenched his hands into fists. "Of course, if the two of you are too busy with other things, we can just forget about it."

The look on his face made it clear just what kind of other things he was talking about. Cullen surged forward, ready to teach the bastard some respect.

Lusahn stopped him. "Settle down, you two. We don't have time for this. Joq, quit being rude and tell me what you've seen."

"I want you to see for yourself." Joq ignored Cullen, keeping his gaze on Lusahn. "I will leave it for you to draw your own conclusions. Once you see what I've seen, we'll make plans. Let's go."

Cullen's gut feeling was that Joq was up to something, but he had no choice but to let Lusahn make the call on whether to trust Joq or to walk away from her mentor. He stepped to the side, allowing the Other male to pass by. He wasn't surprised when Lusahn immediately followed him out into the dim light of the midday star. Even if she wasn't as sure of her old mentor as she'd like to be, her sense of duty wouldn't allow her to duck a difficult situation.

But if Joq was leading them into a trap, the bastard would be the first one to die.

They were being followed. Lusahn even knew who it was; the only question was what to do about it. Larem's suspicions were obviously worse than she'd feared. If he no longer trusted her, then his days as a member of her Blade were over. A Sworn Guardian was only as strong as the Blade that served her; there was no room for doubts and second-guessing. She would have no choice but to ask for his resignation.

If that were the extent of the problem, she'd find some way to live with it. However, the Guild wouldn't reassign Larem to another Blade without investigating what had caused the rift between them. And since Kit and Glyn looked to Larem for leadership almost as much as they did her, they might ask for a new assignment, as well.

It wasn't as if she didn't already have enough complications in her life, the biggest one of which was marching along beside her in grim silence. Cullen hadn't taken his eyes off Joq since they'd started for the eastern tunnels, nor had his hand strayed far from his sword.

Joq wasn't behaving any better. He'd charged off ahead of them, never once stopping since they'd left his house. Why was he so angry? He'd probably guessed that she and Cullen had spent the night together, but who was he to question her decisions? Hadn't he been the one who'd been telling her that she needed a male in her life?

If she didn't know better, she might have thought he was jealous—but how could that be? He'd never done anything that suggested he thought of her that way.

As Joq rounded a bend in the trail, Lusahn took the opportunity to touch Cullen's arm and whisper, "We're being followed."

"I know. He's been dogging our footsteps since we left Joq's house. Do you want me to hide behind those rocks ahead and take him out?"

"No! It's Larem, one of my Blademates. The big question is, why is he following us?"

"Do you think he suspects I'm not one of you?"

Her stomach roiled. "He definitely suspects something, but I have no idea what. I know he doesn't trust Joq."

"Smart man." His dark eyes swept past her in the direction Joq had gone. "I don't, either. He's up to something."

She wanted to scream. "Cullen, I don't need that from you, too. Larem wasn't happy being left outside when I talked to Joq about you. He and I have been friends since childhood, yet I can't begin to guess what Larem is thinking right now. And when he finds out about us, he'll go for his sword."

Cullen's dark eyes sparked with cold fury. Gone was her easy, laughing lover from last night. In his place was the hard-edged warrior she'd faced all those weeks ago. "All the more reason for me to fall back and invite him to the party. Either he's on your side, in which case we can use the backup, or he's on their side, whoever *they* turn out to be."

She froze, unable to go a step farther. "I hate all of this—especially never knowing which of you I can trust!"

Cullen's expression softened as he gently caressed her cheek with his fingertips. "You can trust me."

But she couldn't forget that his purpose in being here was to protect his world from her kind.

"You'll be gone soon, and then where will I be?" She looked up and down the trail. "My mentor has become unpredictable, my Blade doesn't trust me, and my brother has chosen your people over his own. That doesn't leave me much."

Her eyes burned, but she ignored the tears that threatened to spill down her cheek. She was a warrior and would make a warrior's decision. "Bring Larem to me alive. I'll catch up with Joq."

Cullen nodded and stepped off the trail. When she reached the bend up ahead she risked a backward glance to check on her lover, but there was nothing but silence in the air. Drawing her cloak against a sudden chill, she turned and trudged uphill after a man she still badly wanted to call friend.

The boulders offered enough cover to keep Lusahn's Blademate from seeing Cullen. The Other wasn't being all that careful, probably too intent on keeping Lusahn and Joq in sight to worry about covering his own tracks. Cullen planned on waiting until the nosy bastard reached the bend in the trail before tackling him from above. He took off his cloak and dropped it on the ground behind the boulder. There was no way to disguise who and what he was in an up-close-and-personal fistfight, and the cloak would only hamper his ability to move.

Cullen grinned. Lusahn didn't want this Larem guy gutted, but she didn't say Cullen couldn't bruise him up some. He might be calmer than most Paladins, but he still occasionally needed to express himself with his fists. And right now, he had a lot to say to these Other males who had Lusahn all tied up in knots.

It didn't help to know that he was a big part of the problems she was facing right now. Maybe she'd let him hold this guy down while she got in a few good licks of her own. He doubted she'd take him up on the offer, but he wished she would.

The crunch of a boot sliding on gravel had him ducking back down. His quarry was nearby. Cullen held his breath, knowing these Others had senses that were far more acute than his own. He didn't doubt his ability to take this Larem on, but he'd promised Lusahn he wouldn't kill him. A surprise attack from above was the only way to bring him down without crossing swords.

The Other kept walking. Poised to leap, Cullen counted to ten, giving the male time to come up even with the boulder, then made his move. Something gave him away, though, because the Other whirled around at the last second. But he was no match for an angry Paladin intent on destruction.

The Other landed on his back with a satisfying thud as Cullen's full weight slammed into him. Before the Other could catch his breath, Cullen straddled his chest with both of his hands in a chokehold around the Other's throat.

His opponent immediately tried to buck him off, but he froze when he got his first close look at Cullen.

"Human!" he croaked.

"Damn straight I am." Cullen tightened his hold on Larem's throat for a few seconds to make it clear that his intentions were serious. "I've killed enough of your kind to know how to do the job right, so don't push me. I've got no problem with adding one more to the list."

A gasp from behind him had him cursing under his breath. Lusahn had doubled back just in time to hear him. The slide of metal in a scabbard warned him she hadn't come alone.

"Let him up, human." Joq's voice was little better than a growl.

"I don't answer to you, Joq. So either put that sword away or be prepared to use it." Cullen might die, but he'd take company with him. Tightening his grip, he watched Larem's face turn a fascinating shade of red, then darkening toward purple. It was the most color he'd ever seen in an Other's face.

"Let him up," Lusahn ordered, her voice as chilly as their poor excuse for a sun.

He made sure to meet Larem's gaze one more time, reminding him which of them had won this skirmish. He eased back, releasing his sword hand first to give himself a fighting chance if Joq decided to attack.

If Lusahn were to draw her sword, he didn't know what he'd do. He couldn't possibly kill her—and hoped that she felt the same about him. Her eyes met his briefly; they were flat and cold, sending a shiver straight through to the heart of him. Aw, hell, what did he expect? He didn't lump her in with the rest of her kind, but she had no way of knowing that after hearing his threat to Larem.

He made it to his feet without being attacked. Joq still had his sword out, but now it was aimed more in Larem's direction than Cullen's.

Lusahn stepped between them, offering a hand up to her Blademate. Cullen wasn't surprised Larem refused the offer, but the Other's rejection made Lusahn flinch.

"Why were you following us? Explain yourself, and in English." She injected enough authority in her voice to force the male to answer.

His voice was raw, but understandable. "My job is to protect you, Lusahn. Even from yourself." He glared at Joq and at Cullen. "These two will get you executed as a traitor."

"What's to keep us from executing you first? You are of her Blade, not her judge." Joq tried to slide past Lusahn, but she wouldn't allow it.

"And you are not anything, Joq, except a bitter ex-Guardian who will lead her into disaster." Larem tried to shove Lusahn out of his way.

Cullen immediately drew his own sword. "Touch her again, Other, and you'll lose your hand."

That did it. Lusahn threw her hands up in the air in disgust and stepped back to draw her sword. "Fine. Fight it out if you must, but know that the one left standing will face me."

For a long heartbeat, Cullen thought the other two males were going to cross blades, but finally reason won out. Joq eased back a step and Larem did the same. If they were going to behave, he guessed that meant he'd have to, as well. He lowered his sword but didn't sheathe it.

"Now, back to my question, Larem. Why were you shadowing us? How did you even know where to find us?"

"If it hadn't been me, it would have been Kit or Glyn. We all know something is wrong, but we didn't know what, so we've been taking turns watching your house." He shot Cullen another nasty look. "I guess I've figured out what the problem is now." He nodded his head in Cullen's direction. "Why is he still breathing?"

"Because her brother sent me." That was a

stretch of the truth, but Larem didn't need to know that. He directed his next question to Lusahn. "How much do you want him to know?"

"It is too late for secrets now. If he and the rest of my Blade are intent on shadowing my every step, they'll be better off knowing what they are getting into."

Cullen positioned himself next to Lusahn, showing without words whose side he was on. "We know someone in your world is working with people in mine to rob your world of the blue stones. We want it stopped. Barak thought we might be able to work together this one time."

Judging from the shock on Larem's face, he hadn't known that Barak was still alive. He looked to Lusahn for confirmation.

"This is Cullen Finley. He crossed the barrier with a note written in my brother's hand. Too many of our people are dying, Larem. I had hoped to keep Cullen's presence secret, but not because I didn't trust you. If he's caught here, the Guild will execute anyone involved."

"You would share this with Joq, but not your own Blade?" The male's pride was clearly smarting.

"I repeat, Larem: I trust you, but I didn't want to put you and the others at risk."

Joq interrupted. "Either we leave now, or give up for the day. You both have to be back in time to patrol."

Lusahn tried one more time. "I don't suppose you'd consider returning to town and forgetting what—and who—you've seen here today."

Larem's jaw took on a stubborn set. "No. I am your Blade."

She nodded with resignation. "Then you two keep an eye out for anyone else behind us. Joq, you lead the parade."

The four of them moved out in a ragged line, their mood grim and silent.

A short distance later, the trail became too steep for any conversation. Cullen maneuvered to bring up the rear, not trusting either of the males at his back, even if he had to breathe their dust all damn day. He had to admire the ease with which his three companions handled the steep terrain. It was a struggle for him to keep up, the thin atmosphere and the previous night's lack of sleep taking a toll.

What could be at the top of this miserable hillside that Joq couldn't have just told them about? It had better be worth the hike, or he'd take his bad mood out of the Other's hide, no matter how Lusahn felt about it.

It took another fifty yards of hard going before the trail finally leveled out. His three companions waited for him outside a narrow opening into the hillside. Nobody seemed in a hurry to go any farther, but he felt exposed out in the open. Even with his cloak back on, he felt like he stood out.

Once again Lusahn took charge. "So what do you have to show us, Joq?"

"Study the ground around you."

The bastard sure liked power games. Why couldn't he just point at whatever he wanted them to see? Maybe he should wipe that smug look off Joq's face for him. For Lusahn's sake, however, he'd refrain from starting another battle.

It didn't take long for him to see what Joq had found. Footprints—several sets of them that didn't belong in this world, because they were put there by humans. Others wore smooth-soled boots nothing like the athletic shoes that had made these tracks.

"Son of a bitch! So I'm not the first human to cross into your world." He knelt down to better study the prints. "Judging by the size of these, I'd guess three men crossed near here. I wish I could make casts of these prints. I have friends who could trace what brand of shoes have these patterns on them. It's not much to go on, but it would be a start."

"Come inside now." Joq pulled a small blue stone out of his pocket and held it out. Within seconds it began to cast a glow, enough to light their way into the cavern.

Inside, they all blinked rapidly to adjust to the dim interior. When Cullen could see clearly, he cursed. Camping gear was scattered around the small cavern; clearly someone had been staying on this side of the barrier for days at a stretch.

A small section of the barrier ran across the back wall, barely wide enough for one person to walk through. It was unlikely that the Others used it, since they crossed in groups. So where did it come out in his world? It had to be near where he'd crossed, somewhere in Seattle.

Now that they'd seen what he'd wanted them to, Joq backed toward the entrance. "We can't stay here long. There's no telling who's watching the entrance or when the humans will be back."

Joq might be done, but Cullen wasn't. The Other male could have simply told Lusahn about his findings, and she would have believed him. Why had he insisted on dragging both of them all the way up here to see a couple of sleeping bags and some footprints? Granted, the prints looked fresh. If they'd been there any length of time, the wind would have softened their edges, eventually filling them in completely.

He drew his sword and blocked the entrance, making it impossible for Joq to leave.

"Get out of my way, human!" Joq snarled, reaching for his own weapon.

"Not until you answer some questions." Cullen flexed his grip on the pommel of his sword, ready to use it if necessary.

"I don't answer to you."

Drawing herself up to her full height, Lusahn spoke with the full weight of her office. "Maybe not, but I'm a Sworn Guardian. You will answer to me."

Larem immediately positioned himself alongside the Sworn Guardian, his sword drawn and ready to protect her. The shock on Joq's face was priceless. He immediately lowered his blade, all his anger gone. He looked far older than he had only moments before.

"You needed to see for yourselves what has been going on. The humans are not just stealing our light, they are invading our world."

Cullen couldn't let that one pass. "Not likely. Judging by those footprints, there were two, maybe three, in your so-called invasion. Hell, that's not even much of a scouting expedition."

Joq sneered. "Three here, but there's you, too, human. How many more have crossed over without us knowing? Every warrior knows that the best way to defeat an enemy is to know the enemy. What are you doing here, but learning our ways and our weaknesses?"

Did the Other hope to deflect suspicion away from himself by directing it toward Cullen instead? He risked a glance in Lusahn's direction, but her focus was solely on Joq. Larem divided his attention between both Joq and Cullen, his expression too shuttered to read. Cullen didn't give a damn what he thought, but Lusahn might.

"Joq, I've already told you why Cullen came here, and at great risk to himself. These men," she said, pointing at the scattering of footprints with a sweeping gesture, "are the problem, not Cullen. Tell me what you know."

"Very well. You asked me if I knew anything about the theft, and this is what I know. Someone has been using this cave for illegal dealings. Very little goes on in this sector that the Guildmaster doesn't know about." He shot Cullen a narrow-eyed look. "At least not for long. I ran across the tracks in my wanderings, but I haven't actually seen anybody. Not yet, anyway. That's all I know, so now I'm leaving."

Cullen looked to Lusahn for approval. When she gave him an abrupt nod, he stepped aside and watched Joq stomp out of the cave. When the older male was out of sight, her shoulders slumped briefly before she turned to face Larem.

"Now I have to decide what to do about you." Her expression was grim. "I need your word that what you've learned here today won't go any further than this cave. Once we walk outside, you are not to say a word to the rest of our Blade or the Guild until I give you permission to do so."

"Do you think so little of me, that you think I would betray you?" The Other kicked a rock across the cavern, sending it ricocheting off a nearby wall. "I deserve better, Lusahn."

"I don't doubt you, Larem—but you have a family to consider. They have to come first. By dragging you into this mess, I've put them at risk, too. I was trying to avoid that."

It was time to step in. "You also have to know that she had no warning that I was going to show up on her doorstep. If Barak hadn't been injured, he would have been the one to come, which would have made things simpler."

Larem's laugh was nasty. "Simpler because she would have executed him herself for the traitor he is. The question is why she chose to let you live— especially since your people would not have afforded any of us the same courtesy. The one time we crossed to bring back our own traitors, we were met at sword point."

Cullen studied the Other's face. Had he been one of the three who'd fought Devlin while Cullen had faced off against Lusahn in the tunnels near Seattle? Maybe, perhaps even likely, but he couldn't remember. Most Others had such similar coloring that they all blurred together in battle.

And that was a good thing. Wholesale killing was hard enough without knowing the enemy as individuals that you might like—or even love.

"You were allowed to return to your home.

We'd prefer it if more of your people stayed there in the first place."

"Enough." Lusahn sheathed her sword and stepped between them. "We need to get back to town."

She led the way down the hillside, Cullen and Larem following in sullen silence. Going down was easier on his lungs, but the tension was as thick as the dust hanging in the air. He badly wanted to reach out to Lusahn, to offer her the comfort of his touch, but she hadn't shown any inclination to let him be close in the presence of her friends.

Even though he understood her reasons for maintaining distance, it hurt more than it should have based on their short acquaintance. How much worse would it feel like when the moon cycle ended and he went home, the barrier forever between them?

"Cullen Finley, pay attention!"

He stumbled into a halt just short of plowing into Lusahn, who had stopped in the middle of the trail. She was looking at him with a small smile playing at the corner of her mouth. Even Larem looked amused.

"Are you intent on running all the way to town?"

"Figured I need the exercise." He grinned at her, glad to see some of the life back in her eyes. "Seriously, did I miss something?"

"We need to think about the best way to return

to town. I left with one man; it might draw attention if I were to return with two."

Larem spoke up. "It would be less noticeable if he were to walk with me. We can circle around and approach from another direction. I will take him back to your house before joining you for patrol."

Cullen wasn't ready to trust Larem's motives. "What makes that better than you returning to town the same way you left it—alone—while the two of us walk back together?"

"The Guild sometimes watches for patterns in behavior. We want to avoid having them wonder who you are if I spend too much time in your company." A hint of color brushed Lusahn's cheeks. "They are not used to seeing me show much interest in males outside of my Blade and Joq."

Then for her sake, he would follow Larem. "Fine. I'll see you at the house."

"Good. Keep your hood up and your head down. You've grown careless in our company, and it won't be safe for you to do that in town."

For a second she leaned toward him, but then thought better of it. "Be careful, and I will see you when my patrol is done."

He watched as she walked away, looking so brave and confident and so damned alone. When she was out of sight, he looked over to see Larem watching him with barely concealed hostility.

"You will get her killed."

"Anyone who hurts her will face me." Cullen gripped the pommel of his sword, pulling it out a short distance to make his point.

Larem didn't look impressed. "And me, as well. Remember that, human. Hurt her, and you die."

"Fine. We understand each other. Now let's get a move on. I'm in no particular hurry, but you can't afford to be late."

D.J. barged into Devlin's office. "We need to talk."

"Not now, D.J. I'm busy."

"It can't wait." The antsy Paladin paced the floor, stopping long enough to take a knife down off the wall. After flipping it in the air a few times as he crisscrossed the room, he put it back and reached for another one.

"Damn it, D.J., if the government could harness your energy, they could light up the entire West Coast. Quit wearing out my carpet."

"Fine, but we need to talk." D.J. flopped down in one of the chairs facing Devlin's desk without waiting for an invitation.

Devlin looked at the never-ending mountain of paperwork that multiplied geometrically every time he left his office undefended, then sighed. "What's on your mind?"

D.J. leaned forward, a worried look on his face. "I can't find Cullen."

Devlin gave up and set his pen down. "I haven't seen him either, D.J. Maybe he doesn't want to be found."

The other Paladin shook his head. "When he goes off on his own to work, he always checks in periodically. We're supposed to be fine-tuning that software program we've been working on, but he hasn't come in. I e-mailed him twice and tried both his cell and his home number half a dozen times. No answer." D.J. scratched his head. "I even went by his house. No sign of him."

Though D.J. could be a pain in the ass at times, he wasn't one to cry wolf. If he said Cullen was missing, he was.

"Ask around and see when was the last time anyone saw him."

"Already did. No one has seen him since he picked up Barak and drove him to the tunnel. In fact, that snappy new red sports car Cullen just bought is still sitting in the parking garage, right where's it's been for the past day or so."

Now Devlin really was getting worried. Of all the Paladins, Cullen was the most levelheaded one. It wasn't like him not to check in when he was supposed to. Besides, he was damn proud of that car. He wouldn't leave it unattended unless something was seriously wrong.

"Who were the last ones to see Cullen?"

D.J. held up a hand and ticked the names off

on his fingers. "You, me, Lonzo, and Trahern. Barak, of course, since he was there in the tunnel with Cullen. If anyone else saw him after that, I haven't heard about it."

"Did you talk to Penn Sebastian? He's the one who told Barak about Lacey being kidnapped. If Cullen was still with Barak at that point, he'd know."

"Nope, I missed him, and Laurel wasn't letting Barak have visitors yet except for Lacey." D.J. jumped to his feet. "I'll go track down Penn. He may be in the lab with Barak and Lacey. If not, I'll keep looking."

Devlin reached for his pen. "Keep me posted."

"Will do." D.J. slammed the door behind him hard enough to rattle the weapons on the wall.

Devlin winced, wishing that D.J. would learn how to control some of that energy. In battle the man was a whirlwind of a fighter, especially with that throwing hammer he liked so much. But the rest of the time, it would be nice if he could tone it down a bit.

He stared at the door, hoping like hell that D.J. was wrong, and Cullen was just grabbing some downtime. He'd give his friend time to talk to Barak and Penn before calling in the troops. But from what D.J. had said, Cullen had already been missing for almost two days, and the trail was growing colder by the second.

His concentration shot, Devlin shoved the stack of paperwork to the side. Maybe his time would be better spent following D.J. over to the lab. If D.J. was right—and Devlin had a bad feeling that he was—there wasn't a minute to waste.

He picked up his cell, hit the speed dial for Trahern, and waited for his friend to pick up.

"Something's come up. Meet me at Laurel's lab in fifteen minutes." He hung up without waiting for Trahern's response. By the time he reached the outside door, he was running.

Chapter 7

"*W*hat makes your people try to leave your world? I know your star is fading, but we've never understood the why of it all." Cullen sat at the kitchen table, watching Lusahn put together a simple dinner of bread, cheese, and fresh vegetables.

She reached for the plates. "You've never bothered to ask that before, so why now?"

He took the plates from her and set the table as he tried to figure out how to answer her question.

"I guess we were too busy protecting our world to worry about it. The few who get past us go on binges of murdering anyone who gets in their way. We fight like hell to keep that from happening." He picked up the pitcher and filled everyone's glasses.

She set the platters of food on the table. "We've seen a few instances of that on our side, but not many. Most who seek the light manage to cross the barrier. If they don't make it on their first try, they keep at it."

"Why don't you stop them? Can't your Guild do something? Isn't there a cure of some kind?" He didn't mean to sound accusatory, but he'd spent his whole adult life fighting because of her people.

She jerked a stack of bowls off the shelf. "Don't you think we've tried? Why do you think we patrol the caverns? It sure isn't for the scenery!" She slammed the last bowl down. "I do not need your questions right now."

Considering the dark circles under her eyes and the weariness in her slumped shoulders, he could have picked a better time. "I'm sorry, Lusahn." He walked around the table to offer the comfort of a quick hug. "I know it's been a tough day, and last night wasn't exactly restful for you."

She leaned into the warmth of his body and sighed as his arms pulled her close. "You don't hear me complaining about last night, do you?"

"No, and that's a good thing." He pressed a soft kiss against her temple. "I know it was hard facing down both Joq and Larem. How did your patrol go this afternoon?"

"About as usual. We made our rounds and then spent the rest of our shift doing paperwork. I swear someone invents forms just to keep us busy."

He chuckled. "The top Paladin in Seattle has the same complaint. Whether he's requesting a new sword or a pack of pens, the paperwork has to be done exactly right. It takes him hours and hours just to keep up."

Her smile washed away some of the weariness in her eyes. "See? In some ways, we are not so different from your people."

He hid the urge to wince. It had been bad enough to get to know Barak as an individual he both liked and respected. But now he'd met Larem, Bavi and Shiri, and Lusahn herself. How could he look at the Others in the same way he always had— as little better than animals?

A movement at the kitchen door caught his attention. Shiri stood there, thumb in her mouth, her big eyes curious. She seemed unsure of her welcome.

"Come on in, little one." He held out his hand, inviting her to join the two of them.

When Lusahn smiled and nodded, Shiri came at a dead run, letting Cullen hoist her up between the two adults. Shiri tucked her head under Lusahn's chin but held on to Cullen's shirt. His heart did a slow roll as the two females settled trustingly in his arms. A surge of protectiveness washed through him. He would lay down his life without hesitation to keep the two of them safe, and Bavi as well.

Was this what family felt like? For a few seconds he let himself pretend it was real, that he belonged to them and they belonged to him, now and forever. Then Bavi walked in, and the atmosphere went from warm and cozy to cold and angry.

He snarled something at Lusahn, who flinched and slowly turned to face the angry young man. But she made no move to step away from him or to set Shiri down.

"Bavi," she said in English for Cullen's benefit, and speaking slowly for Bavi's, "show respect. We are not hurting your sister, nor are we trying to turn her against you."

Her remark startled Cullen. He'd assumed that Bavi didn't trust him around his sister because he was a Paladin. It hadn't occurred to him that the boy might feel threatened for a whole other reason.

He echoed Lusahn's feelings. "She is your sister, son. Nothing and no one can change that. I appreciate you and Lusahn sharing her with me for a little while."

At least this time Bavi didn't explode or try to drag his sister out of the room. Lusahn finally stepped away, taking Shiri with her. Cullen let them both go, knowing it was important for Bavi to know that Lusahn was on his side, that he and his sister were the important ones in this equation.

Cullen immediately took his accustomed seat at the table and waited for the other three to join him. It felt good to relax at the dinner table, enjoying the simple fare and the company of the three Others.

He frowned. The word *Other* jarred his conscience. They must have a name they called themselves that had more meaning than the one some nameless Paladin in the past had dubbed them with. Later, when the kids were asleep and Lusahn slipped downstairs again, he'd ask her. Well, not right away. He had other plans for them, ones he'd been working on since she'd left his bed during the early hours of the morning. But afterward, when they were both sated and weary, they could talk.

To get things moving in that direction, he picked up the bowl and passed it to Bavi.

Cullen was plotting something. She could see it in the way his eyes followed her every movement and how he managed to brush against her whenever he found an excuse, slowly setting her skin on fire. She ached in places that didn't bear thinking about, since she had chores to complete and children to get off to bed.

The star had barely set, too early to shoo Bavi off to his room. He'd suspect something was going on for sure. He was just beginning to tolerate Cullen's presence in their home; she didn't want to disturb the fragile peace for her own selfish needs.

But as soon as the children were both asleep for the night, she was going to extract her revenge. She hoped Cullen had conserved some of his strength after their strenuous hike up to the east tunnels, or he might not survive the night ahead.

Right now he was sitting at the table with Shiri, watching as the little girl struggled to build a tower of cards. He said it was supposed to be a house, but it didn't look like any building she'd ever seen. Still, it was fun to watch the two dark heads so close together as they celebrated each success and laughed at each failure when the cards came tumbling down.

Even Bavi had hung around, occasionally trying his hand at some of the fancy shuffling that Cullen had shown him. The boy was quick with his fingers, so he enjoyed a greater degree of success than his sister did. Cullen's teeth flashed white against the dark color of his whiskers, which looked scruffier every day he spent in her world. She liked the way his beard softened the sharp angles of his warrior's face.

She couldn't wait to rub her face against his whiskers, liking the way it felt against her skin, and not just on her face. Her body went warm and liquid, remembering a few particular moments from the night before.

Some of what she was thinking must have shown in her expression, because Cullen gave her a heated look and an impudent wink before looking away. Her favorite bowl slipped through her fingers, only luck and quick reflexes saving it from shattering on the stone floor. Naturally Cullen noticed, but he'd pay for that bit of laughter later—although he might just enjoy the punishment she had in mind.

He'd gathered up his cards and began spreading them out on the table in some sort of pattern. Bavi was watching over the top of his book whenever he didn't think Cullen would notice. He'd underestimated the Paladin.

"Bavi, would you like to learn this game?"

Cullen kept his eyes on the cards, giving the boy a chance to consider his answer without being pressured. For a man who had no children of his own, he had a surprising natural ease with them. Shiri, who was generally shy with strangers, had taken to Cullen immediately, and now he was slowly winning Bavi over.

When Bavi glanced in her direction, she gave him an encouraging nod. It was nice to see him willing to risk trusting another adult. Her only concern was that Cullen would be gone in a handful of days. He'd settled into their routine so seamlessly that it was hard to remember that he hadn't always been there, and it was painful knowing that he would never do so again.

She immediately turned back to drying dishes, planning to do some laundry next. Anything to keep from thinking about the future. When she left the room, Bavi was sitting next to Cullen and listening carefully to the rules for playing something called solitaire, a game for one person. Maybe she should learn the game herself. It would help while away the hours once the barrier went down and Cullen Finley returned home.

His lady was sad. Cullen wasn't sure what had put the sorrow in Lusahn's eyes, but he hated seeing it there. One minute she'd been giving him looks that almost had him panting; the next, she had walked out with such a sad expression on her face. Her kids seemed fine, so he had a sneaking suspicion that whatever was bothering her had to do with him.

"You catch on quickly, Bavi. Why don't you finish that game by yourself and then deal another one? I'll be back shortly in case you have any questions. I need to tell Lusahn something."

The boy nodded and pointed to a card for Shiri to move, who giggled at being able to help her big brother play.

It wasn't hard to find Lusahn. She stood at a window, staring out at the silver-white moon in the dark sky. Her arms were crossed over her waist, her shoulder resting against the wall. He paused, unsure of his welcome. After the day she'd had, she might want a few minutes to herself.

She was a warrior, though, and always aware of her surroundings. "The moon is beautiful tonight," she said.

"Yes, it is." He eased closer until her scent filled his senses and he could feel her warmth. "So are you."

"Flatterer."

But he could tell she was pleased. He closed the small distance between them, liking it when she relaxed back against him. The gentle press of her body had a predictable effect on his, but he wanted to offer comfort, not make demands.

"What's wrong, Lusahn? Is it something I did?"

She shook her head. "No, not exactly."

When she didn't go on, he pushed a little bit. "What does 'not exactly' mean? I can't fix it if I don't know what's got you down."

She sighed and snuggled closer. "I was thinking how good you are with Shiri and Bavi. That's a good thing, because they need reminders that adults can be trusted. It seems so natural to have you sitting there with them. Then it hit me how soon you will return to your own world. Shiri will have a hard time understanding where you've gone. I don't know how much she remembers about her parents, but it can't be good for her if the adults she loves keep disappearing from her life."

He buried his face in the dark silk of her hair. "It's no comfort, but it will rip my heart out to leave the three of you behind."

She turned in his arms. "It is some comfort that

you will be leaving your heart here, since you will be taking a big piece of ours with you."

He caught her chin with the side of his finger and tilted it to the perfect angle for a long, slow kiss, one meant to soothe. But holding her, kissing her, even making love to her, wasn't going to be enough to heal the gaping wound that would be his life once he went home.

He couldn't stay without endangering her and the children, even if his honor would allow it. So he'd go home—but he wouldn't be the same man who had so naively crossed the barrier such a short time ago.

When she broke off the kiss, she whispered, "You are only part of what's wrong. I'm upset about Joq, as well as the members of my Blade. I'm angry that someone is robbing my world and my people for something as shallow as money. And I worry about the children. I can't really replace the parents they had."

"I've said this before, and I mean it: you're a terrific mother to them. Remember, the parents they had deserted them." He let some of his anger show. "And I keep thinking I might have been the one to kill them."

She laid a finger across his lips, shushing him. "Once the madness strikes our people, they are already gone. Nothing will stop them from trying to cross into the light of your world."

"What causes them to act that way? Is it some kind of sickness?"

"Not exactly. All we know is that the victims live normal lives up to that point, gradually becoming more and more sensitive to both cold and darkness. Then one day they snap and are driven to try to escape our world. Once that happens, there is no turning back."

That scenario sounded all too familiar: different symptoms, different cause, but the same outcome. Paladins fought the battles they were born to fight, dying over and over with no apparent change in their physiology, until they died one time too many. When that happened, they awoke as ravening monsters, intent on killing anyone who got in their way.

He knew that the Paladins shared a few common genes with the Others, so it was only logical that some form of the same malady would afflict both worlds. Son of a bitch! Why hadn't someone made that connection before now? Or if they had, why hadn't someone told the Paladins?

The answer was obvious. The Regents probably thought it was imperative that the Paladins think of the enemy as monsters, to keep them fighting the Others without question. Maybe the Others *were* monsters once they crossed the barrier, but they certainly didn't start out that way. He had the proof right there in his arms.

"Did I say something to upset you?"

Lusahn's soft voice jerked him back from the dark path his thoughts had taken. He gave her a soft squeeze and nuzzled her hair, soothing his spirit with her feminine scent. He couldn't do anything about his questions until he returned home, so he wouldn't allow them to cast shadows on the short time he had left here.

"No, I'm fine."

She looked unconvinced, but let it slide. "I should get back to the children. It's almost time for Shiri to start getting ready for bed, and Bavi likes to join us while I read to her. The books are too young for him, but I think it brings back memories of a better time."

"You're giving him more good memories, Lusahn. Don't forget that."

She raised herself up to plant a soft kiss on his mouth, one that was full of promise. "I have a few special plans for tucking *you* into bed tonight, too, Cullen Finley."

He squeezed her close again. "I can't wait. In fact, I think I'll head on downstairs and stay out of your way. Wouldn't want to slow you down."

"See you soon."

She sashayed off, leaving him with his tongue hanging out. Damn, that woman sure knew how to move.

• • •

Cullen checked his watch for the tenth time in thirty minutes. What was keeping Lusahn? There hadn't been a single sound from upstairs in almost an hour.

Had she decided against joining him? That didn't make sense. Her last words to him had been full of sultry promise, and she wasn't the kind of woman to play games. If she had issues, she would have been right up in his face about them.

Was there a problem with one of the kids? That would explain her absence, but not the silence. If she needed help, or even if she didn't, she would let him know that plans had changed.

It was time to investigate.

He kicked his shoes off, knowing he could move more silently in his stocking feet. He picked up his sword and started up the stairs. The hinges on the door creaked softly, but there was no reaction. He listened for several seconds, trying to discern any movement in the house.

The silence was damned worrisome.

He eased through the doorway and checked out the kitchen. The dishes had been dried and put away; nothing looked out of place, and the front door was locked. The living room was next. All quiet there, too.

Bavi was right where he should be, curled up and sound asleep in his bed. That left Lusahn and Shiri. He pushed the door to Lusahn's room open.

It was empty, her bed undisturbed. His steps quickened right along with his pulse. Intellectually he knew it was unlikely that anything was wrong, but with adrenaline pumping through his veins, his need to protect was running full bore.

As soon as he peeked into Shiri's small room, he slumped with relief. The little girl was sitting up in bed, flipping the pages of a well-worn book, whispering the story to herself. Lusahn was curled up on the edge of the bed, sound asleep.

He set his sword down in the hallway, not wanting to scare the little girl. When he crept into her room, she looked up from her book and put her hands over her ears and shook her head, her way of telling him not to make any noise.

Cullen smiled at her and mimed picking up Lusahn and carrying her to her own bed. Shiri nodded her approval and obligingly moved away from Lusahn, giving him room to work. He worked his arms around her shoulders and under her knees and swept her up off the bed. She sighed and snuggled into his chest.

With some careful maneuvering, he managed to carry her out of the room without bumping her head on the door frame or waking her up. When he reached her room, he realized he should have turned back her covers first. Luckily, Shiri had followed him and took care of that herself. He couldn't strip off Lusahn's clothes with the little girl watching, so he just removed her boots and pulled the covers up over her.

Then Shiri took his hand and led him back into her room. She handed him the book and climbed back in bed, clearly wanting him to read to her.

"I don't speak your language." He held up his hands, hoping she'd understand what he was trying to tell her.

Shiri smiled, patted the bed beside her, inviting him to sit down anyway. Then she took the book back and pretended to read it to him. From watching her, he realized that she wasn't paying any attention to the words, but that didn't slow her down. He nodded in what seemed liked appropriate places until they reached the last page and she closed the book.

He took his cue from her and stood to awkwardly tuck the blankets in around her. Evidently he did a passable job, because she closed her eyes and settled in to sleep.

That left him the sole person awake, with the long hours of the night stretching out before him. He was too keyed up to sleep, at least in that lonely bed downstairs. His body was almost painfully aware of the woman curled up in the room right across the hall.

Lusahn would probably rip into him in the morning, but there was no way he was going to miss the chance to hold her in his arms. He blew out the light in Shiri's room and picked up his sword out in the hall before making his way to the far side of Lusahn's bed.

He stripped down to his skin and slid in beside her. Moving slowly so as not to wake her up, he eased across the bed to cuddle against her long, elegant back. With his arm across her waist and his face snuggled next to the back of her neck, he gradually relaxed. With the warmth of her body and the sweet scent of her skin surrounding him, he slept.

There was a hand on her breast. She wasn't fully awake, but enough that she knew she wasn't imagining things. And her legs were tangled up with someone else's. The room was too dark to see, but without a doubt it was Cullen Finley who was crowding her almost off the edge of the bed.

She'd planned on spending the night with him, just not in her own bed. That lumpy mattress in the basement wasn't as comfortable as hers, but it did offer more privacy. When had their plans changed?

The last thing she remembered was sitting on Shiri's bed as she and Bavi took turns reading. Then he'd gone off to his own bed. She didn't remember anything after that—especially why she had on all of her clothes, while she strongly suspected her companion was naked.

When she reached behind her to test her theory, Cullen immediately rose up to answer her un-spoken questions. "You fell asleep on Shiri's bed. She came with me to help tuck you in, so I left your clothes on. I didn't want to freak her out."

Sweet man. She stretched and turned to face him. "So what's stopping you now?"

His teeth gleamed whitely in the darkness. "I had to take my own clothes off, lady. I'm waiting for you to do the same so I can watch."

She couldn't help but laugh at his outrageous de-mand. "You won't be able to see much in the dark."

"I've got great night vision and a well-developed imagination." He sat up, leaning against the wall, his hands behind his head. "Go on. I'm waiting."

All right, two could play at this game. She left the bed to light a small candle, casting everything in a soft glow, enough to push the shadows back to the corners of the room. Then she stood at the end of the bed, out of Cullen's reach but where he could see her.

She started by undoing her braids, shaking her head to send her hair cascading down past her shoulders. Then turned her back to him as she bent over and eased her trousers slowly down her legs. He moaned, and she smiled.

She tossed the pants aside and then started on her tunic. One by one, the buttons slipped free, until she could slide the garment off her shoulders and down to the floor. Finally, all that remained was the thin undershirt she wore, and her panties. Before she could remove those, Cullen held out his hand.

"Come here and let me help you with those."

She crawled up the bed, straddling his lap. Judging by the strength of his erection, he had been more than pleased with her little show. He immediately filled his hands with her breasts, gently kneading them, abrading her nipples with the soft fabric of her shirt.

"Kiss me."

His command was a deep growl, his mouth hot, wet, and demanding as their tongues dueled. She rocked against him, riding the ridge of his penis through the sheets and her panties, driving them both crazy.

"I need your skin against mine," he murmured.

She held up her arms, letting him peel her undershirt over her head. He rewarded her by suckling her breasts as she threaded her fingers through his hair and pressed him closer. His whiskers felt softer than before, and she loved the feel of them against her.

His hands followed the curve of her waist down to slip inside the waist of her panties. One hand cupped her bottom while the other eased down the front. She moaned and threw her head back, rocking against the sweet pressure of his fingers. When he delved inside her slick folds to test her readiness, she wanted to howl with pleasure as she strained to break through the pressure building inside her.

"Come for me, Lusahn. I want to feel you come." He increased the rhythm and pressure at the exact right moment to send her over that last hurdle, throwing her into a vortex of sensation.

She collapsed against his broad chest for a few seconds, but only long enough to catch her breath. It was his turn. Or more correctly, hers. Smiling, she inched back down his legs, taking the sheet with her.

"Oooh, look what I found." She wrapped her fingers around the hard length of him and gently squeezed.

Cullen's hips flexed, his reaction pleasing her. She tried it again, this time a little firmer, a little quicker.

"Lusahn, you're killing me." He fisted the sheets as he thrust himself up in her hands again.

"Not yet, but I'm working on it."

She stretched out beside him so that her tongue could join the party. She gave a few quick flicks and then one tantalizingly slow lick from top to bottom. He grew harder, bigger, making her want the whole length of him inside her.

"Again!" he demanded. "More!"

Taking him in her mouth, she pleasured them both by pushing him to the limit.

Finally, he pulled her up and kissed her before turning her onto her back and settling between her legs. He slowly worked his way down her body, stopping to kiss the curve on the underside of her breasts. Then he pressed his lips against the damp heat at the juncture of her legs. Even through her panties, the heat of his breath went right to the core of her.

"Take me, Cullen," she panted.

"I've got a few things I want to try first."

He eased off her panties so he could run his tongue right up the center of her. She almost jack-knifed off the bed at the warm sensation. He laughed, the vibration sending another thrill through her.

Finally, when she feared for her sanity, he rose up over her and slowly thrust inside her. His thick length stretched her almost to the point of pain, but her body quickly adjusted to the sweet invasion.

"Am I hurting you?" He rocked against her gently, pushing in just that much farther.

She smiled up at him and ran her hands up his arms to hold on to the strength of his shoulders. "Not at all. Give me everything you have," she whispered, squeezing him gently with her inner muscles.

That did it. He began moving inside her, picking up speed and power until his hips were pounding up and down, the slap of his flesh against hers adding to the storm building between them.

In a surprise move, he rolled over, hardly

breaking rhythm as he pushed up inside her, his hands playing over her body. She rested her hands on his chest and met each thrust with her own. How could they survive this? It was too much and not enough, yet she wanted more.

"Cullen!"

"I know, honey, I know." His dark eyes smiled as he rolled them back over one last time, and he put even more strength into his passion, this time weaving his fingers through hers, giving her an anchor to hold on to as the world around them burst into streams of color and light.

Then he gathered her up in his arms and let their bodies melt into each other as sleep claimed them both.

Chapter 8

Cullen leaned against the wall to pull on his pants, not bothering with underwear since he was going right back to bed when he got downstairs.

Lusahn stretched and sat up, blinking sleepily. "Where are you going?"

"My bed." He felt around on the floor for his shirt and socks.

"What's the matter? Do I snore?" She stretched out on his side of the bed and watched him pull his shirt on over his head.

"Yep, that's it. You may be beautiful, and you're the best lover I've ever had, but I can't take the noise." He chuckled as he picked up his shoes.

"Beast!" She tossed a pillow at his head. "Seriously, though, where are you going?"

Was that insecurity he heard in her voice? She'd been sleeping so soundly that he hadn't wanted to wake her up to tell her why he was leaving. Maybe he should have.

He sat down on the edge of the bed and captured her hand with his. "I didn't think you'd want Bavi or Shiri to find me in here, so I was going back downstairs before they woke up."

"That was thoughtful of you."

"I try." He kissed her fingertips, one at a time.

"Keep that up, and you're going to have to take all those clothes right off again." She made no move to tug her hand free from his grasp as he stood up.

"Don't tempt me—unless you mean it." He paused at the side of the bed, torn between wanting to avoid upsetting the children and the overwhelming urge to shed his clothes and climb back in.

When she didn't insist he join her, he reluctantly released her hand, knowing it was for the best. "Get some rest. Tomorrow will be another long day."

"Do you know something I don't?" She yawned and stretched, testing his willpower even more.

"No, but tomorrow night is hours away. Keeping my hands to myself all day long is going to put a strain on my—"

"Your what?" she demanded as she deliberately let the blanket drop down. Even in the low light, he got an eyeful that had him groaning.

"It's just plain mean to tease a man like that, Lusahn," he groused. "And you'll pay for it later."

She laughed as she snuggled back down into

the bed. "I hope so, Cullen Finley. I truly do."

By the time he got downstairs, he was too awake to go back to sleep. The sky seemed to be getting lighter, signaling the start of a new day. Rather than waste his time tossing and turning, he decided to work out.

He started with the stretching routine he'd learned watching both Barak and Lusahn. Once he was warmed up, he went through drills using his own sword before giving in to the temptation to try out Barak's blades again.

Would Lusahn care? He didn't think so, since she'd invited him to try them out when they'd sparred together. The weapon felt good in his hand, but working with a single edge was a challenge. Gradually, though, his movements became smoother, more second nature, until he was lost in the sheer pleasure of the dance.

By the time he stopped to take a breather, he'd gained an audience. Bavi sat on the steps, watching him with an enigmatic look on his face. He wished he knew more about talking to a kid, but his experience was limited to young Paladins who already knew the score.

"Good morning, Bavi. I hope I didn't wake you up." Considering where he'd spent the night, he really, *really* hoped he hadn't.

Bavi shook his head. "No, I wanted a drink." He mimed the action to make sure Cullen understood. "I heard you from the door. Came to see."

"A glass of juice sounds good about now." He wiped the sweat off his forehead and started to put the blades away.

"I bring."

Bavi was off and running before Cullen could respond. He came back in just seconds, carrying a tall glass of cold juice. When he reached the bottom of the steps he didn't hesitate to approach Cullen, a far cry from the anger he'd exhibited at first.

Cullen drained half the glass without stopping. It tasted good and went a long way toward restoring his energy. He sat down on the bed, and to his surprise, Bavi joined him.

"Do you wake up this early often?"

Bavi shook his head. "No. I was dreaming."

Cullen wasn't sure he wanted to know what kind of dream had jarred the boy out of a deep sleep, but he had to ask. "What about?"

Bavi's eyes dropped to stare at the blanket on the bed where his fingers were tugging at a loose thread. "My parents. It was a good dream about how we were. You know, before."

Damn, he'd been afraid of that. "You must miss them."

"I know they must be dead." Despite his words, there was a note in his voice that warned Cullen that the boy was hoping he'd contradict him.

Better to be truthful than to lead the boy on, no

matter how much it hurt both of them. "They must be, Bavi, or else they'd be here with you. I know if you were my son, nothing short of death would keep me away."

Bavi's head shot up, his eyes wide. Clearly Cullen's bald statement of the facts had surprised him. "They needed the light."

Cullen nodded grimly. "That's what Lusahn told me. Sounds like it was something they couldn't help."

"I will follow them someday. So will Shiri." The boy went back to fingering the blanket, his shoulders slumped in grim resignation.

What could Cullen say to that, especially if it were true? Lusahn hadn't mentioned that the craving for light was genetic, but it sounded as if Bavi believed that it was. God, how could these people live, knowing that madness followed by death at the hands of the Paladins was all that awaited them?

Without knowing the facts, there wasn't much he could say by way of comfort for Bavi. Someone had to have answers, or else should damn well be looking for them.

"You in the mood to work with the blades? I could use a sparring partner."

He was pretty sure Lusahn wouldn't be happy about it, but he had to do something to put some life back in Bavi's eyes. The boy glanced up the stairs, obviously thinking along the same lines.

"Let me worry about Lusahn, son. If she gets mad at anyone, it will be me." Rather than give Bavi too much time to think about it, he gave him his orders. "Stretch out your muscles, and we'll get started."

With the energy of the young, Bavi whipped through Lusahn's system of stretches in record time. The promise of weapons practice was clearly enough to motivate the male of the species.

"Take this sword and hold it this way," Cullen said, showing Bavi the correct placement of his fingers and thumb on the pommel.

"That's good. You're a natural at this, Bavi."

Next, he demonstrated the first in a series of movements designed to improve arm strength and control. With only a few repetitions, Bavi showed improvement. Then he got cocky and whacked Cullen a good one on his arm. It hurt like hell and had Cullen cursing.

The boy instantly dropped the blade and backed away, his already pale complexion ashen. "Sorry. Sorry. Sorry."

Cullen ignored the stinging pain, more worried about what had spooked the young Other. "It's all right, Bavi. Accidents happen, which is why we use blunted blades. Now come on back and pick up the sword. I want to run through that movement again, to show you where you went wrong. After that, if you want to quit for the day, put the blade away with the care it deserves."

Who the hell had scared the boy so much that a simple accident had him running for cover? Maybe the reaction was left over from Bavi's days on the streets, running from the authorities and trying to provide for his sister. Whatever the reason, Cullen burned to go after *someone* in this dismal world for not taking better care of their children.

Not that his own world was any better. Son of a bitch, why was it always the young and helpless who had to suffer? In the short time he had left in this world, he was going to do his damnedest to make sure Bavi learned the rudiments of self-defense. Hopefully Lusahn or one of her Blade would pick up where Cullen left off, although he didn't much like the idea of leaving the job half done.

Bavi slowly picked up the blade and checked it over for damage.

Cullen smiled and nodded his approval. "Always respect your weapons. These might only be practice blades, but it's an important habit to get into."

"Your arm?"

"Don't sweat it. It stung, that's all. Besides, I heal fast." He held out his arm, where the mark was already fading away. "Now, let's see that movement again."

It took a few minutes for Bavi to get back into the rhythm of things, but finally he was performing the steps smoothly. Cullen had been hearing footsteps overhead for several minutes, so it was time to wrap things up.

"I suspect breakfast is almost ready. Better put the blades away now." He handed his to Bavi, trusting him to handle the weapons with care. When they were safely back in their box, he held out his hand to Bavi.

"Thank you for the workout."

Bavi studied Cullen's hand for a second or two, unfamiliar with the human custom of shaking hands. Cullen reached out to grasp Bavi's hand and gave it a firm squeeze. Bavi immediately squeezed his in response.

"That's it. I don't know about you, but I've worked up a big appetite."

Food was something all growing boys understood. "I think I'll need seconds, maybe even thirds."

Cullen laughed as he followed Bavi up the stairs. "We'd better warn Lusahn to add more food to the pot."

Breakfast was a surprisingly noisy affair. Normally Bavi made sure that Shiri had plenty to eat before diving into his own meal. This time, however, he chattered excitedly about his impromptu workout with Cullen. Lusahn still wasn't comfortable with teaching Bavi weaponry, but she'd never seen the boy so animated before.

Cullen kept up a steady stream of answers to Bavi's questions, but every so often he shot Lusahn a questioning look to see how she was reacting to the sudden change in their relationship. She considered letting him worry a bit, but she couldn't fault him for trying to reach out to Bavi. Nor could she deny a bit of jealousy that he'd been so successful on his first try. Cullen Finley wasn't just good *to* Bavi and Shiri; he was good *for* them, as well.

How would she survive the pain of losing him? The two men she cared most about, Cullen and Barak, would both live out their lives on one side of the barrier while she would exist on the other. What she wouldn't give to make things turn out differently. But even if Cullen were willing to stay, she couldn't hide him in the basement forever. That would be no kind of life for either of them.

"What time do you have patrol today?" Cullen's question jerked her attention back to him.

"I told my Blade to take the day off. I'm going to retrace our route from yesterday."

"Any particular reason?"

She began clearing the table. "I keep thinking we may have missed something yesterday because we were in such a hurry. I'd like time to look around without Larem and Joq hovering."

"I'm coming with you." His voice dropped to a whisper, laced with what sounded like a bit of anger. "I have some questions that I don't want to ask where Bavi might overhear me."

She had no problem with him coming, since she'd need someone to stand guard while she searched the cave. Besides, he might glean some information that she'd miss simply because the cave's inhabitants were from his world, not hers.

"Fine. We should leave soon."

"What about the kids? Will they be all right? Do you always leave them alone so much?"

They'd been alone the past two days without him commenting. What had changed? "Bavi knows how to take care of Shiri. At first I hired a woman to come in, but that didn't work out. They seem happier alone than with a stranger in the house."

"I was a stranger, but you let me stay in the house with them."

True, but she hadn't thought of him as a stranger to her from the first time they'd crossed swords. "I trust you, even if at first they didn't."

Her answer seemed to please him. She brushed the back of her fingers across his cheek, liking the feel of his beard. It was softer now that it was getting some length to it.

"Be especially careful with your hood today. Men of my world don't wear beards."

He scratched his jaw. "I can't wait to shave it off. It itches."

Yet another reminder that soon their paths

would part. "Let's get our things. I'd like to get back by early afternoon; I need to go to the market before it closes."

Cullen frowned. "I wish I could do something to help with the grocery bill, but I'm afraid my money is no good here."

His pride was likely hurting because of his dependency on her for everything: food, shelter, protection, sex. Well, he probably didn't mind that last one, but he was a warrior with a strong male's pride. He wouldn't like not being able to provide for his own needs.

"Your people took in my brother. I may be angry with him for leaving, but I am glad that he found shelter and worthy friends." Barak had never fit in their world anyway. He asked too many questions that had no answers.

"I'll get the cloak and my sword and meet you at the door." Cullen disappeared down the stairs.

What had happened this morning to put that worrisome note in his voice and questions in his mind? Had the boy said something that set off Cullen's protective instincts?

Well, Cullen wasn't shy. Once they were past the boundaries of town, he would tell her what was bothering him. And if he didn't, she'd pound it out of him. She smiled to herself. Many of the males in her world were intimidated by a female who fought well enough to be one of the Sworn

Guardians. Cullen wasn't used to fighting alongside a female, but he obviously didn't find her strength and abilities unattractive. It was just one more thing she liked about him.

He was coming back upstairs, and she'd yet to even buckle on her sword. She hustled down the hallway to find Bavi, who was helping Shiri straighten her bed. Lusahn stuck her head into the room.

"Cullen and I are going on patrol, but we won't be gone all day. When we get back, the three of us will go to market. How does that sound?"

"Yes, let's go!" Shiri immediately started to put her boots on.

Lusahn knelt down to look Shiri in the eye. "Not now, little one. Later, after lunch."

"Now!" Shiri's lip stuck out as she pouted.

Bavi interceded. "Not now. You promised to help me practice the game Cullen Finley taught us, remember?"

Her sunny disposition restored, Shiri gave him a bright smile. "Cards!"

Bavi took her hand and led her down the hallway, promising her that she could deal the first game. Lusahn hoped Cullen's cards were sturdier than they looked, although he probably couldn't bring himself to be mad at Shiri. The little girl clearly had won his heart.

She grabbed her sword and her cloak. She didn't

always wear the cloak while on patrol, but folks tended to see what they expected to. If they saw the two of them walking through town with their weapons and cloaks, they'd assume she was on Guild business with one of her Blade along as escort.

At the door, Cullen stood back to let her go out first, a courtesy her Blade rarely allowed her. She glanced up and down the road before Cullen joined her on the path. All appeared quiet, though she knew better than to assume that no one was watching. Had Larem and the others of her Blade listened to her when she'd told them to stay away today? She hoped so. She'd meant what she'd told Larem about not wanting them to become enmeshed in her problems.

The two of them set off at a brisk pace. She'd feel a lot better when they reached the hills outside town, taking a roundabout way to the caves to bypass the road to Joq's house. She was still angry with him for yesterday.

Their route took them by the Guild. For once, there was no one outside who might have felt compelled to challenge her. The members of the Guild were few enough in number that they all knew one another's business. If she had the day off, she had no good reason to be on patrol. Even if they didn't question her in person, they might report her behavior to the Guildmaster. Right now she wanted nothing to do with any of them—not until she knew who could be trusted. Once she figured out whether the Guildmaster was involved in the theft of the blue jewels, she'd know more what she should do.

Cullen seemed to sense her mood, remaining silent with his hood pulled forward, his head tipped down slightly to keep his face shadowed. After they passed the Guild, they turned west. If Cullen wondered why they were going in the opposite direction of the caves, he had the sense to keep his questions to himself.

She waited until they'd walked for a good distance past the edge of town before beginning a gradual circle back around in the opposite direction, taking a higher route through the edge of the hills. If anyone was following them, she might be able to spot them in the valley below.

"Expecting company?" Cullen leaned in closer, looking down the hillside, squinting against the midday star, when she paused to look down for the third time.

"Not especially, but I wasn't expecting Larem to follow us yesterday, either." She turned back to the path, crisscrossing the hillside to reach the top. "There's not much we can do if my Blade gets it in their heads that I need protection."

"How would you explain me to the other two?"

Cullen sounded more curious than concerned. He wasn't breathing hard, so he was finally acclimating to the air. It would be so easy to forget that he wasn't of her world when he learned to fit in with such ease.

"I couldn't—not in any way they'd believe. And if I told them the truth, they would have to face the same choices as Joq and Larem: turn me in or die at my side." She shivered. It was time to change the subject. "You said you had questions."

Cullen picked up a little speed and kept his eyes firmly on the path ahead of them. She knew he'd heard her, so why the sudden silence? They marched on, neither one ready to be the first to speak. At the pace Cullen was setting, they'd reach the cave far sooner than she'd expected to. Fine. But once they gleaned what information they could from the footprints and the equipment, she'd find out what had him looking so grim.

He was being a jackass, and he knew it. It wasn't Lusahn's fault that he had questions he needed to ask, and she likely had answers he didn't want to hear. He'd crossed the barrier telling himself that Barak's sister deserved better than a hastily scrawled note to tell her why her brother wasn't coming.

The reality was that he had acted on impulse, wanting to see if the Other female was as striking as he'd remembered. She was beautiful, all right— but she was so much more than that. Worse yet,

her people weren't monsters but a group of individuals, some good, some bad, the same as their
cousins in his world.

His belief system had been shaken to the core,
the burden of all the Others he'd killed weighing
him down. Even if he was innocent of the deaths of
Bavi's parents, he was guilty of so many more.

He shoved all that shit to the back of his mind,
where it wouldn't cloud his thinking. He hadn't seen
any sign that they were being followed, but neither
of them knew what they might walk into when they
reached the caves. He hoped Lusahn would be con-
tent with another quick walk-through, because he
had a bad feeling about that place. Some of the
tracks had looked older, which meant whoever it
was had made more than one trip into this world.

Lusahn felt confident that the barrier was stable
for the time being, but she'd also admitted that her
ability to read it wasn't as strong as her brother's. If
she was wrong they could be walking into a hornet's
nest, armed only with swords to face an enemy who
could be carrying automatic weapons. Blades were
effective only when the fighting was up close.

Bullets could kill from a distance, which meant
he and Lusahn were already vulnerable to attack.
He wanted to shove her to safety behind the cluster of boulders they just passed and go on alone—
like she'd let him get away with that! Knowing her,
she'd try to shove him behind the boulders instead.

It was taking some mental adjustments to get used to having a female partner, but eyeing her long-legged gait with pleasure, he had to admit that there were some definite perks.

He recognized the bend in the trail up ahead. They were almost exactly where he'd tackled Larem the day before, and he looked back down the trail again to make sure there was no one in sight.

"I think we're alone this time." Lusahn scanned the trail, both above and below. "I think one of us would have caught sight of anyone following."

"Maybe, but that doesn't mean there isn't a surprise party waiting for us in the caves." He drew his sword. "Let me go first to check things out."

"Why you?" Her sword was drawn, too.

"Because you know the area better than I do, and can circle around from another direction without drawing as much attention."

She wasn't buying it, not for a second. "You can't stand between me and danger, Cullen. It is my world, my job."

"They," he said nodding in the direction of the caves, "are from my world, which makes it my job."

Evidently they each had an equal share of stubbornness. They got into a stare-down match, neither one willing to be the first to blink. Finally Cullen gave in, recognizing the stupidity of paying too much attention to their egos and none at all to the potential danger up ahead.

"Fine. We both go, but be careful."

"As long as you promise to do the same."

She stepped close enough to give him a hug, which was awkward with each of them holding a sword. Even so, just that little bit of contact had him aching for so much more.

"Let's get this over with."

They worked the rest of the way up the hill, alternating the lead. Once the cave was in sight, they watched the entrance for several minutes before making their final approach.

At the mouth of the cave they stopped to listen, but there was only silence. Cullen knelt down to study the ground. "Somebody's been back through here since we left yesterday." He pointed toward several footprints that had been made by the kind of boots he and Lusahn were wearing. "Those are ours, but look here."

She leaned down to study the prints he was pointing to. "Those are human shoe prints, aren't they?"

"Yeah, and they overlap ours here, here, and there."

Lusahn's response was short and pungent, clearly a curse even if he didn't understand the words. "I should have posted guards."

"And they could have stood here on the hillside for days or even weeks before seeing anything." He ducked inside the cave. The camping gear was still piled against the wall, but the air smelled of smoke. Someone had had a campfire burning recently.

"Did you feel the barrier go down?"

She studied the narrow strip of colorful energy shimmering near the back wall. "No, but maybe this area is too small for me to feel from a distance. I'm not as strong as Barak."

Now he cursed. They weren't getting anywhere with this investigation, and his time here was running out.

He went outside to study the footprints again. After several seconds, he realized that while two sets led out of the cave, only one went back in. Someone from his world was still on this side of the barrier. If he could get a good look at the man, he should be able to track the bastard down back in Seattle. Once they had him under surveillance they might be able to catch his buddies, as well.

"We need to follow these tracks. They lead away from the cave in that direction." He had a bad feeling they would lead right to Joq's cabin. For Lusahn's sake, he hoped he was wrong.

Following the tracks took a lot of concentration and second-guessing the man's intentions. Most of the time they had only a fragment of a print to verify they were headed in the right direction. Lusahn had grown quieter, the closer they got to Joq's cabin. Cullen wanted to comfort her, but didn't know how. If her mentor had betrayed her trust so close upon the heels of Barak doing the same, it might shatter her.

When they reached the small rise overlooking the cabin, Cullen stopped. The tracks continued down the dusty path straight toward the front door.

"This might not mean anything, Lusahn."

"It means something, Cullen Finley. Do not try to spare my feelings. If Joq has betrayed my people, he will pay." She shoved past Cullen, ready to march right down to her friend's home.

Snagging her arm, Cullen spun her back around. "You don't know that he has done anything other than show us where my people are crossing into your world. Maybe they tracked him back here."

She flinched. "Do you think they've . . ." Her words trailed off as once again she started for the house, this time with stealth and a drawn sword.

"Let me look first." *In case Joq is dead* went unspoken, but she knew anyway. He made a circular motion with his hand. "Why don't you circle around to see if you can pick up a trail leaving here."

"All right, but know that if Joq is . . ." Her voice cracked. "I will avenge him. Honor demands his killer's death."

If there was one thing a Paladin understood, it was the thirst for his enemy's blood when a friend died too soon. "I'll push back my hood if it's safe for you to come in."

"Don't take too long." She grabbed the front of his cloak and yanked him close for a rough kiss. "Be careful."

"You, too." He kissed her again before giving her a gentle shove in the opposite direction to the house. When he was sure she was going with the plan, he studied the small cabin, looking for any signs of life.

Nothing.

If the bench outside the front door hadn't been lying in the dirt with two of its legs snapped off, the whole scene would have looked peaceful. With no good cover to offer protection, he gave up caution for speed and ran the last few yards up to the narrow window on the near side of the cabin.

The interior of the cabin hadn't fared any better than the bench. He sidled around to the door, almost certain that whoever had done the damage was either gone or dead. For Lusahn's sake, he hoped that Joq had survived the fight.

But if the son of a bitch had done something that would endanger Lusahn, Cullen would gut him.

He spun through the front door, sword at the ready. The inside of the cabin looked as if a tornado had torn through the place, shattering dishes and overturning the furniture. Either there'd been

a hell of a fight, or someone had searched the
place with violent thoroughness.

The only good news was that there was no dead
body anywhere in sight.

"Is he all right?"

Damn it, he'd told her to stay outside until he
signaled her that all was safe! "He's not here, and I
don't remember giving you the okay to come inside."

"I couldn't wait."

There was such sorrow mixed with relief in her
eyes that he couldn't stay mad. He let her look her
fill while he used a broken table leg to poke
around in the debris littering the floor.

"I wonder what he was looking for."

Lusahn did a slow turn around the room. "I
don't know, but I doubt he found it. If Joq had
something of value to hide, he wouldn't have kept
it in the house. This place is too small to hide anything bigger than your fist."

That's what he'd thought, too. "Find any interesting tracks outside?"

"No. Only the one set heading this way, which
looked human. The only fresh tracks leaving were
made by the same person, which makes no sense."

Unless the intruder walked in wearing shoes
from Cullen's world and left still wearing them.
Maybe there was only the one set because the
wearer was Joq? Always more questions than
answers.

"Let's get out of here."

Lusahn protested, "But he could be somewhere close by! We should look."

"All right, but I'm not liking this whole scene. I'll feel better when we get back to the house and the children."

He took off at a slow lope, determined to make quick work of their hunt. The barren countryside offered little in the way of shelter, making the search go quickly. When they met up again near the path back toward town, neither had seen any sign of Joq or the intruder. He hated the defeat in Lusahn's posture.

"Let's go on home and eat something. Afterward, we can make plans."

As the cabin disappeared behind them, Lusahn gave it one last look. "If your people have harmed Joq, they will die on my sword." She brought her chin up in determination.

He gave her a grim smile. "Your enemies are my enemies; my sword is yours to command."

"You are a man who understands honor, Cullen Finley."

"I understand revenge even better."

"Me, too."

"Damn it, Laurel, I need to talk to him." Devlin could have muscled his way into the lab, but he'd never use his strength against Laurel that way. He had too much respect for her as a healer, and loved her too much as a woman for that. Besides, he had no doubt she would exact revenge if he were to circumvent her authority in her lab. She might be smaller than he was, but she was sneaky, and he had to sleep sometime. Payback would be a bitch.

Laurel blocked the doorway, her arms crossed over her chest. "I'll tell you the same thing I told D.J. not more than fifteen minutes ago. Barak's condition is improving by the hour, and I'm not going to let anything interfere with that. I'll call you when he's up to talking."

Devlin ran his fingers through his hair in frustration. He'd benefited from Laurel's fierce protection a time or two himself, but it wasn't fun to be on the other end of it.

He tried again. "I only need to ask him a couple of quick questions, and then I promise I'll leave. He's the only one who might know what's happened to Cullen."

He'd scored a direct hit. "Cullen? What's wrong with Cullen?"

"We don't know. D.J.'s been looking for him since yesterday with no luck." He didn't want to tell her that Barak had been on the verge of returning to his world on a special mission on behalf of the Paladins. She'd skin Devlin alive for endangering her friend.

"What's Barak got to do with Cullen?" Her eyes narrowed, her mouth a straight slash of irritation. "And don't try pulling that top-secret Paladin crap with me."

Aw, hell, he might as well 'fess up. She wouldn't let go of the matter until he did. "Barak was supposed to contact someone in his world to set up a meeting about the flow of those blue stones into our world. Cullen gave Barak a ride to the tunnels. The rest, you already know: Barak took off with Penn to rescue Lacey."

"And?"

"D.J. called Cullen and told him what happened to Barak and that we'd dug him out of the tunnel. As far as I can tell, that's the last time anyone has had any contact with Cullen."

"If D.J. talked to Cullen last, why do you need to talk to Barak?" Her stance was softening, her voice telling him that he was finally making progress in convincing her to let him past the door.

"I need to know what happened between the two of them while they were waiting in the tunnel, before Penn arrived. I've pieced together everything except that." He reached out to trace the curve of Laurel's cheek with the back of his fingers. "I won't stay long, but every minute is important if we're going to find out what happened to Cullen."

She pushed the door open. "Five minutes tops,

Devlin. And if you get Barak worked up, I'll kick you out so fast your head will spin."

He couldn't resist her when she got all feisty. He grabbed her close to kiss her hard and thoroughly. When they came up for air, he took a precautionary step backward, wishing they were somewhere a helluva lot more private and had more time to finish what they'd just started simmering between them.

"I appreciate this. Five minutes, I promise."

Laurel straightened her lab coat, and Devlin followed her into the lab. Damn, he hated the smell of the place. No matter how antiseptic she kept it, the stench of death and pain tainted the air. He'd been strapped down to that steel slab too many times to feel comfortable in the room.

He sloughed off his unease and concentrated on why he was there. Barak looked like hell, but at least he was breathing. That was more than they'd hoped for when they'd dug through a collapsed tunnel to rescue him.

"Where's Lacey?" Devlin asked.

Laurel was studying the readings on one of the machines monitoring Barak's vitals. "Penn dragged her out of here to get some rest. I give her four hours tops before she's back." She adjusted the flow of an IV running into Barak's arm.

Devlin edged closer to the bed. "I'm sorry to have to wake him up."

Barak's eyes fluttered open, and his mouth quirked up in a slight smile. "You should be—but then, you always did hate having your woman fuss over me."

Devlin laid his hand on Barak's. "I'm just glad to see you're still being a thorn in my side."

"Devlin!" Laurel gave her watch a pointed look, reminding him that time was short.

"Okay, okay. I need to ask you about what happened down in the tunnels—before Penn came charging in."

Barak blinked several times, trying to focus on Devlin's face. "Why? What's wrong?"

Laurel answered before Devlin could. "No one has seen Cullen since you and Penn left him down in the tunnel. Devlin's trying to retrace Cullen's steps."

"Do you suspect . . . what is it they call it? Foul play?"

"Right now we don't know what to think. It's not like Cullen to disappear like this, especially leaving his car in the garage for this long."

Barak frowned. "He was proud of his new car when he picked me up. We took the long way to the tunnels so he could show me what it could do."

"I hate to push you when I know you're hurting, but anything you can remember would help." Devlin snagged a nearby stool and sat down to make it easier for Barak to see him.

Barak closed his eyes and drew a slow breath.

"Cullen played cards . . . solitary . . . something like that. And he asked me about Lusahn." He opened his eyes again. "She's my sister—the last family I have. Cullen thinks she is the one he fought in the tunnels."

"I remember that day. She cut his face and sliced his ribs open. Not the sort of thing he'd forget."

"She has considerable talent with a blade. Taught her myself." Barak's voice faded to a soft whisper. "Penn came and attacked me before he realized that they kidnapped Lacey because of him, not me. I wrote a note on the envelope meant for Lusahn, telling her why I couldn't be there at the appointed time, and asked Cullen to throw it across. When I left with Penn, Cullen was still there."

"Time's up." Laurel dimmed the lights over Barak's bed. "If he thinks of anything else, I'll call you."

"All right. I'll be in my office."

Laurel followed him to the door, then fussed with the collar of his shirt the way she always did when she was worried. "I hope you find Cullen, and he's okay."

"Me, too." He smiled in an effort to reassure her, but inside he knew something had gone horribly wrong. His friend was in serious trouble.

Chapter 9

*T*he journey back to town was uneventful, but a growing sense of urgency haunted their footsteps. Something was wrong, maybe even badly wrong.

Once again the approach Lusahn used was a winding, roundabout route, which left Cullen tired and his teeth on edge. His instincts demanded that he pull his sword, ready to defend against a peril he couldn't yet see but could sense. Lusahn was feeling it, too. More than once she'd stopped abruptly and backtracked, without offering any explanation other than the worried look in her eyes.

To distract her, when near-exhaustion demanded they stop to rest by a small creek, he broached the question he'd been meaning to ask since his conversation with Bavi.

"Lusahn, when Bavi and I were talking before breakfast, he said something that bothered me." He waited for her to finish her drink, wanting her full attention.

"What did he say?"

"He's been dreaming about his parents and how things were before they left. He said they must be dead. Rather than give him false hope, I agreed that they were gone, because if he were my son, nothing short of death would keep me away from him. My old man wasn't much of a father, but at least he stuck around until he died." God, he hated thinking about it. Only after he'd been recognized as a Paladin himself had he found out why his father had been the way he was. And that he'd died strapped down and screaming.

"Cullen?"

He shook his head, dragging himself back to the present. "Sorry, I guess I drifted there. I know Bavi's parents sought the light, but he seems to think it's inevitable that he and Shiri will do the same thing."

Lusahn stared up at the pale star in the sky for several seconds before slowly turning to face him. The pain that etched her face told him he didn't want to hear what she was about to say, but he needed to know the truth.

"I told you before that not all of our people have adjusted to the fading of the light. For most, the effect is mild: occasional bouts of depression, irritability, a need to get away from the city. Others have taken to the darkness and actually live in the caves." She looked up at the sky again. "Barak was one who sought solace near the barrier. For a long time that was enough for him. But the ones like Bavi's parents gradually worsen until they become like those you kill to protect your world."

She took another long drink from the stream. "Those who move away from the city, either to live like Joq or in the caves, function pretty well, and they may be the only one in their family so affected. But when a parent seeks the light, it seems the children are prone to do the same. If both parents cross the barrier, like Bavi's did, it is almost certain that their children will as well. That is why none of their blood family would take them in. Imagine the pain of raising a child, loving them, nurturing them, all the while knowing that one day they will seek the light, and in doing so, die."

A tear trickled down her cheek. She swiped at it with the back of her hand and looked away. His own grief had him wanting to rage out of control, to scream at the gods, to gut someone for not putting a stop to the madness before now.

He picked up a handful of rocks and threw them as far and as hard as he could. It didn't help. Neither did the obscenities that poured from his mouth. If he could have offered up himself in their place he would have, and died happy knowing that Shiri and her brother would live long and happy lives.

"Why haven't your people found a cure?" It was

an unfair question, and he knew it. There were plenty of children in his own world who suffered from illnesses that were beyond mankind's ability to heal. But he didn't know those children personally, hadn't held them on his lap or taught them how to hold a sword.

Lusahn gave his question the answer it deserved: none. If it killed him, knowing what lay in store for Bavi and Shiri, it had to be eating her alive every minute of every day. Who could imagine that a simple thing like the lack of adequate sunlight could wreak such havoc in someone's life?

He was about to reach for more rocks when it hit him. Sunlight. His world had bright, beautiful, glaring sunlight. If that's what Bavi and Shiri needed to thrive, he could give it to them. Crossing into his world would be a shock to them, but they were young. They would adapt. He'd make sure of it.

"Lusahn, would more light prevent the disease from taking its normal course?"

"Nothing we've tried has worked. We can light more candles, and a few like Barak have the gift of bringing light out of the blue stones, but none of that has helped."

She started walking, cutting straight across country toward the city rather than following the path.

Cullen caught up with her. "What if I took Bavi and Shiri to my world? If they were given an opportunity to live in the bright sunshine of Earth, would it hold the disease at bay?"

Lusahn rounded on him, her pale eyes blazing with fury.

"What are you saying, Cullen? That we should try to sneak our children across, only to have them die on a Paladin's sword? You might hesitate to kill a child, but would all of your kind feel that way? Or would they hold them prisoner and shove them back across the barrier the first chance they get? That would get us nowhere, and the trauma would likely hasten the progression of the disease."

"Damn it, Lusahn, I'm not talking about saving all of your children! I can't do that any more than I could save all those who suffer in my world. But maybe, just maybe, I can save Bavi and Shiri by taking them back with me."

"You would take them from me?" The anger was gone, replaced by something far more vulnerable. "But I just found them."

"Then come with them—with me." He didn't know which of them was more shocked by his offer, but he meant every word. When he reached out to hold her, she lurched away, shaking her head.

"No! It won't work. Not for them. Not for me." She whirled away and all but ran down the trail.

Cullen stared after her retreating back, wishing her rejection didn't hurt so much. He should be glad that one of them was thinking straight. What did he know about taking care of kids, especially two with so much baggage already? And if he was out of place in Lusahn's world, she'd be lost in his.

A small voice in the back of his head argued that he was wrong. Barak had adapted well enough, and he was Lusahn's brother. He would be there to help Bavi and Shiri. And she wouldn't be stepping across the barrier praying for mercy. She'd have family there—the children with her, and him.

It was the only logical solution to the problems they were facing. The stubborn woman wasn't ready to listen to reason, but he had time to convince her. He set off down the trail, determined to use every moment he had.

Lusahn could hear Cullen stomping down the hillside behind her. She picked up speed, unable to face him right now. Her emotions were a jumbled mess, her stomach churning with anger and hurt, mixed with a small splash of hope.

Could he really save Bavi and Shiri from almost certain insanity? If there was even a breath of chance, she should be packing their belongings and planning her good-bye speech. Instead, she wanted to race home and lock them away before Cullen caught up with her.

They were her family—the only one she had left. If they were to cross the barrier, she'd never see them again. That wasn't going to happen. It was bad enough that Cullen would leave.

She glanced back at the grim-faced man closing in on her. The thought of never again seeing those dark warrior eyes or feeling those gentle lover's hands ripped her breath away.

The cold chill of the afternoon seeped into her bones, her veins, her soul.

Cullen caught up with her at last and marched alongside her in heavy silence, a stubborn set to his jaw that she ached to soothe with a kiss. Maybe later he would let her close enough for that. For now, it was better they concentrate on the problems at hand.

She deliberately approached the city from the far side to avoid the Guild. She wanted her sword in hand, and parading through the heart of the city with her weapon out would draw too much attention. With luck they'd make it to the back door of her house without mishap, but she'd fight her way to the children if she had to.

Cullen held out his hand to stop her when the house was finally in sight. "Wait and watch."

He was right. Charging in without taking the time to scope out a potential trap was just asking for trouble. The two of them edged into the deepening shadows and froze. She wished her vision was stronger, but there was nothing wrong with her hearing or sense of smell. She drew in a deep taste of the air as she closed her eyes to concentrate on listening for sounds and scents that didn't belong. There was something . . . someone. Turning her head slowly from side to side, she narrowed down the potential hiding spots.

"There." Cullen spotted him at the same time she did.

Although the star hadn't set, the day's light was already starting to dim, casting long shadows across the landscape. Their adversary stood in a clump of low trees, watching the back of her house.

"If there's one, there may be more."

She nodded, already scanning the area, watching for sign of any accomplices. It didn't take long to pick them out; there were only a few good hiding places. She was surprised the neighbors hadn't already sounded the alarm.

She leaned in close to Cullen's ear. "It has to be my Blade, since my neighbors would recognize them and not raise the alarm. If anyone else was lurking in the area, they would draw suspicion."

"But your Blade had the day off. What would bring them here?"

"Maybe they found out about the attack on Joq's place."

"How? We would have seen their footprints if they'd been close enough to his house to look in."

His lips settled into a grim line. "Unless the set of footprints approaching his home belonged to one of them."

"But they were made by human shoes," she protested.

He pointed at his own foot. "And I'm a human wearing an Other's boots."

She'd had enough of being called a name that meant nothing. "We are not 'Others,' Paladin, so don't call us that. We call ourselves the Kalith."

Cullen's expression softened. "Kalith it is. What does it mean?"

A sense of irony and sadness weighed her down. "It means 'People of the Light.' It refers to the ability to draw light and warmth from the blue stones."

"I like the sound of that." He smiled and pressed a sweet kiss to her lips. "Now, back to your Blade. We need to find out what they are doing here. I'm all for the direct approach, but you didn't want them to find out about me."

"I still don't. I will draw them into the house. Once we're inside, you can make your way to the basement."

"I don't like it. If they're involved in the thefts, you and the children could be in danger."

"Even so, I think they'd hesitate to attack me— at least until they find out what I've learned and exactly who I've talked to. But if they are part of the problem, they would attack you first before turning on me. I won't risk that."

"And if you find out they can't be trusted, what then? You'll never be safe here."

He was pushing again, wanting her to turn her back on her world and its people.

"One problem at a time, Cullen. For now, I need to get to the children." She looked past him toward the house.

He gave her a gentle shove. "I've got your back. At the first sign of trouble, holler and I'll come running; to hell with secrecy."

She knew he would sacrifice himself for her and for the children. As much as she wanted to think it was only because he was a warrior following his calling, that wasn't cold honor burning in his eyes. It was something far stronger and far hotter. She recognized it because the same strong emotion had settled somewhere near her heart.

"Watch your own back, Cullen Finley. If you manage to get yourself killed, I will never forgive you."

She meant it as a dark joke, but he didn't look at all amused; he looked guilty. What was that about?

Walking away from Cullen, she retreated some distance before making her approach to her Blade, hoping they hadn't already seen her as part of a pair. She still hoped to protect Kit and his brother from this mess she was mired in;

Larem would have to make his own decisions.

Kit stepped out of the shadows as soon as he recognized her. As usual, he smiled. "We were worried about you."

"About what? We weren't on duty today." She kept her voice neutral, not wanting her words to be taken as criticism.

The smile disappeared. "Then you haven't heard. Larem found Joq earlier today. He'd been attacked."

"Is he all right? Has he been able to tell us who did it?" Her concern was genuine, even if her shock wasn't.

"I've been out here since we found him. Larem might know more. He's the one who found Joq and brought him here."

Her instincts went on full alert. "Why not take him to the Guild? He could have gotten medical care there, even though he's not on the roster any longer."

Kit shrugged, his eyes still scanning their surroundings. "Either Joq asked him to, or else Larem thought you'd want Joq here where you could keep an eye on him."

Which was it? She'd give anything to know the facts of the situation before she walked through the door. It was too late to change plans, though, so she had no choice. She could only hope that Bavi and Shiri were all right.

Walking in the door with weapon in hand was only asking for a confrontation. She checked to make sure the sword slid easily in its scabbard and started for the house. The calm before a battle settled over her. Even if the war was to be fought only with words, she was ready.

The door swung open as soon as she reached it. Larem loomed in the doorway, but stepped back as soon as he recognized her. She noted he kept his weapon drawn as she pushed past him, looking for Bavi and Shiri.

"Where are the children?"

"They're in their rooms. I figured that was the safest place for them until we find out who attacked Joq." Larem curled his lip and sneered, "I put him in your human lover's bed."

Her hand itched to smack his face, but it would serve no purpose. "I'll speak with the children, and then I'll check in on Joq. You stay here."

"But—" he started to protest.

Lusahn snapped back her shoulders as her hand went to her sword. "You dare argue with your Sworn Guardian? If you wish to be relieved of duty, say so now. But know if you walk out of that door, you are no longer part of my Blade. And I will post the reason for your dismissal."

Larem hissed in shock. If it got out that he'd refused a direct order, his career in the Guild was over. Hers, too, probably, because they'd demand his version of the events that led to his dismissal. It probably wouldn't save him, but he'd have the satisfaction of taking her down with him.

Right now she didn't care; she had more important things to worry about.

As soon as she crossed the threshold, she knew Bavi's room was empty despite the boy-shaped lump under the bedcovers. Bavi never slept with his head under the blankets; he'd fashioned a dummy out of his bedding to fool Larem into thinking he was asleep. He'd undoubtedly slipped down the hall to his sister's room to be with her as soon as Larem turned his back.

The door to Shiri's bedroom was closed. Rather than barge in, she knocked softly.

"Bavi, it's me. Can I come in?"

It took a few seconds for the door to open. Judging by the sound of things, Bavi had blocked the door with the bed. Ingenious. The boy might be young, but he had the instincts of a warrior. Cullen had been right to start introducing him to the world of weapons.

As soon as the gap was wide enough, she eased inside and closed the door. Shiri immediately leaped into her arms. Bavi stood back, allowing Lusahn and Shiri to comfort each other before speaking.

"You were gone too long!" There was equal temper and fear in his voice.

"I know." She met his gaze head-on, paying him

the respect he deserved. "We didn't mean to be, but things got complicated. Someone tore up Joq's cabin, and we were trying to find out what happened to Joq. I just found out that he's here."

Bavi dropped his voice to a whisper. "That Larem brought him inside, saying he'd found Joq wandering in the city, beat-up and bloody."

"You don't believe him." It wasn't a question; the distrust was right there in Bavi's eyes.

"Something isn't right, but I didn't have a chance to find out what. Larem ordered us into our rooms before I could get a look at Joq." He smiled wickedly. "Larem probably thinks I'm still there."

"I'm sure he does, and you did the right thing by coming in here." She handed Shiri back to her brother. "I need to go check on Joq and see what's going on."

She wished she could speak to Bavi without the little girl hearing, but that wasn't going to happen. "Bavi, you can trust Cullen Finley, no matter what happens or even if what he says frightens you. If something happens that I can't come to you right away, do whatever Cullen asks of you. Do you understand what I'm saying?"

Looking far more adult than a boy his age should, he gave her a solemn nod. "I will trust him."

Lusahn leaned in close to give Shiri a kiss on the cheek. "Be good for your brother, little girl. I love you both."

Bavi surprised her with a hard hug, squeezing Shiri so tightly between them that the little girl squealed in protest. Lusahn ruffled Shiri's dark curls. "Sorry, Shiri, we didn't mean to crush you."

It was time to go. "Block the door behind me."

Back out in the hallway, she closed her eyes to better listen to the sounds in her home. There was one heartbeat near the front of the house, no doubt Larem. The second one below her had to be Joq. She paid special attention to him. If he was beat-up and bloody, as Larem claimed, why was he prowling in the basement like a caged animal?

Bavi's instincts had been right; something was definitely wrong.

There was little chance that she could make it to the steps that led downstairs without Larem noticing, so she went for speed rather than stealth. She made it most of the way down before Larem was behind her, his sword pointed right at her back. Even so, she wouldn't have been worried except that Joq was waiting below her with his own sword in hand.

"You look awfully good for someone who's supposed to be injured."

Joq smiled, showing a lot of teeth. "See, Larem, I told you she was too smart to fall for that excuse. We should have told her it was Kit who was injured. She might have believed that." Then he shrugged. "Of course, it's too late for that, since he's dead."

"I just saw him a few minutes ago, and he was fine." She prayed to the gods that he still was.

Joq shook his head. "You and your human lover killed him not more than five minutes ago. It's a tragedy, really."

"Joq!" Larem shouted. "You never said anything about Kit or his brother having to die!"

"Casualties are part of any war, Larem. Be glad it wasn't you."

Joq's smile sickened her. Tears burned her eyes, and rage burned like acid in her stomach. "You won't survive to spread that story, Joq. If I don't gut you, Cullen will."

The older man's head jerked toward the door, as if expecting the Paladin to come charging in. So he wasn't as confident about his ability to take on the two of them as he wanted her to believe.

"So which of you is stealing the blue stones? If I'm going to die, I'd like to leave this world knowing who my friends really were." She eased down another step, slowly moving her blade back and forth, ready to counter whichever of them attacked first.

Larem answered, "This isn't about the stones, Lusahn. It's about you betraying our people to the Paladins. It sickens me to know you've been spreading your legs for the enemy."

It didn't matter how they knew about how far her relationship with Cullen had gone; she wouldn't let them tarnish what she and Cullen had shared.

Nor would she let his hurtful words spur her into acting rashly.

"Larem, you are a fool. This isn't about honor at all. It's about greed." She was only one step from the bottom now, bringing Joq almost into the reach of her blade. "Cullen wasn't lying about why he was here. Someone has been stealing the stones and coaxing our people into crossing the barrier with them. They hope the stones will buy their way to safety, but they die instead, and the human thieves and the corrupt ones from our side get richer."

Joq's laugh was ugly. "The fools die anyway, Lusahn. Their deaths are senseless; you know that as well as I do. At least if the Guild profits, we get some value for their headlong rush onto the Paladin's swords."

Larem retreated up the steps. "Gods above, what have I done?"

Lusahn took that final step forward. "Say your prayers, Joq. Ask the gods for forgiveness, because you'll get none from me."

"I suggest you do the same, girl. You might have been the best Blade I ever had, but I know how you fight, since I'm the one who taught you."

"But you don't know a damn thing about how *I* fight, Other—and you're about to find out."

None of them had heard the door open, but Cullen stood there, battle-ready, with the promise of death in his eyes.

With a howl, Joq charged Cullen, and the fight was on.

Lusahn charged up the steps, fearing Larem would head for the children. She didn't want to kill him, but she wouldn't tolerate any threat to Bavi and Shiri. Luckily, he'd headed for the front door. She went right after him.

If he reached the Guild to sound the alarm, there would be no time for Cullen to escape to the safety of the caves. She had to buy them enough time.

Luck was with her. Rather than taking the road where the dim lights would have left him exposed, he cut through the yard, hoping to disappear into the shadows.

Lusahn knew the area far better than he did and made better time. When he looked back to see her closing in, he tripped over Kit's body and went flying headfirst into the trunk of a tree. The impact dazed him into immobility. Yanking his hands behind his back, Lusahn used her belt to tie them together, then used Kit's belt to tie Larem's ankles.

She tightened the belts one last time and then stood up.

"Larem, I won't let you turn Cullen in. He's going home to his world. After that, I will stand down as Sworn Guardian. I promise you that."

He managed to roll over onto his back, glaring up at her. "It's not enough. You're a traitor to our kind, just like your brother. I will see to it that the q'Arc name is erased forever."

That wouldn't be hard. She was the only one left, and the Guildmaster would order her execution as soon as Larem got free and reported in. So be it. Right now, she had to get back to Cullen and the children.

"You could have been so much more, Lusahn. With the right male beside you, you could have been Guildmaster someday. Even Joq thought so. Instead you settled for being a whore for that human. You disgust me."

"Right now I'm not too pleased with you, either." She gagged him with a strip of fabric she cut off his tunic, then ran for the house.

The back door stood wide open, the light from the basement spilling out into the darkness. From inside came the clang of two blades in the hands of two master swordsmen. She prayed that Cullen's youth and strength could overcome Joq's years of experience.

She approached the door with care, not wanting to distract Cullen. Her heart settled in her throat when the combatants moved into her sight. Cullen was bleeding badly from a cut on his leg, causing him to move in an awkward lurch. Joq was wounded, as well, but nothing that hindered his ability to outmaneuver his opponent.

She ached to join in the battle, but the room

was too small for the three of them to maneuver without hampering one another's movements. When Joq realized she was back, he made a quick dash to the far side of the room to keep Cullen between them. He lunged forward, swinging his blade in a wide arc aimed right at Cullen's neck. The Paladin roared in fury as he blocked the move and went on the attack himself. Joq danced backward, his feet a blur as he outdanced his human opponent.

Lusahn clenched her sword tightly as she watched her lover fight for his life. With her pulse pounding through her veins, she prayed the gods of her world would protect him.

And if her prayers went unheard, she would finish off Joq herself—making sure he took a long, long time to die.

Chapter 10

Cullen figured he could afford to die, but it would be damned inconvenient. Did Lusahn even know that he could come back if this bastard managed to kill him? The first chance he got, he was going to tell Lusahn every damn detail of his life and demand that she do the same.

His arm ached, and his leg hurt like a son of a bitch, but he wasn't going to let this traitor get the best of him. The Other was a master with a sword, but Cullen had learned from the two best Paladin swordsmen. From Devlin Bane, he'd learned technique and finesse. From Blake Trahern, he'd learned sheer cussedness. The combination was lethal.

Joq's eyes kept flitting from Cullen to Lusahn and back. She was hanging back, staying out of their way, but her mere presence was enough to make Joq sweat. He knew that even if he managed to take

Cullen out, he'd still have to face Lusahn. And with the mood she was in, the best Joq could hope for was a mercifully quick death.

It was time to end this. Cullen waited until Joq glanced at Lusahn again and charged right at the Other, bringing his sword down with all the strength he could muster. At the last possible second, Joq countered, and in doing so, managed to yank Cullen's sword right out of his hand.

Cullen scampered backward, grabbed the little table by the bed, and threw it right at Joq's head. As the Other ducked, Lusahn shouted Cullen's name, and her sword came flying toward him. He snagged it out of the air just as Joq moved in for the kill.

"Are you ready to die, human?"

"Been there, done that. No big deal." Cullen motioned for Joq to come and get him. "Paladins die all the time, Other—but we don't stay that way."

Blood from a cut on his forehead dripped down into Cullen's eyes, temporarily blinding him, but he'd seen enough of how Lusahn fought to guess what her teacher would try. He caught the side of Joq's blade with a crushing blow, knocking him in one direction while the Other's sword flew in the other. Lusahn got to it before Joq could.

They all knew Joq was dead. He just hadn't laid down and quit breathing yet. With sweat pouring off his face and his hands shaking, he pleaded with his former student and friend.

"You don't want to kill me, Lusahn. You and I both know that."

Cullen laughed. After all the evil the bastard had caused, after the senseless deaths of her Blade, Joq thought he could call on their friendship to save him?

"Who have you been working with?" The chill in Lusahn's voice dropped the temperature ten degrees.

When Joq made a slight movement toward the door, Cullen cut him off. When he looked back toward the staircase, Lusahn cut off that route of escape.

"Who have you been working with?" she repeated.

"It was Larem."

"Liar. He wasn't happy about me working with Cullen, but his honor was never in question."

"Not happy?" Joq sneered. "He hated you for choosing a human to bed, when you would hardly let a Kalith male near you. If you needed a lover, you only had to look to your own Blade, or"—his voice cracked—"to me."

The shock on Lusahn's face was painful to see. "You never offered."

For an instant Joq's face softened, allowing the full depth of his feeling to show. "I did, but you chose not to hear."

Then he gathered a cloak of anger and hatred

around himself. "I'm done talking. So what's it going to be, Lusahn?"

"You die, Joq. When Larem gets loose, he'll head straight for the Guild. If the Guildmaster is working with you, he'll execute you to protect himself. If the Guildmaster is still a man of honor, he'll execute you for your crimes. Either way, it won't be an easy death. I can at least save you that."

It was the truth, and they all knew it. The only question was, who would swing the sword to end Joq's life? Cullen wanted to be the one. He'd killed so many Others in his lifetime that one more wouldn't add much weight to his already burdened soul. He'd never had to kill one in cold blood, which was how it felt, now that Joq was cornered and unable to defend himself. But he'd do it to save Lusahn the pain.

Joq grew quiet and still. He looked Cullen straight in the eye, as he bent his head in a quick bow, then went into a full-out charge in a heartbeat. Cullen jerked his sword up and braced himself for the impact as Joq impaled himself on the razor-sharp blade. Lusahn screamed, and time stood still as Joq's hand floundered for support on Cullen's shoulder.

His pale eyes widened in surprise, either at what he saw waiting for him on the other side of death or in shock at the pain. Cullen gently lowered the older male to the floor as Lusahn knelt at Joq's side, tears streaming down her face.

As Cullen pulled the blade free, Lusahn lifted her mentor's head into her lap, cupping the side of his face with her hand.

"Why?" she choked out.

Joq didn't answer, saving his last bit of energy to stare up into her face. Then he slowly turned to Cullen, grimacing in pain at the movement. "Take her away from this, human."

"I plan to."

"Good. She deserves better than darkness."

Blood bubbled out of his mouth as his final breath rattled and then stopped, leaving the two of them shrouded in silence. Cullen wished he could allow Lusahn to grieve for all that she'd lost, but there was no time. Eventually Larem would get free, and then all hell would break loose. They needed to get to the tunnels and the barrier with the children.

Escaping to his world was their only hope.

"Lusahn, we have to get moving."

Cullen's hand came down on her shoulder in comfort, but the urgency in his voice was a reminder that the danger wasn't over. She looked up at her human lover, tears streaming down her face. How could it have gotten this bad so fast? Had it only been a handful of days since Cullen had appeared in her life?

He left her side long enough to yank the blanket off the bed and cover Joq's body. Then he gently picked up Joq's weapon, wiped it clean of blood, and laid it across Joq's chest, a sign of respect. The gesture eased her heart enough that she could stand and step away from the shrouded figure.

Cullen stood at her side. "Remember him as he was, if you can, and that he cared deeply about you."

"You knew?"

"I suspected." He pulled her into his arms.

"Why didn't he say anything?" Although what difference it would have made, she didn't know.

"Maybe he figured if you were interested, you would have picked up on the signals he was sending. Since you always treated him as a valued friend and mentor, he didn't push the issue." He rested his face against her hair. "He settled for whatever you were willing to give."

She smiled. "You wouldn't have settled, would you?"

"Hell, no. I knew from the first that you were worth fighting for."

"But that first time you were fighting *with* me, not *for* me." It felt good to smile.

"And I came after you the first chance I got." His expression turned serious. "I'm not giving you up, Lusahn. This world is no longer safe for you or the children. I want you in my life, but I want you to have choices. When we cross the barrier, I'll take you to your brother if you need time to adjust. But either way, we need to get the hell out of here before it's too late."

He was right. Individually, they were lost and alone. Together they could be a family, even in a strange world.

She hurried to the staircase. "What should we take with us?"

"Weapons, enough food and water to last until the barrier drops, and whatever the children need to make them feel safe."

"You check the kitchen for supplies while I talk to Bavi and Shiri." Shiri would do anything Lusahn asked, but Bavi deserved an explanation and the chance to choose his own life's path.

"Okay, but talk fast. We need to be in the caves before the star rises in the sky."

She ran. When she called out Bavi's name, he immediately shoved the bed from the door. Judging from his pallor, the noise from the basement must have carried upstairs.

"Cullen and I are fine, Bavi, but things aren't good." Turning, she said, "Shiri, go see if you can help Cullen in the kitchen while I talk to your brother."

The little girl skipped out of the room. At least one of them wasn't frightened. Lusahn put her hands on Bavi's shoulders and looked him straight in the eye.

"Bavi, you are the son I've never had, and I love you as if I had birthed you myself. I don't have time to explain everything right now, but I will, the first chance we get. Right now, Cullen and I want you and Shiri to go with us to the caves where the barrier runs through. When it goes down again, we will take you and Shiri across to live in his world, in the light. But I won't force you to go—even though it will kill me to lose you." She looked out the window into the darkness beyond. "This is your home, and you may want to stay."

Bavi followed her gaze and shivered. "Cullen will protect us from his people?"

"He will keep us safe there, and my brother will help. Both of them would lay down their own lives to keep you and Shiri safe, as I would."

"We go, then. A family should stay together." His voice cracked, and he let her pull him close for a brief hug.

When she let him go, he looked around the room, frowning. "I will pack Shiri's books and blanket."

"And a change of clothes. We need to travel light, so only take what is necessary."

"Can I take your brother's practice blades? I will need them if Cullen is going to teach me to fight."

"I'm sure my brother will be honored that you wish to use them, Bavi. I'll go gather my things, too." She stopped in the door and looked back. "We will keep you safe, Bavi. This I swear."

It would be her last vow as a Sworn Guardian, but she couldn't think of a better one to end her career with.

Devlin's office had turned into Command Central. D.J. had set up extra computers. Trahern was in the corner, honing his sword. Lonzo held his cell phone in one hand as he took notes. He'd called in a few favors from a friend on the Seattle police force, but so far all they'd collected was a bunch of negatives.

They knew where Cullen wasn't: his home was vacant; his car was still parked in the garage; and there was no record of him entering or leaving any of the Regents' installations in the whole damn state. That just left the rest of the universe for them to search.

Devlin hadn't slept in over twenty-four hours. His eyes were gritty, his mouth tasted like shoe leather, and his temper was just shy of a full boil. Glancing around the room, he knew he wasn't the only one on edge. They'd all lost friends they'd fought beside, but always in battle or in the lab, when they'd died one too many times. It was part of being a Paladin—the ugly part that came with the job.

But to have one of their own just up and disappear was killing them all. He wasn't used to grasping at straws, but right now he'd pursue any lead, no matter how tenuous.

If Cullen could phone or e-mail, he would have—so either he was dead, or there was no phone service.

No phone service . . . He looked around at all the technology that surrounded them: landlines, computers, e-mail, cell phones. Something about that idea had Devlin sitting upright, poking and prodding it until it hit him.

Son of a bitch, he hoped like hell he was wrong!

He grabbed the phone and dialed Laurel's cell. When she answered, he asked one question that she dutifully passed along to Barak. The Other's answer had Devlin cursing loud and long. When that wasn't enough, he cleared his desk with a sweep of his arm, sending papers and everything else flying.

The other Paladins stopped to stare at him, and he fought to regain control. Cullen had always been the calm one—but if the Professor was where Devlin suspected he was, the man had given up all claims to sanity.

Devlin slowly stood, meeting Trahern's gaze and then D.J.'s, knowing they would take the news the hardest. "You can stop searching. I know where he is."

Lonzo hung up from talking to the police and

joined the rest around Devlin's desk, looking even grimmer. They knew the news wasn't going to be good.

"That crazy fool decided to play hero! He crossed the barrier to confront Barak's sister himself." He had no proof, but it was the only explanation that made sense.

"So what do we do now?" D.J. asked.

"We wait. And if he—*when* he crosses back, we make sure he's safe and sound. Then we kick his ass up and down the tunnels for being an idiot. I get first crack at him, then the rest of you can take turns."

Trahern sheathed his sword. "Sounds good to me. If there's anything left of him when we're done, we should let Laurel have a crack at him for good measure."

"I want someone watching the barrier where he crossed twenty-four/seven. I'll take the first shift. The rest of you go catch some sleep."

"I'll go with you, Devlin," D.J. offered. "When he crosses back, he may need help."

Devlin didn't have the heart to deny D.J. the chance to stand watch for his friend. "Fair enough. Trahern, set up a schedule of two-man rotations. The first one should relieve us in six hours."

"Will do."

After leaving Laurel a message on their home phone, Devlin picked up his favorite sword and headed for the tunnels. He was looking forward to throttling Cullen—right after he welcomed him home.

It was Cullen's turn to carry Shiri, but Lusahn knew she'd have to relieve him soon. Although he'd made good progress in adjusting to the thinner air, he was breathing hard as they swiftly climbed the hillside.

"Let me take her."

She held out her hands to the tired little girl, and Shiri immediately lunged for her. Cullen didn't protest, a clear sign that he was feeling the effects of the climb.

"It's not much farther," she promised, directing her comment to include Bavi. "Just over that rise is the entrance to the caves."

The promise of an end in sight brought a surge of energy to the boy's steps. Once they were inside and out of sight, she'd find a hidden place for the children to rest while she and Cullen took turns standing guard.

She paused to look back the way they'd come. Had Larem worked his way free of his bonds? Please, gods, let him still be tied up and helpless. With the star already rising to cast its dim light over the landscape, the neighbors would be stirring. Even if Larem was still tied up, he wouldn't be that way for long. And as soon as he got feeling back in his legs and arms, he'd run straight for the Guild, screaming for every Sworn Guardian and Blade to join him in the hunt. She shivered.

By the gods, what a tangled mess her life had become! Only days ago, she knew who her friends were and who the enemy was. Now her friends wanted to kill her and her enemy had become her lover, his world her sanctuary. If they lived long enough to cross the barrier.

Life in a new world—the whole idea terrified her. She drew comfort from knowing that Barak had managed to build a life there.

Her feelings about her brother were still mixed. Barak had been her hero when she was growing up, making the pain of his desertion so much worse. Her reasons for hating him had been good ones, but now she was going to need his help to redefine who and what she was. Instead of holding a position of authority and honor, she and her children would be refugees with no roots, no identity.

Her thoughts were as dark as her world had become. Was this what it had been like for Barak? So much darkness that even certain death had been welcome? He must have felt so alone.

Shiri stirred in her arms, reminding Lusahn that she was *not* alone. She had this trusting little girl, her much more cautious older brother, and she had Cullen. She turned her head, needing a glimpse of his face.

When his dark eyes met hers, he smiled, and his warmth had its usual impact on her. There was strength in that face, and honor in his soul. This man alone, of all those she'd ever met, made her feel complete. No matter where their path led them, they would walk it together. With renewed resolve, she marched up the hillside.

Cullen stepped up beside Bavi. The young Kalith had been grimly silent since leaving Lusahn's house. He had to be scared, but he was doing his best not to show it. Maybe talking would help distract him.

"Bavi, I am eager to show you my world."

Bavi took several more steps before speaking. "What is it like, this place where we go?" He shifted the pack on his thin shoulders.

"The colors alone will amaze you. The people there wear whatever colors they want, and the humans themselves have different colors of hair and skin."

Bavi's eyes narrowed, clearly not buying Cullen's story. "That cannot be."

"I swear it is true. The trees are tall and very green, there is a large body of water called Puget Sound on one side of my city, and there are mountains to the east and west."

Bavi gave him an unconvincing nod, and Cullen wasn't sure how much he'd understood. Aware that

Lusahn was also listening intently, Cullen continued, "I have a house with big rooms and lots of windows to let in the light. Right now I live by myself, but there's plenty of room for a family."

He resisted the urge to look at Lusahn. He didn't want to pressure her, but damn it, she belonged with him. It wasn't just the sex, although that had almost blown the top off his head—waking up with her warm body next to his was just as good.

He noticed that the ground had leveled out; they were nearly at the entrance to the caves. He wished he felt better about their chances. He turned to Lusahn.

"Can you feel the barrier from here?"

She closed her eyes, breathing in slowly through her nose and out through her mouth several times before shaking her head. "I'll have to get closer— probably because I'm tired."

"Let's get inside. We're too exposed out here, especially now that the star is up."

Damn, he wished they knew how much time they had before the Guild's forces descended. He and Lusahn both needed some serious sleep before they'd be ready for another battle. The best they could hope for was that the barrier would fail in time for them to escape before the attack came. But his gut told him that trouble was hot on their heels.

"Give me a little time." Lusahn handed Shiri off to Bavi and then pulled a small blue stone from her pocket. Curling her fingers around it tightly, she stared at her hand and frowned. After a bit she stumbled, and Cullen lunged forward to steady her.

She opened her hand and smiled. The stone was glowing. "Now we can see inside."

Neither of the kids seemed impressed by her feat, but Cullen sure as hell was. From the little Barak had told them, the gift for working with the stone was rare among their people.

"I didn't know you had the talent."

"I don't always, but it was worth trying. I can read the barrier better when I'm closer to it, so I thought it might also strengthen my other weak gifts."

He nodded toward the stone. "I wouldn't call that weak. I'd call it a miracle."

His praise pleased her. "Let's step inside the cave. I want to settle you and the children out of sight while I examine the barrier. If I can find a weak spot, perhaps I can weaken it further."

She didn't sound all that confident, but it was the only hope they had. They wearily entered the dim cave, the only light coming from the small blue stone and the barrier itself. It didn't take long for Cullen's eyes to adjust to the poor light. And unless he was mistaken, she was leading them in the opposite direction from where he'd crossed over.

"It is beautiful." Bavi's voice sounded reverent as he stared at the shimmering power of the barrier.

Maybe it was, but Cullen had learned to associate the barrier with blood and pain and too many deaths to appreciate the myriad colors that had Bavi so riveted.

"Make sure neither of you gets too close to the barrier. It may be pretty, but its touch can kill."

Bavi clutched his little sister's hand, positioning himself between her and the danger. The boy had all the right instincts. Maybe police work or even the military would suit him. Cullen would make damn sure the boy got to choose what he did with his life. Being born a Paladin had left Cullen no options other than to pick up a sword and learn to fight.

Lusahn herded them along. "Just ahead is a small room with an entrance that's only one person wide. A narrow strip of the barrier runs across the back."

Which meant Cullen could hold off any attackers while she worked on weakening the barrier. Without being asked, Bavi settled his sister away from the entrance and joined her on the floor, then talked to her in a soft voice as he peeled a piece of fruit to share with her. Cullen positioned himself near the entrance, listening for any sign of pursuit. Lusahn stripped off her pack and drew her sword before running through an abbreviated version of her usual warm-up routine, maybe to help her focus. When she was done, she faced the narrow band of the barrier, standing with her feet apart and holding her sword raised in front of her.

After some time passed, Cullen quietly asked, "Getting anything?"

She nodded slowly. "The energy feels stretched and thin."

Despite the chill in the air, sweat had beaded on her face, the only sign of the strain she was under. Once again, she settled into silence. He didn't push her, but time was their enemy. A few minutes later, she stepped back, her shoulders slumped in defeat.

"I can't bring it down. It's definitely weaker, but not weak enough."

Cullen wrapped his arms around her, holding her close. "Why don't you sit down with the kids for a few minutes and eat something?"

"I need to try again."

"Not until you've had something to eat and drink. You need to keep up your strength." Then he played his trump card. He nodded toward Bavi and Shiri. "*They* need you to keep up your strength."

She gave him a weary nod. "All right—but only for a few minutes."

A few minutes might be all they had. He returned to his post, wishing there was something else he could do besides listen for approaching footsteps.

As he stared out into the darkness outside the small cavern, he gradually became aware of a change in the barrier behind him. The colors hadn't changed, but its normal soft buzzing sound had increased in volume several times over.

He looked back to find Lusahn already back at the barrier, standing with her feet braced and holding out one hand mere inches from the shimmering colors. The colors were changing, fading in and out, as she chanted under her breath. He couldn't understand what she was saying, but all he cared about was that it was working. The barrier was weakening.

But not in time.

"Lusahn?" he whispered, drawing his sword. "They're coming."

She immediately stepped away from the barrier, joining him at the entrance after muting the glow of the blue stone. "How much time do we have?"

"Minutes at best. Get the kids closer to the barrier and pray that it goes down before Larem and the rest get here."

She shook her head. "No, you go with the children."

His temper flashed red-hot. "Like hell! I'm not leaving you to face those bastards alone!" No matter how good she was with a sword, she'd be one woman against who knew how many of her former friends.

Lusahn stood her ground, her pale eyes glaring at him. "If there's time, we will all cross to your world. If they find us before that happens, either of us can hold them off long enough for the children to reach the safety of your world—but Shiri and Bavi won't be safe if they arrive alone, or with just me. The Paladins will either kill us or shove us back across the barrier. *You* are the only one who can guarantee my children safe passage to my brother."

He hated the convincing logic of her arguments. The Sworn Guardians and their Blades weren't bothering to muffle their approach, meaning they had come in number. It was only a matter of time before Larem and his buddies found them, and then the fight would be on. He and Lusahn together could hold them off indefinitely, but that would leave the children on their own.

The barrier flickered, but then immediately stabilized. Son of a bitch! What were they going to do?

"Go try to bring it down again. If you succeed, we'll send the children through first, then me, then you."

Before she could respond, a group of her people passed by the narrow entrance to the cave. They hadn't spotted the opening—the passage was narrow and hidden by several large rocks—but once they turned back, they couldn't help but see it: the glow from the barrier would illuminate the entry. Cullen flexed his hand on his sword hilt, wishing he had a gun with him.

"I'll try again." Lusahn motioned for Bavi and Shiri to stand next to her. "Stay still until I tell you to move, and then hurry. Cullen will make sure you get to safety."

Shiri asked, "Where will you be?"

Lusahn met Cullen's gaze over the girl's head. "I'll be right here behind you, little one." She hugged Shiri and then Bavi.

Fear for this brave, beautiful woman made Cullen's heart ache. He wrapped her in his arms and kissed her. "I love you, Lusahn q'Arc. Come share my world."

Before she could answer, the Blade returned. A shout was all the warning they got that their hideaway had been discovered.

Cullen pushed Lusahn behind him as he prepared to fight. "Try the barrier!"

They stood back to back, each prepared to do battle: her with the gifts of her kind, him with all the skills of a Paladin. He prayed that their combined efforts would be enough to turn the tide. But if the fates decreed that this be his last battle, then he would gladly lay down his life for this woman and these children.

"If you cross without me, make sure they know you are Barak's sister. Demand to see him and Devlin Bane—remember that name. It might make the difference between life and . . ." He let his words trail off when he looked at the two children. Huddled against Lusahn's legs, Shiri had tears streaming down her face, her eyes wide with fear. And her brave brother, a child himself, had his thin arms wrapped around his sister, as always trying to shield her. The two of them already knew far too much of death and violence, and it made Cullen sick at heart.

Once he had them safe in his world, he would do his damnedest to make sure that neither of them ever had to fear for their lives again. But he had to get them there first, and barring that, he needed to make sure they knew who could be trusted.

"Devlin Bane will see that you find your brother. He's a man of honor, one I'm proud to call friend."

"Devlin Bane," Lusahn repeated as she positioned herself to attack the barrier again.

The first Kalith suddenly stood in the entrance, and the Other shouted in surprised shock as Cullen knocked his sword aside and ran him through. The dying Blade looked impossibly young as he bled out. Cullen felt a mix of guilt and relief that the body made it that much harder for the next fighter to force his way into the cavern.

It didn't slow him down for long, though. This one was older, more likely a Sworn Guardian. He approached Cullen with deadly intent, and the two of them locked blades.

"Lusahn, sometime soon would be good," Cullen shouted as he fought to keep the Other away from Lusahn and the children.

"A few more seconds." Her voice sounded tired but triumphant. "It's almost down."

That was good—it had been a long time since Cullen had faced a more skilled opponent. And as long as the bastard kept Cullen occupied, it left the entry wide open to more Other warriors to enter. He forced the Guardian to retreat a few precious steps, and with a quick lunge, he drew blood. The Other retreated with a jagged wound on his sword arm, cursing in his own language. Cullen was about to go for the kill when the barrier suddenly flashed and flared.

"It's going down!" Lusahn yelled. "Get ready to change places—I'll hold them back."

Lusahn brought her sword up in time to force the Other to fight her, instead of Cullen. "Get the children across!"

Cullen reluctantly let her take his place. He urged Bavi and Shiri closer to the barrier, ready to shove them to safety as soon as the barrier failed. He tried to ignore the clash of metal on metal and the sound of Lusahn's ragged breathing as she fought on.

When he couldn't stand it any longer, Cullen

rejoined the fight. Between the two of them, they drove the Guardian back out of the entrance just as the barrier flashed and then blinked out.

Cullen quickly pushed Bavi and Shiri closer to the opening, and shouted, "Lusahn, it's time!"

She nodded and started toward them. But before she could reach them, Larem charged into the cavern with another Guardian and his three Blademates, all with swords drawn. Hatred had twisted her former friend's face almost beyond recognition.

"Lusahn, surrender or die!" Larem never gave her a chance to comply before going on the attack. The Guardian and his men moved to surround her, cutting off her retreat to Cullen and the children.

"I don't want to kill you, Larem!" She was the better swordsman, and they both knew it. But her reluctance to kill him hampered her, whereas he clearly had murder in mind.

She tried to draw the fight away from Cullen and the children, to give them time to escape to the safety of his world, but saw him starting to rejoin the fight.

"No! Cullen you have to cross!" She forced Larem back with a flurry of thrusts. "Go before it's too late!"

"No!"

"You promised to keep the children safe! Leave before we both die."

As three more of her kind pushed through the

opening with death in their eyes, she met Cullen's gaze one last time. "I love you, too, Cullen Finley. Never forget that."

Then she screamed out a war cry and rushed into battle.

It felt as if his heart was being ripped out of his chest as he followed Bavi and Shiri to safety. He screamed his throat raw for Lusahn to follow, her image blurry through the tears streaming down his face.

Chapter 11

*C*ullen fell to his knees as the barrier snapped back in place. Bavi and Shiri stared in terror at the sight.

"Where's Lusahn?" Bavi held Shiri in his arms, looking very young. He dragged his gaze from the shimmering wall of energy to Cullen. "Why isn't she here?"

How could he answer that? He'd never run from a battle in his life, even against overwhelming odds, but that's exactly what he'd just done. His stomach churned as he fought to catch his breath.

"She held back the Guardians and Blades so I could get you two to safety. She'll follow as soon as she can." If she could hold off her attackers until the barrier fell again. How likely was that?

"What do we do now?" The boy's voice cracked.

A gruff voice answered the question. "You'll explain where the hell you've been, and what these kids are doing here."

Damn, he *must* be messed up if he hadn't noticed Trahern and several other Paladins standing a few feet away. Instinctively, he stepped between them and the children.

"Get Devlin. I need him and Barak as soon as possible. Then I'll explain everything." He put his arm around Bavi's shoulders. "I also need a safe place for my friends here."

Trahern's icy glare warmed up only fractionally when he looked at Shiri and then Bavi. He nodded and stepped over to a landline phone on the wall, then punched in a series of numbers.

"Devlin, our long-lost buddy Cullen just showed up, looking a little worse for the wear and with some interesting company. He says he wants to talk to you and Barak, if he's up to it." He held the phone away from his ear while Devlin yelled loud enough for Cullen to hear him from across the tunnel.

"Fine, Bane, I hear you. I'll bring all of them." Trahern hung up. "All right, Cullen, you heard the man. He'll call Lacey and have her bring Barak in." He glanced at the other Paladins. "The rest of you stand guard in case the barrier goes down again."

Cullen cleared his throat. "Trahern?"

He glanced at Cullen. "You got something to say about that?"

Aware that he was crossing a boundary that would change his life forever, he nodded. "Barak's sister, Lusahn, is on the other side. If it goes down, let her cross and call me."

The big man rolled his eyes and shook his head. "This explanation of yours better be damned good. Okay, men, if a female crosses, don't kill her unless you have to."

Cullen wanted to protest, but Trahern was only doing his job. He and Lusahn hadn't thought to make plans if they were separated, but she'd know to surrender to his friends. It was her *own* kind that had him worried. She couldn't hold off multiple Guardians and Blades forever, and they could afford to keep sending in fresh opponents until she was too exhausted to fight. He could only pray that they would take her prisoner rather than execute her immediately.

He swung Shiri up in his arms and took off at a run, with Bavi and Trahern right behind him. The faster they got to Devlin, the faster they could form a plan to rescue his woman.

Devlin Bane was seriously pissed off, and clearly didn't care who knew it. "Damn it, Cullen! You were where? Not here, where you were supposed to be. Oh, no! Instead, you went off on some self-appointed, harebrained mission to deliver the mail in an alien world! Goddamn it, what the hell were you thinking? We had a plan, you idiot!" He slammed his hands down on his desk. "Do you have any idea what an uproar you caused around here? We even had the police searching, and every Paladin in Seattle was pulling double duty trying to find you. All we knew was your car was left parked outside, and there was no sign of you anywhere."

He stopped to draw another breath. "If Barak had died in that tunnel, we would never have guessed that you'd do something so damn—"

The phone rang, interrupting the tirade.

Devlin listened to the caller, then hung up. "Barak's here."

The door behind Cullen opened, and Barak limped into the room. For a man who'd been seriously hurt only days before, he looked pretty damn good.

"Cullen!" The normally reserved Kalith crossed the room and laid his hand on Cullen's shoulder as if needing the physical touch to accept what he was seeing. "I am greatly relieved to see you alive and well."

Cullen cut right to the chase. "Barak, the Guild captured Lusahn."

Barak's pale complexion went ashen. "Do you know that for certain?"

Cullen raked his fingers through his hair, his whole body aching with exhaustion and worry. "I don't know much of anything for certain. The last I saw her, she was fighting Larem. She wouldn't let me help because I had to protect her children."

"Children? What children?" Barak sank down on a chair. "I haven't been gone *that* long."

"She adopted two orphans whose parents sought the light. They're with Laurel and Brenna right now. Lusahn said Bavi and Shiri would need your help adjusting to this world."

Devlin took control of the conversation again. "Enough of the warm, fuzzy family stuff. You owe us an explanation, Finley."

The urge to get back to Lusahn was riding Cullen hard, but he couldn't save her alone. To get the help he needed, he had to explain, to convince them there was no choice but to stage a rescue.

He leaned back in his chair and stretched out his legs, weary to the bone. "Devlin, that female Other I fought that day in the tunnels with you turned out to be Barak's sister, Lusahn. No matter how hard I tried, I couldn't get her out of my mind. When Barak ran to save Lacey, I was left with a choice: toss his note across the barrier and hope that Lusahn wouldn't ignore it, or take it across and hand it to her myself."

Barak stared at Cullen as if he'd sprouted a second head. "And if she'd been waiting there with her Blade?"

"When the barrier failed, I could see that she was alone." He smiled grimly, remembering that moment when he didn't know if she'd kill him or not. Looking back, she might think her decision to spare him had been a monumental mistake.

"I told her what had happened to Barak, and that I was there to set up a meeting with her about the theft of the blue stones. The barrier popped right back up, cutting off my only escape route. She took me home with her because she knew it would stay up for at least several days." He glanced at Barak. "She said her gift for reading the barrier wasn't as strong as yours."

"Tell me more about this gift." Devlin glared at Barak, who ignored him.

Barak looked shocked. "She invited you into her home? That would be a betrayal of her oath as a Sworn Guardian."

"She had no other place to stash me that would be safe. The next day, she took me to meet Joq."

"Who is this Joq?" Devlin asked.

This time, Barak answered. "He was her Sworn Guardian before she became one herself." He paused to formualte an answer that would make sense. "He would be a leader entrusted to train those who would then serve as his aides. Once Lusahn had proved herself in the service of the Guild, she took vows as a Sworn Guardian and headed her own Blade."

Cullen picked up where Barak left off. "A Blade is made up of three trusted warriors whose job is to protect and fight for the Sworn Guardian. Joq trained Lusahn and then retired, so that she could replace him as a Sworn Guardian. The Guardians and their Blades patrol assigned areas to keep the peace."

Devlin looked for confirmation to Barak, who nodded.

"Joq took us up to the hills to a cave that humans have been using as a campsite. I'm sorry to say that Joq turned out to be one of the traitors, although he tried to keep that from Lusahn. He wasn't happy to see her with me."

Devlin asked, "Why? Because you're human, or did he have other reasons?"

Leave it to Devlin to see right to the heart of the matter. "He was in love with her himself, but she never saw him that way. In the end, he impaled himself on my sword to keep from being turned over to the Guild." He shuddered at the memory. "He'd already killed two members of Lusahn's Blade; the third one led the charge to capture us."

Barak and Bane were so wired, they almost trembled with it. He'd certainly gotten their attention. "Lusahn and I had already realized that the only hope for us and the children was to come back here. She held off the attack long enough for me to get the children across, but the barrier was restored before I could get back to help her."

"You left my sister to face the Guardians alone!" Barak's words were deadly quiet, laced with anger.

Cullen met his gaze head-on. "Yes, because we had the children to protect. Now that they're safe, I'm going back for her."

No longer able to sit still, Devlin was up pacing the floor. "Like hell you are! You're lucky you made it back alive. I won't risk losing you again."

Cullen played his trump card. He slowly rose to his feet and made sure he had Devlin's and Barak's undivided attention before speaking. "If it were Laurel and Lacey at risk, nothing short of death would keep you from going after them. You can't deny that, because it's exactly what you both did."

"But she's—"

Cullen closed the distance between himself and his leader and friend, fists clenched, ready to fight. "Watch what you say, Bane, or we're going to have one of those 'discussions' of yours. Only this time, I'm going to be the one doing all the talking."

The anger faded from Devlin's green eyes. "Oh, hell, you love her."

"I love her." Cullen looked at Barak. "And she loves me. Once I get her safely to this side of the barrier, we plan to build a life together. She'll want your blessing."

Barak shook his head. "Lusahn will not forgive me for abandoning our people."

"She didn't hate you for abandoning your world, Barak. She hated you for abandoning *her*. She'll get over that if you give her half a chance.

But before that can happen, you've got to get me back across the barrier."

"She may already be dead." There was as much sympathy as truth in Devlin's reminder.

It killed his heart to admit it. "Maybe she is, but I have to know the truth. And every minute we stand here talking is another one she's in danger."

When neither man responded, he drew the line. "Make up your minds now whether you two are going to help me, or get the hell out of my way—because nothing is going to stop me from going back. Barak, I'll understand if you're not up to coming, but you'll have to bring down the barrier for me."

"You can do that?" Devlin looked sick. "Why haven't I known about this?"

Barak stood to meet Devlin head-on. "I refused to use my gift for my people. I wasn't about to use it for yours." He turned to Cullen. "I'll need to get my sword. I didn't expect to need it when Devlin called me to come."

Cullen let out a long breath. "Are you sure you're up to it? The terrain is pretty rough from where we cross, down to the town."

"She's my sister. I would crawl if I had to."

Cullen understood the feeling. "Then change your clothes while you're at it. You'll stick out in those jeans, over there." He grinned and slapped Barak gently on the shoulder.

Barak smiled back. "Fine, and you go shave. My people don't wear beards." He limped out of the office.

When Cullen turned around, Devlin was already taking his favorite sword down from the wall. "Will black pants and a shirt be good enough for me to pass?"

Ordinarily there was no one Cullen would rather go into battle with than Devlin Bane, but not this time. "I can't let you do this, Devlin."

"Why the hell not? You're not going back there with only Barak as backup."

"There's no person I'd rather have with me than you, but your looks are too distinctive to pass for a Kalith male. There's some variation in build among their people, but I didn't see one of them your size."

Devlin understood that sometimes the success of a plan hung on small details. "Okay, but you're still not going alone. Do you want D.J. or Lonzo?"

"Lonzo would fit in better, but don't tell D.J. I said so."

"I'll handle D.J. Is there anything else?"

"You know that if we're captured, it'll go hard for us."

"So don't get caught." Devlin opened his office door and shouted, "Trahern, get your worthless ass in here."

"Are you going to ask him to go?" Trahern was

tall, but not quite as massive as Devlin. He wouldn't stand out as much.

Devlin shrugged. "That would be the plan, but you know Trahern. He's a loose cannon and will do what he damn well feels like."

Trahern sauntered in. "What's up?"

"Cullen's in love with Barak's sister. Someone has to go with him to break her out of an Other jail and bring her back here, or we'll never hear the end of it."

Trahern gave Cullen a curious look. "You sure like to play dangerous games. You'll be lucky if Barak doesn't slice and dice you for messing with his sister. I'd better come along to make sure that doesn't happen."

Cullen's eyes burned, and he quickly blinked the sting of tears away. These two men were the brothers he'd never had by birth. The three of them had fought together, bled together, and dragged each other back from death far too many times for them to leave him to face his worst nightmare alone.

But watching Trahern strap on his weapons, ready to risk everything for him . . . there were no words for that kind of friendship and loyalty.

Devlin checked his watch. "We'll meet back here in an hour. That should give you time to get changed and bring Lonzo up to speed. I'll get D.J. back here to keep an eye on things. I'd send more of the men with you, but we can't leave the barrier undefended."

Cullen nodded. "It will better with just four of us; we can pass for a Sworn Guardian and his Blade. As long as we keep our faces covered, we should be able to get close to the Guild without drawing attention."

Trahern gave him a considering look. "What's it like over there? I've always figured it must be hell itself, from the way they fight to get out."

Cullen closed his eyes and pictured the desolate landscape. "It's all cold and gray, everywhere, all day. Their star is dying, and not all of them adjust to the lack of light. Those two kids I had with me lost both of their parents to our swords." He thought about Bavi's staunch protection of his little sister. "The disorder sounds genetic. If Bavi and his sister had stayed in their world, we would have ended up killing them, too. I couldn't let that happen."

Trahern slipped one last knife into a sheath in his boot. "Why don't you stretch out on the couch and catch some shut-eye until we get back? You look like hell—especially with that scruffy beard."

Cullen shook his head. "I'll head for the gym and take a quick shower and shave, first."

"See you in a few, then."

Devlin waited until Trahern was gone to give Cullen a considering look. "I don't know how all of this is going to play out, Cullen. The Regents still aren't happy about Barak, although most of the Paladins are okay with him now. Even that hothead Penn Sebastian is all right about him and Lacey. But having a Paladin show up with an instant family of Others will likely be more than the organization will accept."

Cullen would cross that bridge when he had to. Right now, all that mattered was rescuing Lusahn. Once he had her safe, they'd work out their future together, with or without the Regents' approval.

Devlin was still waiting for some kind of response.

"I can't breathe for wondering if she's—" His throat choked up; he couldn't get the words past the pain.

His friend's big arm settled around his shoulders. "We'll get her back, Cullen. Right now, that's all that matters. The rest is small potatoes."

"I've never known anyone like her. She's as good with a sword as any Paladin, and I know it. But leaving her facing that bunch of crazies is ripping me apart." He could still hear the clash of their swords and see the killing rage in their eyes.

If she was dead, so was his heart. It was that simple.

Larem prowled the small cell next to hers, his endless pacing driving Lusahn crazy. He was outraged that the Guildmaster had arrested him, but what had the fool expected? In one night, the Guild had lost two members of her Blade, a former Sworn Guardian, and numerous men in the caverns as they'd fought to capture her.

Did Larem really think that the Guildmaster would be satisfied with only *her* life in payment?

She still didn't know if the Guildmaster was involved with Joq and the humans. If he was, anyone who'd had contact with Joq would be suspect. In that case, Larem would be lucky if his entire clan wasn't declared forfeit. She wished with her whole heart that this whole nightmare would just disappear.

That wasn't completely true. No matter what happened, she couldn't bring herself to regret allowing Cullen to live when he'd crossed the barrier. Closing her eyes, she let the soft brown of his dark eyes and his bright smile chase the shadows from her thoughts.

Her warrior heart had found a kindred spirit in his. She would hate to have lived out her life without ever knowing the feel of his body against hers and inside hers, the warmth of his breath on her skin, or the joy of knowing that a man of such strength loved her. If the gods decreed that they share so few days together, at least they had been good ones.

She hurt for Bavi and Shiri. She hoped that they

didn't find their new world too frightening. They both trusted Cullen, and he would see that they were safe. She was sure Barak would help, too. Even though her brother had made choices she didn't understand, his strength of character would not have changed. He would reach out to her children and hold them in his heart for her sake.

"Why are you smiling, Lusahn?" Larem pressed his face against the bars on his cell, distorting his features almost beyond recognition. "Do you want to die? Because if that's what you wanted, you could have saved us all a lot of trouble and let Joq finish off you *and* your human lover."

"Joq was the traitor, Larem. Not me."

"So you say, but I've seen no proof of his betrayal. You, on the other hand, not only allowed a human to live, but you let him fuck you."

She ignored him, not willing to let his anger tarnish her memories of what she and Cullen had shared.

"Your own kind wasn't good enough for you." Larem lunged against the bars, rattling the cage they were in. "Any one of us would have served you, had you been interested. Were you blind to how Joq felt about you?"

Yes, she had been, a fact she regretted. Love couldn't be forced, but she should have been more sensitive to his feelings. But how was she supposed to have known that he thought of her as more than a favored member of his Blade? He never said a word. There was plenty of blame to go around, not all of it hers.

The door at the end of the passage creaked on its hinges. Larem immediately flopped back down on his cot, pretending a disinterest he certainly didn't feel.

She remained where she was, staring at the blank wall and wondering if the order for her execution had come through. By force of will she kept her hands from shaking. Inside, though, her control fractured, the pieces all sharp edges and painful. Footsteps marching in unison passed Larem's cell to come to a crisp stop outside hers.

Only after several seconds passed did she slowly raise her eyes to face the intruders. Had they drawn straws to see which of her former peers would have the dubious honor of escorting her? If so, was this the winner or the loser?

"Lusahn q'Arc, I am Sworn Guardian Berk. You will accompany us to the Guildmaster's office." He kept his eyes focused just over Lusahn's head, obviously determined not to make eye contact.

"Tell him I'm busy this afternoon. Maybe I can fit him into my schedule tomorrow."

One of the Blademates didn't quite hide a quick grin before wiping his face clean of all expression. The small slip pleased her. But his youth reminded her of Kit, and once again her spirit sank through the rough floor.

"He will see you now." This time there was more force behind the words, the Guardian determined to carry out his duty with force if necessary.

She'd had enough of fighting so she stood, staying clear of the door until they pushed it open wide. She fell into step with the group, marching smartly in their midst with her shoulders back and head held high. She had been one of them, willing to die to protect those in her care. That hadn't changed.

The Blade halted outside the Guildmaster's office, only the Sworn Guardian escorting her inside. The Guildmaster didn't look up from the stack of paperwork on his desk—another move in the game to show who was controlling the situation. Finally, he set down his pen and moved the pile to one side. He folded his hands on top of his desk as he stared at Lusahn.

"Thank you for bringing her, Guardian. You may wait outside."

"Do you want me to restrain her, sir?" The Guardian pulled a length of rope from the inside pocket of his cloak.

The Guildmaster stared at Lusahn's rumpled appearance and shook his head. "I think we can trust her to behave for the moment."

What choice did she have? If she attacked the Guildmaster, she was dead. Of course, chances were that her death was already scheduled. Her eyes burned, but she'd spilled all the tears she was going to. She would meet her executioner with dignity, even if she was no longer a Sworn Guardian of her people. They could strip away the title and trappings of the office, but not the training and strength that had made her good at her job.

When the Guardian left the room, the Guildmaster leaned forward, resting his elbows on his desk, his fingers intertwined. "You've been busy, Lusahn. Adopting strays, smuggling a human into our world, and killing your mentor, not to mention your Blade."

"I did not kill the members of my Blade. Joq did that. And in point of truth, I did not kill Joq." Although it had been her sword, she had not administered that final blow. Cullen had saved her that much.

"But you don't deny allowing a human to take refuge in your home, along with those strays you took in."

Before, she would have honored this man's position as head of her Guild and accepted his censure without a murmur, even if he was wrong. Not this time.

"Bavi and Shiri are not strays. They are children, *our* children. It is not their fault that their parents sought the light. I took an oath to protect the citizens of our world. There was nothing in that oath that allows me to pick and choose those whom I would serve."

"Very noble, Lusahn," her leader sneered, clapping his hands in a mock salute. "How convenient to stand behind your oath when it serves your purpose, but ignore it when you'd rather take a human to your bed than execute him."

He was right, and they both knew it. But there was more to it than that. "Someone on this side is working with humans to steal the light from our world. The Paladins mean to put a stop to it, even if it means working with us, their sworn enemy."

He swept his hand across the desk, scattering papers everywhere. "And how do we know this? Did you bring the messages they sent to me, your Guild-master? No, you kept them secret. Did you report the human when he came across? No, you hid him for your own purposes. Whose word did you trust? Your brother, who it turns out did not die when he crossed the barrier, but has joined forces with the enemy?"

She remained quiet for the simple reason that he was right. All of those things were true, but they weren't the truth as she knew it—not deep down inside, where it counted. Yes, she'd held on to the note because it was addressed to her, a private request from brother to sister. Barak had survived in the human world, but they'd both paid a terrible price for his decision. Telling the Guild that he'd survived would have accomplished nothing. He'd already been declared a traitor. Confessing his whereabouts would only confirm it.

But most of all, Cullen wasn't just any human. From the time they first crossed swords, she'd known that. Even at the cost of her own life, she would not have betrayed him and what they'd found together.

The Guildmaster's eyes narrowed. "Even now, you think of that human rather than your duty and your people. Yet here you sit, condemned to die, and where is he? Back home with the rest of his murdering kind, probably bragging to all his friends about what fools we all are. Considering all you have lost, Lusahn, I would say you struck a poor bargain in letting the human live."

Her blood ran cold hearing that she'd been condemned before she'd even walked into this office, without a chance to defend herself or explain. She slowly rose to her feet, taking pride in the flicker of fear in the Guildmaster's eyes. Did he really think she would attack?

"I am still a Sworn Guardian. As such, I cannot lift my hand against those weaker than I am. That includes you." She placed her hands palm down on his desk and leaned forward, enjoying the effort it cost him not to back away. "But know this. If you were working with Joq to steal the light from our world, there will be a reckoning."

Leaving him to sputter, she executed an about-turn and walked with dignity out of the office. Without a word, the Guardian Berk and his Blade fell in beside her, silently escorting her back to her cell.

When the door swung shut she slumped back against the wall, letting its cold strength support her. She'd put on a good show for the Guildmaster and the Guardian and his Blade, but now there was nothing left to do but make peace with her gods and wait.

"Lusahn!"

She ignored the harsh whisper, turning her back to the noise and tugging her threadbare blanket up higher over her shoulders.

"By the gods, Lusahn, will you wake up!"

Her eyes were slow to open, feeling gritty and dry. She sat up, trying to make sense out of the shadows outside of the cell. A male form stood at her cell door, one that looked vaguely familiar.

"I was asleep." Finally, after hours of tossing and turning and listening to Larem berate her from his cell next door.

"Obviously, but now is not the time." The male's voice was threaded with impatience and some humor. She recognized him now; it was the same Guardian who had come for her earlier.

Was it time for her execution? The Guildmaster hadn't mentioned a time. The middle of the night would be the perfect time if he wished to keep her death a secret from those who had known and respected her. So be it. She reached for her cloak and gathered her dignity.

"I am ready to die, Guardian Berk."

"Don't use my name! And as far as dying goes, I'm not here to execute you. We need to talk before the drugs I slipped your roommate wear off and he wakes up." The sound of a key turning in the lock sounded unnaturally loud in the darkness.

She backed away from the door as Berk stepped into the cell. Her hand automatically reached for her weapon, forgetting for a heartbeat that she no longer carried it strapped to her waist. She remained poised to fight, but Berk made no move to attack. Instead he lit a small candle, its flickering light barely dispelling the shadows.

What was he up to? He motioned for her to sit, and then sat on the opposite end of her narrow cot.

"I'm risking a lot just by being here, Guardian q'Arc. I hope that you will understand when I ask that you not tell anyone about this visit."

She shrugged. "Who would I tell? Larem is no longer a member of my Blade, and the Guildmaster is not interested in anything I have to say."

Berk cocked his head to one side. "Does that

surprise you? About the Guildmaster, I mean."

As sad as it made her feel, she had to admit it didn't. "Not really. Either he's involved with the thefts of the blue stones, or he's afraid to investigate for some reason."

"He's more interested in keeping his job than he is in finding the truth."

"Why are you here?"

"Because I'm tired of seeing our people robbed by those who should be protecting them. I knew about Joq's greed, but I hadn't been able to catch him in the act. You evidently had better luck."

She blinked rapidly, trying to dispel the surge of pain at the mention of her friend. "I don't know that I would call it luck. I trusted him."

His betrayal had hurt even more than Barak's. Her brother had been an outspoken critic of the Guild's policies, so it hadn't come as a complete surprise that he would eventually turn his back on them. But Joq had been more than just her friend and mentor. He'd been her hero, his honor and loyalty to the Guild beyond question.

She'd been a fool to trust him, and her entire Blade had paid the price for her mistake.

"He was a Sworn Guardian. He should have lived his life above reproach. It is hardly your fault that he didn't."

Berk's words offered only cold comfort, and this was getting them nowhere.

"What do you want of me?" Her days of blind loyalty were behind her.

He accepted the change of subject. "Do you have any information that will help us put a stop to the thefts?"

"Us? Who are you talking about?"

"I will not reveal the identity of my associates. We cannot risk your trying to buy back your own life at the cost of ours." He faced her more directly. "Had we known that you would be willing to assist in uncovering the culprits, we would have approached you sooner. I regret that we found out too late."

"Because I'm to be executed?"

He turned away abruptly. "That isn't what I meant. We would have liked to have met your human, to see what we could do to help."

She had nothing to lose by being honest. "My brother is working with the Paladins, trying to slow the theft of the blue stones. Because of the rumors that the stones can be used to purchase safety in the human world, more and more of our people are trying to cross the barrier. It's a lie, but desperation drives people to accept the risk. The Paladins will continue to protect their world, but even they tire of killing so many of our kind."

"Did they have any information that would help identify those involved on this side?"

"No, but Joq led us to a cave in the hills above his home that humans have been using as a base. If you have someone good at tracking, he should be able to follow the trail from Joq's home right up to the cave. There were items there from the human world, and tracks from their shoes."

"Is there anything else?"

"No. Before we could investigate further, Joq lured my Blade to my house and killed all but Larem. We barely got my children across the barrier before I was captured."

"I would like to speak with your human."

"You can't. He's gone." The pain almost crippled her.

"But he'll be back." Berk smiled, his teeth gleaming whitely in the dim light.

"Why would you say that? What have you heard?" She didn't want to cling to false hope.

"This human was a warrior, was he not? A male worthy of the title?"

She nodded.

"Then he will be back for you. His honor will accept no less than that."

Chapter 12

Larem stirred, causing both of them to go silent. Her Blademate moved around a bit before settling down. When he snored loudly, Lusahn couldn't help but giggle. Berk chuckled softly and stood up.

"A reminder that time is passing, and I must be gone. I will investigate the cave in the next few days." He stared at the wall for a bit before turning to face Lusahn. "I regret that I cannot take you out of here with me, but that would have dire consequences for too many others."

She couldn't argue that. "I will draw comfort from knowing that someone will put a stop to the thefts."

"I hope your human friends don't delay too long in coming for you." He reached inside his cloak and pulled out a dagger. "In case they do not make it in time, I offer you this. If it were me, I would take pleasure in denying the Guildmaster his spectacle."

She accepted the weapon, though it was doubtful that she would use it. Suicide held no honor in her mind, and her honor was all that she had left, but the gesture touched her heart.

"Thank you for this, and for the conversation as well. I wish you success with your investigation."

He turned the key, locking the door behind him. "Try to get some sleep, Guardian. All is not lost—not yet."

When Berk was gone, she stretched out on her cot and stared into the darkness. Along with the knife, Berk had given her hope, a fragile but precious gift. She filled her mind with the image of Cullen's smile and drifted off to sleep.

Each minute lost was one less Cullen had left to rescue Lusahn. If he possessed the gift to bring down the barrier, he would have done so hours ago, and to hell with the consequences. That thought brought him up short. No matter how strong his feelings for Lusahn were, he couldn't forsake his duty. To destroy the barrier would endanger his friends and those he was sworn to protect.

But not knowing if Lusahn was alive and unharmed was slowly killing him. Devlin had insisted on taking Cullen home with him to settle Bavi and Shiri in with Laurel, Lacey, and Brenna, who had volunteered to watch the children. Cullen wondered if they had any idea where some of their menfolk were headed sometime in the next couple of hours, but he doubted it.

He kept his eyes on the Seattle skyline. "Do they know?"

Devlin didn't have to ask who Cullen was talking about. "Not for certain, although they'd have to suspect—especially since Barak is going with you. They all know he's never helped defend the barrier from our side."

"Maybe I should go alone." He had to offer, although a solo mission would stand a greater chance of failure.

"Like we'd let that happen. We were lucky you got back at all." Devlin gunned the engine and passed a slow truck. "Besides, Lusahn risked a lot for you and for us. She doesn't deserve to die." He reached out and put his hand on Cullen's shoulder. "You'll get her back."

Cullen appreciated the comfort. "You'll like her, you know. She's loyal and fights to protect those she cares about. Beautiful, too. There's this special way she smiles when—" Cullen suddenly realized where that train of thought was taking him and stopped mid-sentence.

Devlin let out a bark of laughter. "Man, oh, man, you've got it bad."

"Look who's talking! You get moony-eyed whenever Laurel walks in." The teasing eased the knot in his stomach.

"Welcome to the club, then." Devlin chuckled and shook his head in wonder. "You, me, Trahern, and Barak—who would have guessed we'd ever find women who'd put up with us?"

"Feels good, though, doesn't it?"

Devlin turned serious. "Sure does."

As soon as Devlin pulled up in his driveway, the front door flew open. Bavi and Shiri came barreling out, running straight for Cullen. He knelt down, arms open, and gathered them in. Shiri buried her face against Cullen's chest while Bavi stepped back after only a brief embrace. This all had to be overwhelming, especially without Lusahn to anchor them.

"Are you two all right? I'm sorry to have left you for so long."

"We are fine. The women"—Bavi jerked his head in the direction of the house—"fuss over us like Lusahn."

Cullen stood up, holding Shiri in one arm while he reached out to ruffle Bavi's hair with the other. "Let them. It will give them something to do while we're gone."

Bavi nodded in that too-adult way of his, his shoulders back. "I would go with you if Shiri did not need me."

"I know, but your duty is to protect your sister,

Bavi. I can concentrate on returning to Lusahn, knowing that you are here for Shiri."

Before he could say more, a car and a small pickup pulled up. Lonzo parked on the street and joined the group, his duffel slung over his shoulder. Lacey Sebastian climbed out of the truck, followed by Barak. Bavi stiffened at the sight of the Other male. As Barak approached, the boy looked to Cullen for guidance.

"Bavi, I'd like you to meet Lusahn's brother, Barak q'Arc. I'm proud to consider him a friend."

If Barak was surprised by Cullen's declaration, he gave no sign of it. Instead, he stopped in front of Bavi and bowed slightly. "I would be honored if you would accept me as an uncle."

Bavi studied the older Kalith for some time before answering. "If Lusahn says yes."

Barak smiled gently. "Then that will be one of the first questions I will ask my sister when I see her."

Laurel and Brenna had followed the children out of the house, and stood next to Devlin and Trahern while Lacey hovered behind Barak's shoulder. All three were smiling, but their expressions looked brittle as they tried not to show how worried they were.

The men weren't unaffected, either. Devlin was holding his lover's hand. Trahern casually draped his arm around Brenna's shoulders and pulled her in close to his side. Cullen felt like hell for dragging his friends into this mess, but he stood a better chance of freeing Lusahn with their help than he would have alone.

Cullen gave Shiri another hug. "You two will be safe here with the women and Devlin. I know he looks tough, but he'll protect you with his life. If either of you need anything, don't hesitate to ask him." He winked at the boy.

Bavi mustered up a brave smile. "We will wait here."

"Good. We'll be back with Lusahn as fast as we can."

Trahern gently pushed Brenna's hair back from her face and brushed his lips across hers. Barak cupped Lacey's cheek and stared down into her eyes before stepping away. Laurel immediately crossed the short distance to where Cullen stood and hugged him. "Be careful out there. We just got you back."

"I will. We all will." And if they didn't hit the road soon, he was going to explode. "We need to go."

The four men loaded the duffels with their weapons and cloaks before climbing into Trahern's truck. The women and children huddled together as they waved at the men. As far as Cullen knew, it was the first time in recent memory that a group of battle-bound Paladins had received a send-off by those who loved them. He liked knowing that someone cared.

When they were out of sight of the house, he asked the hard question. "Are you all sure you want to do this?"

Trahern shot him a sardonic look. "Why the hell not? These days anyone can be an international traveler, but intergalactic? Now that's something a man could brag about."

Barak laughed, but Devlin protested. "You go shooting your mouth off, Trahern, and the place will be crawling with tourists. It will spoil it for the rest of us."

"Sorry, boss. I wasn't thinking."

They rode in silence for a few minutes before Cullen asked, "Barak, where are we going to cross? I have a feeling the Guild will have guards posted at the usual spots."

"I know, but I don't think we have much choice. There are other places, but my people don't use them because the barrier is too stable."

Cullen turned to look at Barak in the backseat. "How about the place that Joq's contacts from this side have been using? I don't know where it leads to on this side, but in your world it opens into a cave in the hills above Joq's house."

Devlin interrupted. "We don't have time to hunt for a new crossing unless that mojo Barak's been hiding from us can feel where it is."

Barak ignored the jibe. "When we get down in the tunnels, I'll see what I can detect. Much will depend on the barrier itself."

Collen nodded. "Fair enough."

Trahern pulled up to the entrance of the underground parking lot and waited for the garage door to open. As they drove into the dark interior, Cullen looked back at the disappearing light and wondered if he would live to see it again.

"Why don't you shut up, Larem, and save your strength? Nothing you say to me will change anything."

Lusahn shut her eyes and wished she could shut off her hearing as easily as her sight. Whatever Berk had slipped into Larem's food the night before had made him deathly ill as soon as he woke up. He'd spent the entire morning dividing his time between berating her and hovering over the foul-smelling bucket in the corner of the cell.

"I no longer have to take orders from you, former Sworn Guardian." His remark might have stung more if he hadn't immediately had to dive for the bucket again.

She tried not to laugh at his misery, but it was hard. When she looked at Larem now, it was like looking at a stranger. The handsome friend she'd always known had disappeared into the husk of bitter anger in the next cell.

Pretending Larem no longer existed, she thought about Bavi, Shiri, and Cullen. If she tried hard, the pain at their loss didn't overshadow the good memories. After Barak first disappeared, she'd felt ungrounded and so alone. The two children had filled many of the empty places in her heart and in her life. And then Cullen came along with his Paladin swagger and dangerous smile. How had that man managed to capture her cautious heart so quickly?

Despite what Larem and the Guildmaster thought, it hadn't been all about the great sex. She smiled. Maybe it had been, but the sex had only been one way to experience the wonderful connection that had snapped into place between them from their first meeting. None of her kind had made her melt with a simple touch or a smile.

What they had shared was strong and good and so perfect. As long as she concentrated on Cullen, she could hold off the despair that had Larem in its grip. Slowly she lost herself in the memory of loving Cullen—his touch, his taste, his scent.

The door at the end of the room slammed open, jarring her out of her hard-won peace. She waited until the intruders stopped outside her door before forcing her eyes open. Berk was back, his face impassive. If she didn't have the knife he'd given her tucked away in her mattress, she would have thought she'd dreamed his midnight visit.

"The Guildmaster wishes to see you again."

When Berk unlocked her door, she reluctantly followed him and his Blade back to the Guildmaster's office. The silence seemed heavier this time, as if they already knew what fate awaited her on the other side of the Guildmaster's door.

She didn't bother to knock since she was expected. Once again, the Guildmaster was more interested in the paperwork on his desk than one former Sworn Guardian.

When he looked up, there was a definite chill in his expression. "So, Lusahn, are you ready to face the consequences of your actions?"

"What consequences are those, Guildmaster? Are you talking about the murder of my Blade by my former Sworn Guardian? Or the loss of two children I love as my own? Or the fact that the light in our world is dying, and someone is helping that along?"

The atmosphere in the room grew even colder. He held up a piece of paper. The print was too small to be read from across the desk, but the official seal at the bottom looked ominous. She'd never seen an order of execution before, but a cold wash of dread told her that she was looking at one now.

The Guildmaster smiled and tossed the paper

across the desk. "Go ahead and read it. Or if you'd rather be spared the details, I'll sign it now to save time."

More to spite him than because she really wanted to read her own death sentence, she picked up the elegantly written paper. She slouched in her chair, striving to look casual and unconcerned as her eyes began scanning the venom he had etched on the paper in ink as black as his heart.

Laughter threatened to bubble up out of her, but she forced it down. Hysteria would do nothing to help her situation, and would only convince her former leader that he'd won.

She savored each word, considering its weight and meaning before moving on to the next. It was amazing to see how many crimes she'd committed without realizing it. If the Guildmaster had been able to accuse her of causing the eventual death of their star, he would have. It was tempting to suggest he add it to the list, but the date and time of her execution had yet to be filled in.

There was no use in pushing him, especially if Berk was right about Cullen trying to rescue her. Her pulse raced at the thought; then the Guildmaster jerked her back to reality.

"If you're done memorizing that paper, hand it back. I need to finish it." He dipped his pen in the open ink bottle on his desk, enjoying his moment of power.

Staring straight into his eyes, she considered wadding the paper up and tossing it into the fire across the room. Too many years of sitting at a desk would have slowed him down enough to give her time. Then she thought about how satisfying it would be to rip the horrific words to shreds and toss them in his face. In the end, she let the paper flutter down on his desk as she stood up and walked away.

"Aren't you curious about your appointment with death?"

"Not particularly." She turned to face him one last time. "But know this, Guildmaster. Someday soon, it will be you sitting in one of those cells and waiting to die when the people realize what you've done."

He sneered. "Me? I've done nothing."

"Exactly. You've done nothing for the people you've sworn to serve, while their world is raped by greedy men from both worlds. And that is the biggest crime of all."

Then she walked out. When his Blade wasn't looking, Berk nodded at her, giving her his unspoken approval.

"Sworn Guardian, shall we see you safely back to your cell?"

"I would appreciate it, Guardian. I grow weary of the Guildmaster's games." They walked up the stairs in single file and silence.

When the cell door clanked shut, Lusahn lay on

her cot and lost herself in her memories. If they were all she had, at least they were good ones.

"Damn it, Cullen, if you don't quit that pacing, I'm going to hobble you." Devlin sat against the tunnel wall, his legs stretched out before him. "Let's catch some shut-eye while Barak works his mojo."

"Fine. Call me if anything changes."

Devlin opened one eye. "Don't go far. You may have to move fast."

"Yes, Dad. And I'll look both ways before I cross the damned street."

Cullen stalked off down the tunnel in search of some privacy—or maybe something to punch. Barak had been staring at that same spot in the barrier for almost three hours. So far, there'd been no change in the bright shimmer of energy. Cullen knew better than to interrupt him because the first time he'd tried it, the pale-eyed Kalith had threatened to do everybody a favor and gut him with the dull side of his sword. Trahern had offered to help him.

Fine. Their women were safe at Devlin's house, while Lusahn could be . . .

He couldn't think about that. Not until Barak brought down the barrier.

He paced down the tunnel, feeling his pulse race. If he didn't get control of himself, he was going to pass out. The others would figure it was exhaustion and some serious jet lag from changing worlds, but the truth was, he'd been fighting all-out panic ever since the barrier had snapped back into place, separating him from the one woman he'd ever loved.

Lusahn, with her silver-streaked hair and thickly lashed pale gray eyes, spoke to his heart in a way no one else ever had. What he wouldn't give to be holding her in his arms again, or better yet, to be showing her with his words and his body how much he loved her. He planned on taking some serious time off to do exactly that.

But first, they had to rescue her. They didn't have much of a plan, other than impersonating a Sworn Guardian and his Blade. None of them except Barak spoke the language, which made him the best candidate for the Guardian role. The rest of them would march along in formation and try to look as inconspicuous as possible.

For the first time in hours, he smiled. How likely was it that Blake Trahern, one of the biggest, baddest Paladins ever, could fade into the background? But as long as they kept their faces shadowed in their cloaks, they could pass for a Blade— until the fighting started.

It was time to see if Barak had finally made some progress in weakening the barrier. As Cullen returned down the tunnel, he heard Devlin and Barak talking.

Barak's words were coming fast and furious. Although Cullen couldn't make out what he was saying, the excitement was clear. He started off at a ground-eating lope. Devlin was starting in Cullen's direction, but he stopped when he saw him coming.

"Finley, get your ass back here if you want to go after your woman."

Cullen sped up. The barrier was clearly weakening but it might not stay that way for long.

Barak stood with his hand held palm out toward the barrier. Cullen and Lonzo positioned themselves half a step behind him on either side, while Trahern stood behind them in grim silence. Warriors to the bone, all were ready to hike through hell to do battle if necessary.

Barak shuddered as a section of the barrier slackened and died. "Hurry! It will not stay down long."

He led them through in a rush. It snapped back in place a heartbeat after Trahern cleared the ragged hole in the energy field. The four of them clustered together, adjusting to the change in temperature and light.

Barak tilted his head to one side and then the other. "We're not alone in the caves." He pitched his voice so that it wouldn't carry far beyond where they stood. "Give me a minute to check where they are."

He didn't stay gone long. "If we are careful, we should be able to reach the outside without a problem. Beyond that, I cannot guarantee anything."

Cullen clapped him on the back. "You got us this far. It's a start."

"Keep your hoods pulled forward to shadow your faces. As chilly as it is, no one will question that. And—"

"Enough already!" Cullen snapped. "Let's go get her!" Before he totally lost it. He tried to push past, but Barak got right up in Cullen's face, his pale eyes flashing in anger.

"Don't forget that Lusahn is my sister, Cullen Finley. You've already jeopardized her life. Don't make it worse by rushing things now." Then he slowly moved out, the rest of them falling into formation behind him with their hands on their weapons.

The battle would soon begin, and there was no one in any world Cullen would rather have at his side. He trusted these men with his life—and even more important, he trusted them with Lusahn's.

Chapter 13

*T*ime was a slippery thing. Had she been locked in this cell for two days? Two nights? It was difficult to tell with no windows and the limited light, and the hours seemed to drag.

Sleep only came in fits and starts, her dreams haunted, leaving her as tired when she woke up as when she'd gone to sleep. Mostly it was a weariness of the heart.

When the door opened, she didn't bother to look. Either they were coming for her, or they weren't. She wouldn't cower, and she wouldn't beg for mercy.

But the footsteps stopped at Larem's door. The scrape of a tray being pushed under the door echoed loudly. Breakfast. Or maybe it was lunch. Since they fed them the same thing at every meal, it didn't matter. But since they still bothered to feed them, perhaps it wasn't yet time to die.

Her tray arrived next, shoved under the door with no comment. Ever since Berk had drugged Larem, she ate only a little and then waited to see if she felt ill. So far, the bland soup had had no side effects.

Maybe it was silly to even worry about someone trying to drug her or poison her. She would soon be dead; what did it matter how?

Larem stirred and then picked up his tray. All hope for sleep gone, she did the same. After a few spoonfuls she started to set the tray back down on the floor, planning on shoving it back out of her cell.

"Eat more of that. You need to keep up your strength."

Larem's unexpected remark startled her. She set the tray beside her on the cot again. "Why do you care if I eat or not?"

Larem kept his eyes on the far wall. "Worrying about you is an old habit."

"I can take care of myself." Even if it hurt to feel so alone.

Some of the anger drained out of Larem's expression, to be replaced with . . . sadness? Or was it regret? "I won't disagree with that. No matter what has happened in your life—the loss of your parents, the loss of your brother, and now the loss of all that you've worked for—you still march on, head held high."

He slowly turned to face her. "Have you ever allowed yourself to really need someone, Lusahn? Or doubted yourself? If so, I've never seen it. It makes it hard for ordinary men to keep up with you."

He sounded curious rather than angry, but his words still cut through her. Was she so cold? Of course she had doubts and fears; who didn't? And she *had* needed someone, but hadn't found him in this world.

"I've had doubts, Larem. Never about the loyalty of you or my Blade, but about the Guild and how things are done. From what I've seen here, I was right." Especially the Guildmaster's greedy madness. "I needed my brother, but he left our world because of those same doubts. I needed my parents, but they died. And I need Cullen Finley." If Larem couldn't deal with that truth, too bad.

"You still feel that way after he deserted you, leaving you here to die?" Larem sounded more like his old self, protective of her.

"Cullen didn't desert me. We were taking the children to the safety and light of his world, and one of us had to hold off your attack long enough for them to escape. I could do nothing for them in Cullen's world, but he could. It was the right decision."

"Will he come back for you?"

Lusahn shrugged and looked around at the thick stone walls that surrounded them. "Thanks to you, we didn't have the time to plan that far ahead.

I won't hold it against him if he doesn't. It is enough that he saved my children."

"Why would he do that, when he is one of the butchers who slaughters our people?"

Lusahn shot him a surprised look.

"I remember Cullen from when we fought our way back to the barrier that time the four of us got trapped on the human side. Even then, you acted strangely about him. You could have killed him then and didn't."

"He and his friend allowed us to return to our world, Larem. That is hardly the mark of a crazed killer. If *our* world was being attacked every time the barrier failed, we would kill those who threaten us. They are warriors, just as we are."

"Were, Lusahn. We are but shadows that will soon fade into darkness." Then he slumped over on his cot, facing the wall, and pretended to sleep.

She understood his despair, but to give in to it meant that the Guildmaster and Joq's accomplices had won. For that reason alone, she nurtured the small hope that Cullen would indeed come after her. But even if he didn't, she wouldn't have died for nothing. Her children stood a chance of thriving in the light. Her brother would know she'd forgiven him.

And the memory of Cullen's love would carry her through whatever lay ahead.

• • •

"Why can't we have some light?" Trahern complained. "I'm tired of stepping on the back of your heels."

The passage was so dark that if they didn't stay close, it would be easy to get lost. They all had better-than-normal human night vision, but Barak had them all beat. He marched ahead as if they were taking a stroll in broad daylight instead of inky darkness.

Barak answered, "The Guardians and Blades who patrol these caverns do not generally use lights. If they do, they use one of the blue stones, which we don't have. If we want to blend in, we must function as they do."

"Finley, you're going to owe me big time for every damn bruise I get," Trahern grumbled.

Cullen grinned. "Maybe Brenna will kiss your boo-boos and make them all better when we get home."

"Shut up, Cullen." Trahern cursed again when he bumped into the wall as the tunnel made a sharp turn.

What were they walking into? Were Larem and his buddies lurking in the darkness up ahead, or waiting for Cullen to charge out of the cave?

This whole expedition could turn into one major cluster fuck. But if the other three decided they were on a fool's mission and turned back, he would go on alone.

"We need to stop." Barak's whisper was barely a breath of air as he came to an abrupt halt.

All of them heard the voices coming toward them, and the approaching Blade were carrying light with them, as well. Someone else had the gift for the blue stones.

"We should keep moving, but let me do any talking." Barak started forward again.

Well, duh. That was obvious, since the rest of them didn't speak his language. They'd gone no more than ten yards when a Sworn Guardian and his Blade came into view. Barak put on the swagger that Larem and Joq had worn like a second skin. The four of them moved to the side to allow the approaching Blade to pass, but the other Guardian stopped and drew Barak aside. They talked for a minute before the Guardian signaled his Blade to move out.

Barak said something curt to the Guardian and his Blade before they left. When they were out of sight, he signaled them to resume their march, continuing on in silence until they reached the mouth of the cave. Outside, the cold silver light of the moon did little to lessen the darkness or the chill of the night air, but it felt damn good to be out of the choking, closed-in caves.

A short distance down the trail, Barak stopped and looked back. They were alone.

Cullen took one more look around before speaking. "What's wrong? What did that Guardian say to you?"

Barak looked worried. "He questioned our patrolling the same area that he and his Blade had been assigned, then complained that the other Blade had taken a break and hadn't come back yet. He suggested that we patrol the trail down to the valley, because with the mood the Guildmaster is in, he'd blame everyone if some crazy human made it past the caves."

Lonzo said, "So they are expecting Cullen."

"I think so. He also grumbled about all this unnecessary duty because of a Sworn Guardian who had been arrested and was awaiting execution. As of this evening Lusahn was being held prisoner, along with the sole surviving member of her Blade."

"Larem."

"It would have to be." Barak's expression turned grim. "But the execution order has been signed and could be carried out any time the Guildmaster decides to. All the Sworn Guardians and Blades have been ordered to do extra patrols, just in case someone is crazy enough to try to rescue her."

"It's no more than we expected." Trahern was staring all around them, studying the barren terrain of Barak's home world.

Lonzo had drawn his sword, holding it down at his side. "So what do we do now?"

"Nothing's changed. We walk in formation to the Guild and do whatever's necessary to get Lusahn out of there," Cullen replied.

Trahern asked Barak, "Do we have time to get there before your sun comes up?"

Barak studied the sky. "Yes, I would think so. However, it would be impossible to get her away from the Guild and back to the barrier before dawn."

Cullen had already reached that same conclusion. "And if we broke her out, we'd have to find a place to hole up until nightfall, and with every Guardian and Blade searching for us." He considered their options. "So the best bet is to hide first, break her out after the star sets, and then make a run for it."

Blake added his two cents' worth. "But every hour we delay makes it that much more likely they'll execute her before we can get to her."

Cullen's temper was frayed to the breaking point. "Damn it, Trahern, don't you think we know that! But what good would it do to stage a raid on the Guild in broad daylight? And you can see for miles in this wasteland; we'd be sitting ducks."

Lonzo stepped between them. "Can we take this argument somewhere else? We're too exposed on this hillside."

Paladin tempers always ran hot right before battle. Until they were safe, it would take a lot of effort to think clearly beyond the need to fight, even if it was with each other. Cullen shoved his anger back under lock and key.

"We've got two options. We can head for Lusahn's house, although they'd be more likely to look for us there. Or we could spend the day at Joq's cabin outside of town. We'd have farther to go to reach Lusahn at nightfall, but we'd have a clear view of anyone approaching the cabin. It has the added advantage of no close neighbors."

Trahern looked past Cullen to Barak. "What do you think?"

"I'd say Joq's is the best option. We can skirt the town, reducing our risk of running across another patrol. They'd be expecting us to head toward town, not away from it."

Cullen nodded. "Let's get moving. Standing on this ridge is making the back of my neck itch."

"Stay close. I wouldn't want you to walk off the side of the trail. You'd get to the bottom faster that way, but you wouldn't enjoy the trip as much." Barak gave them one of his fleeting smiles and led the way.

They automatically fell into their Blade formation and hiked down the hillside, stopping every so often to rest, since Lonzo and Trahern weren't yet acclimated to the thinner atmosphere. Each time, Barak would reach out with his extra-sensitive hearing to make sure they weren't being followed. So far, luck was with them.

By the time they reached the bottom, none of them were in the mood to talk. Barak led them to a small spring so they could drink their fill of the cool water. Despite a strong mineral aftertaste, the drink, combined with some cold water on his face, restored Cullen's energy for the rest of the long journey. As they followed a twisting route through the low, rolling hills, he tried to figure out how long it had been since he'd last slept through the night.

Two days? Three? It didn't matter. He'd stay up round the clock for the next week if that's what it took to get Lusahn back. But once she was safely back in his world, he was going to take her straight to bed. And they even might eventually get around to sleeping.

Barak cuffed him on the back of the head. "I've seen that look before. That better not be my sister you are thinking about, human."

It was too dark for Cullen to see Barak's face clearly, but the Other's voice held a touch of anger. "That's not for you to decide."

Barak's shoulders snapped back, and his chin lifted in challenge. "I am the only male she has left to stand for her. By our customs, you must approach me for permission to court her."

Cullen curled his hands into fists, ready to emphasize his point of view with them if it became necessary. "It's a little late for you to play big brother, don't you think? You were the one who left her alone."

"Not because I didn't care."

"Tell *her* that."

"I will, but that doesn't change anything. If you'd stayed on your side of the barrier, she wouldn't be in this mess. She is not for you to dally with."

That did it. He grabbed up a handful of Barak's shirt and jerked him forward. "I don't *dally*, Other, not with Lusahn! I'm risking my life, my friends' lives, and my career, because I can't stand the thought of living one more day without her. I love her and she loves me. Deal with it."

It took brute strength for Trahern to muscle them apart. He held Barak with one hand and Cullen with the other. Lonzo moved in close to offer his support should it become necessary.

"Cullen, cool it! We're all walking on a razor's edge here."

"Then tell Barak to stay out of my business!" He pushed against Trahern's hand, letting him know that he would go through him to get to Barak if the bastard didn't back off.

"Shut up, and I will." Trahern glared down at Barak. "You're one to be talking! You didn't stay on your side of the barrier either, and you sure as hell didn't pay any attention when Penn Sebastian told you to leave his sister alone."

Cullen could hear Barak's ragged breathing and his own pulse racing. Both of them wanted the same thing—Lusahn to be safe and happy—even if they didn't agree on all the details. And Trahern was right. While they were standing there arguing, the sky had grown lighter. The star would soon clear the horizon, bathing the countryside with its dim light. It was time to get to cover.

He stepped back, ending the confrontation. "Let's get moving. Joq's cabin should be just beyond that next rise."

Barak jerked his head in agreement before walking away. Cullen let him get a head start and then followed. He'd play nice with Barak if he could, but no one was going to come between him and Lusahn. No one.

The cabin was much as it had been when he'd last seen it. There were several sets of tracks in the area around the cabin, but nothing that would help identify who had been there. All he could tell was that they all appeared to be made by the same kind of boots that Lusahn and her friends wore.

Inside, the place was still trashed.

Cullen said, "Let's sleep in shifts. You all get some sack time, and I'll wake one of you to relieve me in two hours."

Trahern shook his head. "No way. You're running on empty, Finley, so you go first. The rest of us will take shifts and let you sleep."

Cullen wanted to argue but Trahern was right: he'd been living on adrenaline and worry for too long. Only a fool would risk blowing his mission out of pride.

"Good idea."

Barak finally spoke. "Eat something first. You'll sleep better, and it will help restore your strength. I'll see what Joq has that's still good."

It didn't take long for him to lay out a simple meal of fruit and cheese. While he did that, Trahern and Lonzo righted some of the furniture and made room for them to sit at the small table.

They ate in silence, each lost in his own thoughts. From the expression on Trahern's face, Cullen figured he was thinking about Brenna and wondering if he'd live long enough to see her again. Barak probably had some of the same thoughts about Lacey. Cullen had to wonder how it felt to be back in his home world after months away. Did he feel as much a stranger in it as the three Paladins?

When he'd eaten, Cullen stood up. "I'll find a spot to crash. Wake me when you need me."

He climbed up to the small loft overhead. It didn't feel right to stretch out in the dead man's bed, so he made a pallet on the floor. As he drifted off to sleep, he hoped the hours would pass quickly so they could get down to the business they came for.

"Cullen, damn it, wake up!"

He stirred a bit, trying to ignore both Lonzo's voice and the boot he kept prodding Cullen with. Cullen burrowed back into the pillow and ignored his friend.

"I'll give you thirty seconds to get moving before I dump this bucket of water on your head."

A few drops of water splashed on his face and ran down his cheek onto the blanket. When he didn't immediately sit up, those were followed by a trickle of water. By the time he mustered the energy to push himself upright, Lonzo had the bucket tilted and ready to pour.

"How long did I sleep?"

"Barak says the star will set in about two hours."

Cullen climbed slowly to his feet and stretched. "Anyone come snooping around?"

"Not that we've seen. While you slept, Trahern and I took a few turns around the perimeter, hoping to get used to this atmosphere."

"Yeah, that, combined with the lack of light and the permanent chill in the air, makes this the perfect vacation getaway." He met Lonzo's gaze. "I'm sorry I let things get out of hand with Barak earlier. It can't be easy for him to be back here, even if it's to rescue his sister."

"Don't sweat it. I think Trahern's reminder that Barak pulled the same thing with Lacey helped him see reason."

"And how do you feel about me and Lusahn?" Cullen concentrated on pulling his boots on, not wanting to see what Lonzo's long silence meant.

"It isn't a path I would have chosen for you, and it won't be easy. Our job was hard enough when all we knew about the Others was that they were murderous whack jobs. But now Barak plans on marrying a Paladin's sister; you're thinking along the same lines about Lusahn; and those two kids had all of us wrapped around their fingers in about five seconds flat."

Lonzo walked over to the small window under the eaves. "You'll be fighting an uphill battle with the Regents and even a lot of the Paladins, but your real friends will accept her because they care about you. I'm more worried about how this will affect your ability to do your job."

Cullen reached for his sword and strapped it on. "You're not telling me anything I haven't already been thinking about, but there's nothing I can do about it now. Once I've got Lusahn safely across the barrier, I'll worry about the details."

Trahern joined the party. "They're more than details, Cullen. Devlin and I talked while we were waiting for Barak to bring down the barrier. This is going to do more than rock the boat. The Regents are bound to find out about this little excursion, and we'll be lucky if they don't ship the lot of us off to the four corners of the world. They like things quiet and under the radar. Instead, one of their own died in a car bomb, two lawmen were murdered outside the installation in Missouri, I brought a civilian in without permission, an Other is living among us, and Devlin moved in with our Handler. I don't know how much more they'll sit still for before they go ballistic."

Trahern's pessimistic thoughts didn't help Cullen's mood, even if he shared the same thoughts. The best they could do was take things one step at a time.

"Let's go see if there's anything left to eat and iron out our plan."

They climbed down the ladder to the kitchen, to find Barak had been one step ahead of them. The last of the fruit and cheese was spread out on the table, along with a few bottles of Joq's beer.

Cullen took a swig and almost choked. "Lusahn mentioned that Joq's new hobby wasn't working out too well, but this tastes like he was trying to poison himself."

"You never did have much of a stomach for alcohol." Trahern upended his own bottle and guzzled about half of the vile stuff. "This needs to age for a while, but otherwise it's okay."

Lonzo sided with Cullen. "You could let this stuff age until hell freezes over, and it would still taste like piss."

They all looked at Barak to judge his reaction. He took a sizable drink, then pushed the bottle across to Trahern. "I don't know about the rest of you, but I'm not willing to stick around on the chance that stuff might improve."

Trahern finished his bottle, but didn't reach for more. "How soon are we out of here?"

"If we leave shortly before the star goes down, we should reach town about the time the Guardians and their Blades normally change shifts. Though things aren't being done normally, people are used to seeing the patrols head for the Guild about that time of day. So we won't draw as much notice then."

Lonzo reached for another piece of cheese. "That makes sense. Have either of you ever been inside the Guild?"

Cullen shook his head. "I've only been by it a couple of times. It's a two-story building near the edge of town. It's also one of the few that stays lit up twenty-four/seven."

"Any other good news?" Lonzo had his sword out, checking the blade.

"They don't have guns, and we do." Cullen pulled his out of his waistband and checked the magazine. Three pistols weren't much of an advantage against superior numbers, but any edge would help.

"Good. For a minute there, I thought we were in trouble." Lonzo sheathed his sword and pulled his pistol to give it a thorough going-over.

Trahern walked from window to window, looking for any sign of activity. "It's still quiet out there. Shall we, gentlemen?"

Cullen blocked the door. "I've said it before, but I want to say it again before things get hairy. I appreciate you all being here for me. For us."

"Aw, gee, Cullen, don't get all mushy on us. I can't fight when I'm teary-eyed." Trahern tucked his gun out of sight and put on his cloak.

Lonzo pretended to blot tears from his eyes. "Yeah, what he said."

As they started down the dusty trail, Barak pointed out landmarks to Trahern and Lonzo to help them get their bearings, since they'd hiked to Joq's in the dark.

"If we get separated, you want to head for that switchback trail winding up the rise. It will lead you right back to the caves where we crossed. Once you're inside, stay there out of sight. When we're all there, I'll bring the barrier down again."

"We need a backup plan in case the whole thing

goes sour," Cullen stopped and turned to face Joq's cabin. "If you go that way toward those foothills, you'll find another trail. At the top is the small cavern that someone from our side has been using to camp in. I'm guessing that means the barrier there isn't too stable, or they wouldn't be able to cross back and forth. If the first cave is crawling with Sworn Guardians and Blades, that's where we should try next."

Barak reluctantly nodded. "I don't know that area as well, but I agree that it would have to be unstable for the humans to use it regularly. It might even be a safer choice, since my people don't use it."

Trahern stared toward the mountains. "Lonzo and I are just along for the ride. You two decide, and we'll be fine with it."

"Does anyone else know about that back way, Cullen?" Barak asked.

"Only Larem, who followed us up there. Joq did, but he's dead."

"If we do the unexpected we stand a better chance of survival, so I say we use the back way." Barak looked at the others for confirmation.

Lonzo and Trahern nodded.

"Then we're set. We should reach town just after dark. We'll head for the Guild as if we were reporting in for the shift change, bust Lusahn out of her cell, then hightail it to the cave above Joq's place." Cullen knelt down to draw a map in the dust. "Here's the main street through town, and the Guild is on this corner."

He extended the line out of town. "We make a break for the hills and head for the cave up above Joq's." He pointed to where the cave was located. "If we get separated, we rendezvous there. Any questions?"

"No. Let's get moving. I feel like we have a target on our backs." Trahern pulled his hood down further over his face. "I'll be glad when we shake the dust from this place off our boots. No offense, Barak."

"None taken. After all, I left this world behind myself."

Trahern moved off to walk on Barak's right. "I don't blame you one damn bit."

As they drew closer to town, Cullen found himself growing calmer. This was it. Either they would succeed or they wouldn't.

If he had to guess their odds of success, he'd put them around 30/70. If luck was with them, maybe as much as 50/50. But with the Sworn Guardians on full alert expecting an attack, the element of surprise was gone.

All they could hope for was that their impersonation of a Guardian with his Blade would hold up until they reached the Guild. Once inside, they could throw off these confining cloaks and fight their way to Lusahn. That would probably be the easy part. But once the alarm was sounded, they'd have only a narrow window of opportunity before all hell broke loose.

What happened after that was anybody's guess.

Laurel gently picked up Shiri and carried the sleeping girl into the guest room, while Devlin sat with Bavi. The two of them had been playing cards for hours, but Devlin didn't mind. The boy was obviously scared, but when he'd spotted the deck of cards, his face had lit up. Evidently Cullen had spent enough time with the kid to teach him how to shuffle and play solitaire.

Judging by the stack of buttons sitting in front of Bavi, the boy was a natural-born card shark. He'd cleaned out D.J, Laurel, and Lacey. Devlin suspected the two women had let Bavi win, but he knew D.J. had been playing for keeps. It wasn't in his aggressive nature to go easy on an opponent, so he played and fought full-out, all the time.

Bavi set the deck down, his eyes straying to the window and then back to the door as if he could will Cullen and Barak's sister to suddenly appear. Devlin sipped his coffee, feeling bad for the boy, but he didn't have much experience in comforting kids.

He gave it his best shot. "Those three men who

went with Barak are among the finest warriors on this planet. And judging from what I've seen, Barak is right up there with them. If anybody can do the job, it's them."

Bavi's light eyes met Devlin's briefly before he picked up the cards again and began shuffling them. He handled them pretty well, considering how badly his hands were shaking.

"If they don't come back, what will happen to my sister and me?" He kept his gaze firmly on the cards. "We die?"

"Hell, no!" Devlin slammed his cup down on the table, slopping hot coffee on his hand. He forced himself to calm down. Bavi was skittish enough without Devlin scaring the hell out of him.

"Nobody's going to die, Bavi. I have every faith that Cullen and the others will bring Lusahn back safely. But if they don't"—he leaned forward for emphasis—"I promise you and Shiri will be taken care of."

"Why?"

Damn. "Because Cullen matters to me, and you matter to Cullen." He jerked his head in the direction Laurel had gone. "I won't lie to you. I'm a warrior, and shit happens, so I can't promise that I'll always be here. But Laurel is a woman of honor, and she would love you two like her own."

The more Devlin thought about it, the more he liked the idea of her having someone else to fuss over. Although his test readings were still holding steady, and a couple had even improved some more, that was no guarantee that he wouldn't cross the line the next time he died, and that would be it.

Suddenly, he was hit with a powerful urge to hold Laurel in his arms. They both needed the comfort of cuddling in bed, especially after some life-affirming lovemaking. He forced a lighter note into his voice. "It's about time for bed, don't you think? Would you like something else to eat first?"

Bavi's face lit up. "More of the bright things?"

Earlier, Laurel had shared her secret stash of sugary cereal with the children. Devlin had a fondness for the stuff as well, which is why Laurel had to keep it hidden. He was pretty sure he knew where she was keeping it now, and if they hurried, they could have it in their bowls and covered with milk before she caught them.

He gave Bavi a conspiratorial wink. "Sure, but don't tell Laurel. You get the milk while I get the cereal."

Bavi was up and heading for the kitchen before Devlin could move. Laurel might have Devlin's head for raiding her supplies, but he knew she wouldn't begrudge Bavi the sweet treat.

As the two of them chowed down, Devlin thought of his friends trapped in that other world and hoped they didn't get themselves killed. He'd lost too many friends over the years, and it was always hard to take. But Cullen, Trahern, and Barak deserved their chance at happiness with their women.

Gods above, she was weary of this whole situation. It was the second time in only a few hours that the Guildmaster had ordered Lusahn to come to his office. He seemed to think that she had some inside knowledge about Cullen's alleged plan to rescue her.

She'd told him the first time that she had no way of knowing any such thing, since she hadn't spoken to anyone but him and her cellmate since they'd dragged her into the Guild. He obviously hadn't believed her, since he'd let her stew for a few hours before calling her in again, then sending her back to her cell.

If Berk had been around she would have asked him what was going on, but she hadn't seen him since the day before. She hoped nothing had happened to him; her people needed Guardians like him. She would have liked to call him friend if she'd found out about his secret group before Cullen had arrived on the scene.

But it was too late to think about such things; the Guildmaster had finally announced his plans for her execution. It felt strange to be able to count down the remaining hours of her life. The star would set soon. When it arose in the morning, it would be the last dawn she would ever see.

She hoped she could walk to her death with dignity to maintain the honor of the q'Arc name. Until then she would stand vigil, savoring her past since she had no future.

Chapter 14

The town was spread out below them. With nightfall imminent the townspeople made their way home, ready for their day to be done. Cullen motioned for Barak and the other two Paladins to follow him back a short distance.

Lonzo leaned against a boulder and crossed his arms over his chest. "What's up, Professor?"

"If we wait a short while longer, the streets will empty out more. I know that time is critical, but I'd rather we not endanger civilians if we don't have to." Even if he didn't give a damn about the Others, Lusahn would. Trahern and Lonzo looked at each other and then shrugged.

Barak nodded his approval as he walked by. "I'll stand watch."

Darkness gradually settled over them, the faint moon hovering over the far horizon. Even when it rose to its highest point in the night sky, it would do little to light their way. In town that wouldn't matter, because streetlights lit the road in front of the Guild. Once they had Lusahn and were running for the caves, the darkness would help shield them from hostile eyes.

Barak returned and spoke to Cullen, keeping his voice low. "The streets are empty except for a few stragglers and the patrols."

"Then it's time."

Each man prepared for the battle ahead in his own way. Barak stared up at the moon, murmuring under his breath. Lonzo and Trahern rechecked their weapons with ruthless efficiency, while Cullen stared down at the Guild, fighting the urge to charge down the slope screaming for the blood of the Others who dared threaten his woman.

"Got the fidgets, Cullen?" Trahern's silver eyes glittered in the cold light. "You're the calm one, remember? D.J. and Lonzo cornered the fidget market years ago."

It was easy to remain calm when the only life he'd been risking was his own. Cullen glanced at his friends. Was this how Devlin felt when he sent his fellow Paladins into battle against overwhelming odds? If so, he could keep the job.

"Let's move out," he said.

The four of them formed up as a Guardian and his Blade returning from patrol. They kept their eyes on the road ahead, occasionally glancing to the left or right, alert to any threat.

A few blocks from the Guild they met another patrol; both the Guardian and two members of her Blade were women. Tall and rangy, they moved with the same arrogance Lusahn had. The leader got right up in Barak's face.

Not for the first time, Cullen wished he spoke the language. When the woman suddenly barked what sounded like a question in his direction, Barak stepped between them and growled something right back at her. For a minute they teetered on the edge of disaster, but then she backed off and walked away, her Blade right on her heels.

Cullen crowded in close. "What the hell was that all about?"

"She thought we were here to relieve her squad. I told her we'd been out hiking through the countryside all day and were on our way to report in." He turned his light-colored eyes in Cullen's direction. "She didn't like you staring at her."

"I wasn't."

"You were—but I told her it was my job to discipline a new recruit. Remind me to beat you later. Now let's get moving."

As they walked along, Cullen asked, "They really do that? Beat their recruits?"

"I was joking. She was sizing the three of you up for a good time some night, and asked if I thought you'd be interested. I told her that you were spoken for."

Trahern chimed in. "Hey, Cullen, what is it about you and the women on this side of the barrier? You were never that lucky at home."

"Jealous?" he teased. You only had to see Trahern with Brenna for ten seconds to know that the man was permanently out of circulation.

"Shut up—our target is dead ahead," Lonzo said.

Cullen checked the slide of his sword and that his gun was within easy reach. They'd agreed to use their blades first and the guns only as a last resort, since the noise would draw attention.

As Barak set foot on the bottom step that led up to the Guild entrance, a man in a Sworn Guardian uniform stepped out of the shadows at the top. He had his sword drawn and stared down at the four of them. After a hesitation he started down the steps, coming to a stop in front of Barak.

"It's been a long time, Barak q'Arc. What took you so long?" The Kalith male's smile started off slow, then spread into a wide grin.

"Berk?" Barak's grim expression lightened as he looked the man over from head to toe. "Since when do you wear the uniform of a Sworn Guardian?"

The stranger shrugged. "Someone had to take

up the cause when you left. Not that I blamed you for leaving. They gave you no choice."

"No, they didn't."

Berk looked past Barak at Cullen and the other two. His eyes widened slightly. "Interesting Blade you have, Barak—but then, you always did have a different way of looking at things. Or perhaps I should say, more balls than good sense."

"She's my sister."

Berk nodded. "And I respect your sister too much to let her die when the star rises."

The blood drained out of Cullen's head. They had barely arrived in time. If anything had delayed them a few hours more, Lusahn would have died never knowing that he'd come for her.

"Fine. We'll follow you, but make one false move, and it will be your last," Barak said.

Trahern and Lonzo flanked the man, giving Berk no room to escape as he sheathed his sword and led them a short distance down the street and into the shadows between two buildings. When he was sure they were safe from prying eyes, he studied the three Paladins.

"So, which one of you is this Cullen Finley who has caused such an uproar?"

Cullen stepped forward. "I'm Finley."

Berk's pale eyes were calculating. "She thought you'd have the good sense to stay on your side of the barrier."

Cullen glared at the Other male. "She thought wrong."

"Obviously." Berk grinned.

Cullen leaned in close, his hand grasping the hilt of his knife. "It won't go well for anyone who interferes with us."

The male stood his ground despite facing three Paladins armed and primed for battle. "I am not your enemy, human. At least not on this night. Tomorrow . . . who knows?"

Cullen's gut feeling was that the Other could be trusted, at least for the next few hours. "I can live with that. Where are they holding her?"

"In the cells upstairs, toward the back of the building."

That matched what Barak had told them earlier about the layout. The offices for the Guardians and their Blades were on the basement level. The Guildmaster and his associates had more luxurious offices on the main floor, and the second floor was reserved for storage and the occasional prisoner.

"How many Guardians and Blades are inside?"

"Too many for you to get past without questions or bloodshed."

Trahern leaned in close, forcing Berk to take a step backward. "You might be squeamish about a little bloodletting, Other, but we're not."

"I will help you free Lusahn if I can, but not at the expense of Guardians and Blades who are only doing their job. There's been enough of their blood spilled."

"If you've got a better plan, lay it out for us. Otherwise, get your Blade out of harm's way, because we're going in after her," Cullen said.

"Back off, Finley! Now isn't the time for threats." Barak shouldered between his old friend and the Paladins. "He could have betrayed us back there on the steps and didn't. Let's listen to what he has to say."

"There's another way into the building through the window on the second floor at the back, near the cells. I will unlock the window and make sure it will open easily for you. More than that, I cannot do."

Lonzo made a show of patting down his pockets. "Damn, I must have left my rope and grappling hook in my other pants."

Berk sighed. "All right. I'll take one of you into the Guild with me and upstairs to the window. From there, you can drop down a line. We must hurry now, before I'm missed."

"I'm the obvious choice to go with him." Barak pulled his hood back over his head.

Cullen shook his head sharply. "Like hell you are. If something goes wrong, you have the best chance of getting Lonzo and Trahern back across the barrier. If the Guild catches me, they might think I was acting alone."

Lonzo and Trahern exchanged glances. "We don't like it."

Paladins were used to fighting side by side in a type of battle where brute strength meant more than tactics. Watching a friend go into battle alone went against everything they stood for.

But Cullen wasn't going to back down. "I don't see that we have much choice. I'll go in with Berk. Give us ten minutes to get that window open. If you don't see any action, wait a few more minutes and then get the hell out of town."

Leave it to Trahern to get stubborn. "Damn it, Cullen, Devlin would—"

"Devlin's not in charge here, Blake. I am. Besides, Lusahn's my woman, my responsibility." Cullen turned to Barak. "Though she's your sister, she's sitting in that cell because of me. I'm going in after her."

The silence was as dark as the night sky as he waited them out.

"Ten minutes and not a minute more, Finley, but we won't be leaving. We'll be coming in, guns and swords drawn." Trahern already had his gun in hand. "God help anyone who stands in our way."

Cullen studied each man's face one more time, knowing there wasn't anyone he'd rather march into hell with.

"All right. Let's go."

"Follow closely, human, and I don't have to tell

you to keep your mouth shut and your head down," Berk warned him.

Cullen made eye contact with his three friends one last time before falling into step beside Berk.

As they marched down the street and up the steps to the Guild, Cullen stayed a step behind and slightly to the side, imitating a Blademate.

Berk reached out to open the door. "If I say something to you, just nod. We will draw less attention if we act comfortable with each other's company."

Cullen nodded and followed him through the entrance. Inside, blue stones set in wall sconces cast the room in bright light. If the small stones were valuable, what were these fist-sized chunks of brilliant crystal worth? And how like the bureaucracy to use more than their fair share of the badly needed light, while the people walked in darkness and lit their homes with candles.

They'd only gone a short distance when Berk abruptly stopped by what turned out to be a storage closet. Feeling dangerously exposed, Cullen stood in the hallway trying to look casual while Berk rummaged around inside. When the Other warrior finally came back out, he thrust a coiled rope into Cullen's hand.

So far, they were making progress. Then they passed by an open office, and a voice called out. Berk stiffened and then braced himself before turning back. He gave Cullen a pointed look, telling him without words to stay the hell out. Like he couldn't figure that out for himself?

Cullen stood at attention against the wall. Berk and the Other were arguing, judging by the sharp edge to Berk's voice. He hoped Berk could extract himself before their ten minutes were up and Trahern went all Rambo on the Guild's ass.

A trickle of sweat slithered down Cullen's spine, and he concentrated on judging the time by counting his heartbeat. If Berk didn't come out in the next minute, he'd have to reach the window on his own. The worst that could happen was that someone would challenge him, and they'd have to die.

So either Berk came out in ten more heartbeats, or Cullen was leaving without him. He counted them down: ten, nine, eight, seven, six— Then Berk reappeared. Thank God; he really hadn't wanted to go exploring on his own.

The Other stalked by, the rigid set to his shoulders and jaw verifying that the conversation hadn't been a pleasant one.

"We must hurry," Berk whispered.

Well, no shit! While Berk had been being raked over the coals, they'd lost precious time. If they didn't get the hell out of town soon, they'd lose the cloak of darkness long before they reached the caves.

Berk stopped before an intersection and held

his hand up for Cullen to stay back while he scouted ahead. When he saw the way was clear, he waved Cullen forward and around the corner. The staircase was ahead on the left.

Despite the armed guards, Berk headed right up the steps. They almost pulled it off, but at the last second the young guard barked out a couple of words, no doubt an order for them to halt.

Berk went up two more steps, then turned to face down the guard. When he responded, he didn't raise his voice but evidently he didn't need to. The guard immediately backed down, sounding apologetic. Berk continued up the stairs without looking back, and Cullen did the same, feeling like he had a target painted on his back.

Berk pushed the door at the top of the stairs open, then loped down the hall with Cullen close behind. He stopped in front of a window, unlocked it, and jerked the bottom sash up as far as it would go.

"The cells are on the opposite side from here. Release Lusahn and lower her down this wall. Your friends should be there to catch her, and then you." He held out a small bundle wrapped in dark cloth. "If you don't know how to pick the lock, Lusahn should. The key would have been easier, but I didn't think it was worth the risk of stealing it."

Cullen accepted the package and then held his hand out to Berk, surprising himself as much as the Other with the gesture. "Thank you for your help, Berk. I won't forget it, and Paladins have long memories."

Berk grasped Cullen's hand in an awkward grip. "You haven't made it to safety yet, Cullen Finley."

"No, but we might not have made it this far without your help. You'd better get out of here before someone gets curious."

Berk nodded. But before he'd gone two steps, he turned back with a stricken look on his face. "What are you going to do about Larem? If I'd had more time, I would have drugged his food. If you leave him behind, he's likely to raise an alarm."

"I'll let Lusahn decide how to deal with him."

Berk smiled sadly. "He was her Blade; it won't be easy for her. Make her happy, human. She deserves that much."

For the first time in hours, Cullen smiled. "I plan to."

Larem had been quiet for hours. Even his barbed comments would be preferable to the awful silence that gave her too much time to think about dying.

She hoped Bavi and Shiri were adjusting to their abrupt change in worlds. They'd both already been through so much. And she hoped Cullen wasn't suffering too much for leaving her behind. He'd done the right thing by taking her children to safety, but he had a warrior's heart, and retreat would sit badly on his conscience.

A noise caught her attention. She cocked her head, trying to pinpoint what had disturbed her. It came again from across the room. Someone was messing with the door to the cellblock. Were they trying to open it without making any noise? Why didn't they just barge in? Prisoners weren't entitled to any privacy.

Finally, the door opened far enough for a cloaked figure to slip through. At first she ignored the Blade, but then she realized there was something familiar about the way he moved. The dim light from the candle across the room made it impossible to pick out many details, but could it be . . . ?

She froze, unable to move, unable to breathe, unable to hope. If her eyes and mind were playing an ugly trick on her, she couldn't bear to know. Instead she waited, afraid to blink for fear the intruder would disappear.

When he stopped to check Larem's cell, she almost convinced herself that her eyes were lying to her, that Cullen Finley wasn't standing a short distance away.

But even before he looked in her direction, she rose to her feet, drinking in the sight of him. The chill that had surrounded her heart melted in an instant. She must have made a small noise, because

Cullen's head whipped around to face her. He shoved back the hood of his cloak and smiled that slow, sweet smile that made her pulse race and her skin tingle. They both reached the door of her cell at the same time. She grabbed his hands, and even with the cold metal bars between them, she could feel his warmth, his love.

Cullen broke off their kiss far too quickly. "My friends and your brother are waiting outside," he whispered, but even that soft sound caused Larem to stir.

"What about him?" Cullen was carefully unwrapping something rolled in a piece of cloth.

There was no easy answer—if Larem awoke, he was likely to scream for the Guardians. If he slept through their escape, the Guildmaster would likely focus all of his fury on his one remaining prisoner.

Rather than think about him, she asked, "What are you doing?"

"A Guardian named Berk slipped me these to pick the lock. He said if I didn't know how, you would." Cullen looked up from the wires and tools in his hand, his dark eyes twinkling. "Interesting talent for a Sworn Guardian to have."

His teasing helped distract her. She reached out to rifle through the tools. "Joq taught me. He said that picking locks took concentration and a light touch, good skills when it came to investigating."

Cullen's laughter was silent. "Sounds like you liked poking that pretty nose of yours in places it didn't belong."

"That was a side benefit." She reached through the bars and positioned the picks just so. Then, with her eyes closed, she began the delicate process of undoing the lock.

Cullen used the rest of the tools to work on Larem's door, and Lusahn tried not to think about why. Cullen had already killed Joq so that she didn't have to end her mentor's life. It wouldn't be fair to ask him to deal with Larem, too, just because she still felt something for her childhood friend.

Everything went smoothly until the lock on Larem's door suddenly gave way, and the door swung open before Cullen could catch it. The screech of the metal hinges jerked Larem out of a deep sleep. Warrior that he was, he went from groggy to full alert in an instant.

"What? Who?" The second he recognized Cullen, Larem charged forward. Cullen met Larem's attack head-on.

Lusahn's lock finally clicked open, and she rushed into Larem's cell, trying to help Cullen without becoming entangled in the fight herself. Finally, she picked up the bucket and slammed it into the back of Larem's head.

The blow slowed Larem down enough that

Cullen was able to shove him down onto the hard stone floor. He held him there with a knee on his chest and his hands around Larem's throat.

"Lay there and stay quiet, Other, or I'll gut you right now." Cullen's lips were curled back over his teeth, the promise of death in his eyes.

"I'm a dead man anyway, human. Who do you think will die in her place?" Larem glared up at Lusahn. "What honor she had died the day you first crossed the barrier."

"Shut the fuck up," Cullen snarled, and slapped Larem across the face.

When Larem started to speak again, Cullen pressed a knife to the Other's neck, then looked up at Lusahn. "Here are the choices. I could knock him out, but if he regains consciousness too soon, we're all in danger. So either I kill him now or he goes with us. What's it going to be?"

Chapter 15

*C*ullen jerked the Other to his feet, keeping pressure on the knife. His instinct was to end Larem's miserable life—any other choice only complicated things, and their chances were already slim.

But one look at Lusahn's pain-filled eyes stopped him. Even though the male's blood would be on his hands, Lusahn would carry the burden of her Blademate's death on her soul.

"Take this rope," he told her as he tossed it to her. "There's a window on the other end of the building. Do you know the one I mean?"

"Yes, it faces the back of the building."

"That's the one. We'll use the rope to climb down so we don't have to fight our way out of this place. With luck, we'll be in the hills before you're missed."

Larem said proudly, "If you're going to kill me, I'd rather die here."

Lusahn got right in his face. "Quiet! You have no say in the matter. Enjoy the ability to breathe while you still have it."

"You tell him, honey." Cullen grinned. "And remember this, buddy: if it comes to killing you, *I'm* the one who decides if you get to die quickly or if it will take an eternity. Not her, not you. Me. Understand?"

Larem jerked his head in agreement. Good. Now maybe they could get the hell out of Dodge.

"Let's go." He shoved Larem out of the cell ahead of him, his pistol in the Other's back.

Lusahn led the way to the window. The temperature in the storeroom had dropped from the chill of the night air. They had to get out before someone noticed the cold air and came to investigate. He handed his knife to Lusahn so she could keep an eye on Larem, then leaned out of the window to look for Barak and the two Paladins.

One of the shadows behind the next building moved as Barak revealed himself to let Cullen know they were there and waiting. He waved them closer, figuring on sending Larem down first and then Lusahn. If Larem tried to pull anything, Cullen could count on Trahern to take care of the problem with brutal efficiency. After they were safely down he'd start down himself, hoping to close the window behind him.

"Come on, Larem, you go first."

The Other grabbed the rope as Cullen braced himself to lower the male down to the ground. He half expected Larem to make a last-ditch effort to sound the alarm by making noise on his way down, but his descent was almost silent. When he reached the ground, the Paladins quickly surrounded him and led him away into the darkness.

"Okay, honey, it's your turn."

Lusahn gave him a quick kiss, then swung her legs over the windowsill and used the rope to walk herself down into her brother's waiting arms. When they moved out of the way, Cullen wound up the rope and looped it over his shoulder. Leaving it behind might implicate Berk, and he had no desire to cause problems for the Kalith warrior. He eased himself outside and slowly lowered himself to hang from the sill.

For the life of him, he couldn't figure out a way to close the window from the outside without risking a nasty fall and a lot of noise. Hopefully whoever discovered the open window would think it had been left open by mistake. Bracing himself for the impact, he pushed back and dropped. He hit the ground with a teeth-jarring impact, but otherwise intact.

Trahern loomed up out of the shadows. "You cut it pretty damn close, Cullen."

"We ran into a complication." He looked past Trahern to where Lonzo had gagged Larem with a strip of cloth.

"Yeah, we noticed. What are you going to do with him?" Trahern's silver eyes glittered coldly in the darkness. "Devlin won't like you bringing an extra across with you."

"Tell me something I don't know. Maybe we'll think of an alternative on the way."

"You know what the best alternative is." Trahern's hand went to the pommel of his sword. "I'll take care of it if you can't."

His friend meant well, but it was hard not to be insulted by the offer. Cullen could kill, and Trahern damn well knew it. They'd fought together against the Others often enough, sometimes back-to-back against overwhelming odds. But Larem was the innocent in this mess. If Cullen had stayed on his side of the barrier or if Lusahn had taken him prisoner like she should have, Larem wouldn't be in disgrace and likely under the same death sentence as his Sworn Guardian. As much as Cullen hated the Other male, he didn't want to have to kill him.

But he would if there was no other choice.

"Let's move out. We're heading for the cave above Joq's place, Lusahn."

Trahern gave Cullen one last hard look and then nodded. "Come on, Lonzo, let's keep our new friend company." Then he shoved Larem out in front of him.

Lusahn's emotions were in turmoil as they slipped from shadow to shadow, trying to make it out of town without incident. The only constant comfort was Cullen. There had only been time for a quick hug before following her brother away from the Guild. But Cullen held her hand as they walked, never letting go unless the path became too narrow to walk together.

She concentrated on his touch rather than letting herself think about the two Kalith males in their party. Barak had hugged her, and she'd automatically hugged him back before she remembered how much he'd hurt her. His risking everything to come for her, though, would go a long way toward bridging the gap between them.

And Larem—her friend, her Blademate, and now her enemy. Now wasn't the time for solving problems, though, not until these brave men were safely back on the other side of the barrier. That was another puzzle she had no answer for. Why had the other two Paladins risked their lives for hers?

Like all of her kind, she had grown up hearing about the monsters who lurked on the other side of the barrier, killers who relished their jobs, dancing in the blood of her people. Cullen certainly didn't fit that description, and she had to think his friends weren't all that different from him.

Barak came to a sudden halt. "Everybody get down! There's a patrol coming this way." He led them into a cluster of boulders and ducked down.

Lusahn knelt between Cullen and his cold-eyed friend. The third Paladin had control of Larem, with a knife held at his throat, telling her Blademate without words that if he made a sound, it would be his last. She closed her eyes and prayed that the gods would guide Larem wisely.

The soft crunch of the passing Blade's boots echoed in the night. The Sworn Guardian leading them seemed more intent on returning to town than on watching for invaders, and they continued on without pausing.

Cullen waited until they were well out of sight before signaling to continue. Exhausted, Lusahn kept planting one foot in front of the other; stopping would risk everyone's life, not just her own.

Finally they reached the small stream where she and Cullen had stopped only days before. Barak led them a short distance off the path and then collapsed on the ground to rest. The others took long drinks of the cool water before joining him.

Cullen dropped down beside Lusahn, wrapping his arm around her shoulders and pulling her tightly against him. "Did my friends get a chance to introduce themselves?"

She mustered up a smile for the two Paladins. "No, there wasn't time."

"The tall one is Blake Trahern. Lonzo Jones is the one keeping Larem in line."

Each man nodded in her direction at the mention of his name. Lonzo reminded her a bit of Cullen, but the one with silver eyes had an air of danger that set him apart even among his own kind. She shivered, not entirely from the night air. Were all human males so intense?

"How much farther?" the one called Trahern asked.

Barak studied the dark outline of the hills to the east. "Another hour, maybe two, depending on how heavily patrolled the area is. If we keep having to avoid them, it could take longer."

Lonzo Jones spoke up. "Would it be better if we separated? A smaller group might find it easier to avoid detection."

They all looked to Cullen for a response. She hoped they stayed together, knowing he would worry about his friends if they weren't with him. Besides, no one should have to deal with Larem alone.

Cullen mulled it over. "I'd rather stick together in case we have to fight our way to the top. Lusahn isn't armed, and neither is Larem. That leaves four swords to protect six people."

"Now that we're out of town, is there any reason we can't use our guns if we were cornered?" Trahern asked.

"Only the noise factor. If we start blasting away, every patrol in the area will know right where we are." While he spoke, Cullen toyed with Lusahn's braid, as if he needed to be in constant physical contact to believe she was really there.

She knew just how he felt. If her brother and the other men hadn't been there, she would have been all over him, touching and tasting, absorbing his warmth into her soul.

"We should get moving." She stood, and the others followed suit without complaint. They had to be as tired as she was, but the driving need to reach safety provided a surge of energy.

The climb grew more strenuous as they started winding their way up the steep hillside. The path that Joq had shown them would have been easier to follow, but they would also be more likely to run into a patrol. It was hard to find solid footing in the darkness, but Barak had an uncanny knack for finding the easiest way through the terrain.

Though she was grateful, his skill reminded her how much her people had lost when he'd chosen to leave their world. And now she was no better than he was, choosing her heart's needs over duty by following her Paladin lover across the barrier.

A shower of gravel rained down from above. Cullen shoved her against the hillside, covering her body with his, as the rest of their party drew their weapons and sought shelter among the rocky out-croppings.

For several seconds, the night was silent. Then, in a rush of running feet and battle cries, a Guardian charged into their midst with his Blade spreading out behind him.

Lusahn reached for her sword, only to come up empty. Cullen tossed her a knife and then engaged the Sworn Guardian. Barak had infused his energy into the blue stone inlays in his sword, which gave off swirls of blue light in the darkness. Her heart was in her throat as she watched him fight. She had always known he was good, but his skill had visibly improved in the time he had spent in the human world.

Barak used the flat side of his blade to strike a ringing blow to his opponent's head, who collapsed on the ground. The Blade warrior would likely live to fight another day; she hoped the rest of them would be as lucky.

No one was having an easy time fighting on the steep hillside. She noticed Larem trying to sidle away from the group and was tempted to let him escape, but where would he go? Even if he managed to journey to a distant town, the Guildmaster would eventually find him.

She charged after Larem and grabbed his arm. He tried to fight free, but her knife at his throat took the fight out of him.

Barak joined Cullen in fighting the Guardian, and it wasn't long before they had him cornered. Neither of them moved in for the kill, confusing their opponent. He clearly expected to be fighting for his life; instead, he was herded step by step back toward his remaining two Blade members. Their proximity further hampered his ability to fight.

"Drop your sword, Guardian," Cullen growled as he danced forward, forcing the Kalith warrior to retreat until he had nowhere else to go. "I'd rather not kill you, but I will."

Trahern and Lonzo had taken their cues from Barak and Cullen, disarming rather than killing the Blademates. Their leader was still armed, but bleeding from a slash on his sword arm. His expression was grim with pain and defeat, but he finally dropped his sword and held out his hands. His Blade did the same.

Cullen held him at sword point until Barak and Lonzo could find and confiscate their remaining weapons. They had a nice little stash piled on the ground when they were done.

Breathing heavily, Cullen looked around. "Lusahn, why don't you borrow one of their swords? I'd feel better if you were armed with more than a knife."

She left Larem's side and checked out the three captured swords. After trying them for fit, she picked the one the Guardian had been fighting with. He started to protest, clearly not happy at the loss of a favored weapon. But when Cullen brought the tip of his sword up in the male's face, he shut up.

She removed his scabbard and belt from around his waist and strapped it onto her own. "Consider it a loan, Guardian, rather than a theft. I promise to take good care of your sword, and I will try to leave it behind when I no longer have need of it. It's the best I can do."

The male glared at her, then turned his venom in Cullen's direction. "You won't live long enough to reach the barrier, human."

"We've made it this far. No reason to think we won't make it the rest of the way." Cullen pulled out the rope he'd been carrying and cut several lengths of it. "Let's truss these turkeys up."

Trahern and Lonzo made quick work of binding the prisoners, and Cullen was relieved that his friends had accepted his decision to spare the Kalith warriors' lives. It was the right thing to do, but he hoped it didn't come back to bite them on the ass before they reached safety. He told himself that he'd done it for Lusahn's sake, knowing that each life lost in freeing her would weigh heavily on her. But the truth was that he couldn't kill them in cold blood. They didn't deserve to die for protecting their world and doing their job. If they crossed the barrier, intent on murder, he would draw his sword. But not today, if he could help it.

Barak had already started up the slope, with the rest of the group following at regular intervals. Even Larem was climbing without needing Lonzo's sword to prod him along. Lusahn waited until Cullen picked up the last of the captured weapons. He slipped a couple of the knives into his belt, and bundled the rest under his arm.

When they'd gone a short distance, Lusahn looked back to where they'd left the warriors tied up. "Thank you, Cullen." She rose up on her toes to kiss him. "For them and for Larem, I thank you."

"Yeah, well, I can't promise it will happen again. I'm almost out of rope." Part of him was serious, but the small joke helped lighten the worry in his lover's eyes.

That was when he realized that the star was rising. The unrelenting darkness had faded to a shadowy gray, allowing him to see details that had been only dim shapes a short time before. They could travel faster as the path in front of them became clearer.

It also meant that their enemies would have an easier time tracking them. They were less than two miles from the caves, but the Guildmaster would have ordered the Sworn Guardians and their

Blades to heavily patrol anywhere the barrier was exposed. His gut told him there was still blood to be spilled before they reached safety.

About thirty minutes later, with the star shining dully overhead, they reached the top of the ridge. Barak was puffing from exertion almost as badly as the Paladins, and Cullen teased, "Barak, one would think you were human from the way you're gasping for breath."

It was hard to tell if Barak's nasty look was directed at Cullen, or at his sister for laughing.

Larem shifted his weight from side to side, largely ignored since no one had any good ideas about what to do with him. Devlin was going to have Cullen's hide for showing up with yet another stray, especially one who was likely to bite the hand that saved him.

Cullen sighed. "Weapons check."

When Lusahn automatically drew her sword and examined the edge of the blade, Trahern and Lonzo both stopped to watch her. Cullen didn't blame them. She was a beautiful woman, and the added confidence of her warrior training shone like a beacon, drawing their eyes to her strength.

Barak pulled a small sack out from under his cloak. "This may be our last chance to eat." He handed out cheese and some fruit that had seen better days. "Sorry it's not more."

Cullen waved off the apology. "At least you

thought to snag some food. It never even crossed my mind."

Barak's eyes flicked to Lusahn and then back to Cullen. "You had other, more important matters to consider."

If this moment was the last peaceful one Cullen could share with Lusahn, he wanted some privacy. "The rest of you go on ahead. Lusahn and I will be along in a minute."

Trahern's mouth quirked up in a knowing smile while Lonzo rolled his eyes and shook his head. Barak frowned but prodded Larem, who was shooting daggers in Lusahn's direction, into moving out. Cullen stepped in front of her, placing himself between her and the bitter male.

Though they couldn't linger for long, if he didn't kiss her in the next fifteen seconds, he would explode. He reached out for his woman.

Chapter 16

*L*usahn looked at him and then backed up a step. Smart woman: she recognized a male who was thinking with the wrong part of his body. Now wasn't the time, and this dismal hillside certainly wasn't the place, but his body burned to have her. A few scrapes on his bare ass from sand and gravel would be a small price to pay.

"Oh, no, Cullen. Don't think I'd . . . that we'd . . ." She kept backing away until he had her cornered against a boulder.

"Just kiss me, Lusahn. I'll settle for that."

She held out her arms, pulling him in for a kiss that started off sweet but didn't stay that way. His woman knew what she wanted from him and exactly how to get it as her tongue danced and dueled with his. Her hands stroked up and down his arms and then his back. Finally, temptress that she was, she teased his mouth with the tip of her tongue as her wicked, wicked fingers stroked the front of his pants, tracing the length and shape of him until she had him groaning for mercy.

He lifted her onto the rock and stepped between her knees, pressing her back until their bodies fit together. The sweet crush of her breasts against his chest and the damp heat of her body's craving for his was heady stuff. He tried to hold on to the shreds of his self-control, because one of them had to cling to sanity. But, damn it, why did it have to be him?

It took every bit of his resolve to wrench his mouth away from hers. Staring down into her silvery eyes, he brushed a lock of hair back from her face.

"You know I love you." It wasn't a question, but a statement. "You're mine; the kids are mine. That's the way it's going to be."

She nodded with a sweet smile. Her hand caressed the side of his face. "Your whiskers are back. I like them."

"I'll grow a beard, if that's what you want."

Her fingers brushed back and forth across his stubble. "I want."

He stepped back. "But we've got to get moving before your brother comes looking for me with his sword." He offered her a hand up. "Did I really see that thing glowing in the dark?"

Lusahn nodded. "Another of his gifts."

"What other tricks does Barak have up his sleeve?" Cullen asked, then grinned at the confused look on Lusahn's face. "Never mind. There'll be plenty of time later for you to learn our expressions."

Her smile was a little sad. "I hope so, Cullen Finley. I would like that."

Life in his world would be complicated, their union causing far-reaching ripple effects throughout the Regent's organization. But he didn't give a flying fuck about that, as long as he woke up with Lusahn's face on the pillow next to his every morning.

"Let's go home." He took her hand as they started the last leg of their journey.

The early morning was quiet. Too quiet. Lusahn caught Cullen's arm, stopping him. The two of them had caught up with the others a short time before, then moved up to take the lead. She trusted her brother's ability to fight, but it had been too long since he'd last patrolled their world.

She motioned the others closer and said quietly, "They're waiting up ahead in those rocks."

The cold-eyed one studied the terrain ahead. "What do you see that I don't?" He sounded more curious than doubtful.

"Because that's where I'd be." She drew her borrowed sword. "Once we pass that next turn, the cave will be in sight. Rather than scatter the patrols, trying to figure out which cave we sought or which path we chose, they concentrated on protecting the targets themselves."

"Makes sense."

She walked over to Larem and removed his gag. "Will you fight for us or against us?"

Cullen moved up behind her, but made no comment.

"I swore an oath to protect you, Lusahn. I will honor that oath." He held out his bound hands.

She cut his ropes and handed him two knives that she pulled from Cullen's belt. Larem accepted the weapons with a nod of his head.

Cullen pushed past Lusahn to confront Larem. "You betray her, and you die."

Larem's answering smile was nasty and bitter. "I'll see to my own honor, Paladin. You see to yours." Then he assumed his usual position guarding Lusahn's back.

It felt good to have her old friend where he belonged. The wounds between them were too deep to be healed quickly, but it was a start.

Everyone now had their swords in hand. Since the need for silence was over, the three Paladins also held guns, the promise of death in their eyes. These men had risked everything for her and her children. She could do no less for them.

"Now we fight!" She charged forward, hoping the surprise attack would slow their opponents' reactions.

Then the Guildmaster stepped out of the shadows. He spent so much time behind his desk, it was easy to forget he'd been a formidable warrior. Three Sworn Guardians and their Blades formed up around him. The odds could have been worse. If he'd held back additional Blades in reserve, they would deal with that when the time came.

"Lusahn, I see your human did come back. How unfortunate for him. He escaped our Blades one time. It won't happen twice." The Guildmaster scanned the rest of her group, his eyes widening in surprise when he saw Barak. "By the gods, I'm surprised you found the courage to return, Barak q'Arc. We all thought you'd sought the coward's way out of his responsibilities by seeking the light. Yet instead of serving your people, you aid their enemies."

"My actions are not for you to judge, Guildmaster. Look to your own conscience about the disappearance of light from this world. Do these males of honor who serve you realize that you condone the theft of the blue stones, either by your involvement or your inaction?" The writing along Barak's sword flared brightly in the gray light.

The Guildmaster staggered back a step at the display of power. When the Paladins snickered, his face flushed hot and angry. The Sworn Guardians held their positions, but two of them looked toward the Guildmaster with disapproval.

Lusahn knew the Blades would follow their Guardians' lead without question, and she added to Barak's pressure on the Guildmaster.

"Did you also tell them that you condemned not just me, but also my Blademate without a trial, gloating as you did so? Larem was guilty of nothing but holding true to his oath. Do they know that you were prepared to see us dead, rather than carry out your true duties to the people of Kalithia?"

"Silence, woman! You speak of things you have no knowledge of." He brought up his sword, taking a half step forward.

She continued undaunted. "These warriors from the world of light have seen our people clutching the blue stones in their hands, hoping to buy their way into the light. My former Sworn Guardian Joq admitted that he was involved, having given up on the Guild in disgust. These are the truths I know."

She met the gaze of each Guardian in turn before saying, "I am a Sworn Guardian of my people, Guildmaster. Do you wish to challenge that?"

Bellowing in rage, he charged forward. She met his attack head-on, and the battle began. The two-to-one odds made it hard to maneuver, but the confined area hampered their opponents as well.

The Guardians had chosen their position well, making it difficult for Cullen and his men to fight their way through to make a run for the cave.

The Guildmaster caught her sword with a blow hard enough to rattle her teeth, but she stood her ground. When Cullen tried to sweep in from the side to engage her opponent, she shouted for him to back away. This fight was hers, and hers alone.

All her anger over the rape of her world and all of her fear over facing life in a new one poured through her and into her sword. Her mouth curved in a smile that showed lots of teeth and had nothing to do with joy as she led the Guildmaster in the intricate dance of death.

One of the Guardians and one of his Blademates teamed up to fight Cullen. Caught between the blur of their swords, he couldn't fight his way clear to help Lusahn. His head told him that she was capable of defending herself, but his heart wasn't listening.

This time he would not stay his hand from striking a killing blow—not with the woman he loved fighting for her life. He took out his two opponents in quick order. Neither was dead when they hit the ground, but they would be if they lifted their weapons again.

He tried to nudge Lusahn to the side, ready to take on the Guildmaster himself, but she would have none of it. Battle fever had claimed her, and he would only hamper her if he insisted on staying in her way.

"Cullen!"

Lonzo had taken a nasty cut to his shoulder; a stream of blood ran down his arm. The Guardian lifted his sword high, ready to swing it in an arc that would separate Lonzo's head from his body. There would be no coming back from that. Cullen lunged forward to block the downward stroke of the blade, but couldn't get there quickly enough.

Bile rose in his throat as he braced himself to see his friend die for good, when a startled look crossed the Guardian's face and he collapsed to his knees, then fell facedown in the dust. Cullen and Lonzo stared down at the body, trying to make sense of what had happened. Larem stood behind the dying Guardian, holding the knife he'd just shoved hilt-deep in the male's back.

Larem's eyes looked every bit as dead as those of the warrior's crumpled on the ground before him. Then life flooded back into his face as he grabbed Lonzo's sword from his hand and charged back into the fight.

Cullen tried not to resent the way Lusahn accepted Larem's presence at her side. He wrapped Lonzo's good arm around his own shoulder, then inched past the fighting, trying to get to the cave beyond.

"Follow as you can!" he hollered, hoping he'd be heard over the clash of metal and voices raised in challenge or pain.

One by one, the others moved past their opponents, who were greatly reduced in number, retreating toward the cave. Inside, Cullen eased Lonzo down onto one of the abandoned sleeping bags, then sliced off a piece of the bag to press on the open wound. Right now his friend was in more danger of bleeding out than from any possible infection.

"I'll be back."

Lonzo mustered up a smile. "I think I'll wait here."

"You do that." Cullen headed back out to help the others; if Lonzo was up to making bad jokes, he'd survive.

Trahern and Barak were playing rearguard, holding the Guardians and the few Blades still standing at bay while Lusahn and Larem went after the Guildmaster with deadly intent. The fool didn't realize he was backing straight into Cullen's sword until the point of it hit his back.

"Freeze and drop your sword, or these are the last words you'll ever hear." Cullen gave his blade a nudge to show the bastard he meant business. "It won't take much to convince me that both of our worlds would be better off without you."

The Guildmaster immediately dropped his weapon. "Don't kill me! I'll call off my men."

"Tell them to leave the area. We'll be keeping you with us to make sure they stay gone."

The Guildmaster nodded, his head bobbing up and down like a yo-yo. "Retreat! Retreat!"

The Kaliths clustered together and backed down the path, helping their wounded and leaving their dead behind. Trahern held his position until he was sure they were gone, at least for now.

Cullen didn't care what they did once everyone had reached the safety of the cave. The entrance was narrow enough for two to defend indefinitely while Barak brought down the narrow strip of the barrier.

"Anyone hurt besides Lonzo?" he asked.

"Nothing that won't heal on its own." Trahern leaned heavily against the entrance, his gaze moving constantly over the terrain.

Barak had taken charge of the Guildmaster, forcing the older man to kneel against the wall. "Move and you die," he growled. Then he looked toward Cullen. "Give me a minute to catch my breath, and I'll start working on the barrier."

Cullen hoped that it wouldn't take hours this time. The sooner he shook the dust of this world off his feet, the happier he'd be. He looked around for Larem and saw him sitting down next to Lonzo, with Lusahn wrapping a strip of cloth around his ribs. Evidently the Guildmaster had managed to get in one good stroke before they'd brought him to bay.

Cullen didn't like seeing Lusahn fuss over the male, but he'd cut the bastard some slack for saving Lonzo's life. It gratified him greatly that as soon as she tied off the bandage, she was up and heading straight for his arms.

He buried his face in her hair, breathing in her scent and sharing his strength with her. "We'll be home soon."

"Good."

An hour later, they were still in the cave, the barrier glowing brightly. Barak was doing his best, but with no success. It didn't help that he hadn't fully recovered from his run-in with Mount Rainier only a few days before. Even if he'd been at full strength, the barrier was unpredictable.

Cullen joined Trahern on guard duty at the entrance. "Think they'll be back?"

Cullen scanned the hillside, looking for any sign of the vanquished Guardians. "Yeah, they'll be back and bring all their buddies with them. They might not give a rat's ass about their precious Guildmaster, but they won't take being bested on their own turf lightly."

Trahern glanced back into the cave. "We can hold out here for a while, but without food or water, Lonzo's going to be in pretty bad shape."

A movement in the cave caught Cullen's attention. Lusahn stood glaring at her brother, who was shaking his head.

He joined them. "What's the problem?"

"Him. He's about to fall over on his face, but he won't take a break and he won't let me help."

"Why not, Barak?"

"It's never been done. To bring it down, you have to mold your energy signature to match the barrier's own. It can't resonate with two."

"How do you know, if it's never been tried? You're both tired, but maybe together you'll be able to bring it down."

The slide of steel made them all look toward the entrance. Trahern was back in battle stance. "They're coming."

The Guildmaster broke his sullen silence. "Your blood will run like a river, human—but I gave orders that my three be captured alive. Her death will be a public spectacle, along with her brother's and her Blademate's."

That did it. Cullen walked over and shut the bastard up with a solid right hook. The Guildmaster's head hit the cave wall with a satisfying thud.

Lusahn smiled her approval as she held out her

hand to Barak. He stared down at it before slowly enfolding it with his own. "Everything else has changed in my life, sister. Why not how we work the light?"

Together they turned to face the energy field and held out their free hands. Cullen stared at the beauty of his lover's face reflecting all of the colors that shimmered and shifted in the barrier. Almost immediately he could see a change in the colors, as they began to fade and stretch.

"It's going down!" he shouted as he heard the clash of Trahern's sword against the swarm of Others trying to force their way inside the cave.

He couldn't afford to add his sword to their defenses, not with the wounded needing his help. Larem managed to push himself up, but Lonzo had trouble getting his legs to support him.

"I will get him across," Larem said. "Go help your friend."

The offer surprised Cullen, but he didn't argue.

Knowing better than to surprise Trahern when he was in fight mode, Cullen shouted, "Trahern! I'm coming up beside you."

Trahern automatically shifted to the left, making room for Cullen to fight at his side. "How much longer?" he asked.

"It shouldn't be long now." He hoped.

"Good, because my dance card's full, and there's more of the bastards coming up the hillside."

"It's down!"

At Lusahn's shout of triumph, Cullen risked a quick look behind him to see her shove Lonzo and Larem across while Barak remained frozen in concentration. Then she drew her sword and joined them at the entrance.

"Get ready to run on a count of three!" Cullen ordered. Though his arm felt about to fall off, he did his best to push the determined Others back.

"One—two—three!"

First Lusahn retreated, followed by Trahern. Cullen backed up until he was almost to Barak. "Now you, Barak! I can't hold them off much longer."

Barak nodded, still chanting under his breath and stepped across. When Cullen broke for the other side, the Others were but a step behind him. He dove headfirst across the line, where ready hands grabbed him, pulling him to safety.

The Guardians skittered to a halt, unwilling to pursue their quarry across the divide. Barak and Lusahn raised their voices in unison, and the barrier snapped back into place.

They were home at last.

God, Cullen couldn't wait to get home with Lusahn. Yeah, sure, Devlin had good reasons for being seriously pissed. Cullen's disappearance had been especially hard on his close friends; then, too, it hadn't been easy for Devlin to sit home while his friends faced unknown dangers in the Other's world. He also regretted adding to Devlin's hassles with the Regents.

They'd been given a short reprieve, since the Regents had announced a major reorganization right about the time Cullen had led the rescue party into Kalithia. But it wouldn't last long. A new Regent would soon take over the Pacific Northwest region, and once the new top dog took office, they could all expect changes.

He'd be lucky if they didn't kick his ass out of the organization, but he wasn't going to worry about that yet.

"We're here," he told Lusahn as he turned into the driveway. When they climbed out of his car, she seemed relieved to have her feet back on solid ground. Still, she looked around the neighborhood with great interest as he led the way to the front door.

The damn key wouldn't go in the lock, maybe because his hand was shaking so much. When he finally got it to work, Cullen pushed the door open and let Lusahn walk in ahead of him.

As she walked into the living room, her face lit up. Turning slowly, as if being careful not to miss a thing, she smiled, her eyes sparkling with obvious delight.

"So much wood!" She trailed her fingers along the mantel over the fireplace. "And the colors!"

She liked it. That was very good. He'd tried to imagine how his home would appear to Lusahn, whose world was so stark. Because he spent so much time in the dark world of the tunnels, he'd furnished his home in the bright colors of a summer's day: blues, greens, and sunny yellow. He was happy there, yet he'd also felt that something was missing.

Now he knew exactly what that had been: her. He'd been waiting for this moment his entire life.

He dropped his keys on a side table and headed straight for Lusahn. She stepped right into his arms and kissed him.

Now they were finally alone together, he relearned the fit of her body against his and the way her breast was the perfect fit for his hand. She did some exploring of her own, the whisper-soft touch of her fingers fanning the flames between them.

"Would you like to check out the bedroom next?" He traced kisses along the curve of her face to that spot behind her ear that always made her moan.

She pushed back and looked up at him, a worried look on her face. "We should talk before Lacey and my brother bring Bavi and Shiri home."

"Why?"

"Your friend Devlin wasn't happy about Larem coming with us."

"No, but he'll get over it. Besides, Lonzo's already offered to let Larem go home with him when Laurel releases the two of them from the lab."

No one knew how all of this would shake out, but a few things were not debatable. First and foremost, Lusahn and the kids were his family now.

"Tell me the truth, Cullen. How much trouble are you in for bringing us here?" She rested her forehead against his chest.

"I don't know, and I don't care. Whatever the future holds for us, we'll face it together. As soon as we get your paperwork straightened out, we're going to get married—even if I do have to ask your brother for his blessing." He kissed the end of her nose, making her smile. "You will marry me, won't you?"

"Yes. With or without my brother's blessing." Then she grabbed the front of his shirt and tugged him forward. "So, are we going to check out that bedroom or not?"

"Yes, ma'am."

Then he swept his warrior woman up in his arms, and carried her down the hall to his bed.

**Turn the page for a preview of
Alexis Morgan's brand new series
featuring the Talions!**

Coming soon from Pocket Star Books

It wasn't hard to pick out the crime scene. Ranulf parked half a block away to gain some perspective on the area surrounding the club. There wasn't much to see, just the charred bones of the building jutting up against the skyline, giving mute testimony to the violence that had consumed it. The gods had been smiling on the club's clientele that no one had died in that inferno.

The people had been the target and the building just collateral damage. It all added up to the perfect menu for a rogue's banquet: terror, pain, panic, and death. The bastard would be riding high for days or even weeks from the high he'd have gotten. Except Kerry Logan's heroics would have shortchanged him by keeping the death toll to zero.

A gutsy woman, whether she turned out to be Kyth or not. He only hoped that her bravery didn't come at too high a cost. If the rogue found her there'd be hell to pay, but that wasn't going to happen. That's what Judith had called him out of seclusion for. He'd work with the devil himself to save that woman's life; it was the least he could do to reward such bravery.

He climbed out of his car and headed down the sidewalk toward the club. Closing his eyes briefly, he listened for the sound of heartbeats. No one was close enough to get in his way. Starting from the sidewalk, he circled the building, studying the details. The fire had started in the front near the door, convincing him that he'd been right about the arsonist's intent. Block the exits and people died.

The stench of wet ashes and charred wood clogged his

mind and his senses. In his youth, the scent of wood smoke had meant safety, warmth, and home. This smell was different: acrid with the tang of burnt human flesh. It was as if pain was a memory forever burned into blackened bits and pieces of wood that surrounded him, drawing him like a bee to pollen. He'd tasted its like often enough, but only secondhand from a rogue's cache of energy. This was too recent, too direct, too enticing.

Clasping the amulet at his throat, he felt its power thrumming and burning, reminding him of his duty. He forced one foot forward, the other following reluctantly until he came full circle around the building. He moved closer to the outer wall, seeing everything and focusing on nothing, letting his mind roam freely as he processed the scene on multiple levels—scent, taste, even sound. Echoes of the event still hovered in the air for someone able to hear them.

Ranulf cocked his head to one side, as he traced the path of a back hallway into what had been the dance floor. He closed his eyes and listened to the fading notes of music as they were drowned by a rising crescendo of panic and screams. He couldn't see but faint traces of the events as they'd played out. In many ways sight was the weakest of his senses, but he could hear and he could feel.

A single column of wood still held up the remains of the roof overhead. He trailed his fingers along the ebony surface, soaking up the memories held in the charred remains. Heat. Flashing lights. A woman. Not just any woman, but one of his kind had stood by this column. His pulse sped up, keeping time with the driving rhythm left behind by the music.

She was Kyth, one with nearly pure blood in her veins. Anything less and her impression wouldn't have remained so strong. He followed her essence, the trail at times confusing because she'd crisscrossed the room multiple times that evening. In one place, he could feel where she'd knelt and then walked away, burdened with something heavy. Perhaps one of the victims she'd snatched from the licking tongues of fire?

Enough. He'd found out what he'd needed to know about the woman. Now that he'd tasted her scent and her essence in its purest form, the urge to find her and keep her safe overwhelmed him with its intensity. His chest hurt with the need to roar out a warning to anyone who came near her to tread carefully as his muscles bunched up, ready to fight, and his eyes burned bright with his power. With no opponent in sight, he had nowhere to go with the sudden burst of aggression. Standing in the burnt-out shell, he shook until he yanked himself back from the precipice of violence.

Son of a bitch. If she affected him this strongly with just an echo of her being, what would she do to him in person? Damned if he didn't want to find out—and soon.

However, it was Sandor's job to bring the newly discovered Kyth into their society; Ranulf's to take out the arsonist. Sandor was the light; Ranulf, the dark. The younger Talion wouldn't appreciate Ranulf's interference in what he saw as his duty, but too bad. When Ranulf had himself back under control, he dug out his cell phone and hit Sandor's number on speed dial. It rang half a dozen times before the Talion bothered to answer. Ranulf considered disconnecting just so he could ignore Sandor's call in return, but that would be petty.

"What?" Sandor sounded distracted, so perhaps the delay hadn't been intentional.

"She's definitely Kyth."

"Have you seen her?"

He had Sandor's full attention now, judging from the excitement in his voice. "No, I'm still at the dance club. The fire was two days ago and I can still feel her here."

"If she's that strong, how have we missed her all these years?"

Theirs was a dwindling race. To find a Kyth of Kerry Logan's strength would be a valuable gift to the gene pool, but Sandor was right. If they hadn't known about her, then there might be more of her family as yet undiscovered. Dame Judith would be beside herself with excitement.

"I'm still looking for a trace on the arsonist."

"Thanks for letting me know," Sandor said before he disconnected the call. He'd even sounded as if he'd meant it. Would wonders never cease?

After another trip through the ruins, careful to avoid the places where he sensed Kerry Logan had stood, Ranulf returned to the parking lot back on the hunt. It was unlikely the firebug would have risked his own life by spending much time inside the club. No, he would have wanted a front row seat to watch the entertainment he'd arranged for himself. The question was, where? There were several buildings close enough to have afforded him an unobstructed view without the risk of being seen. Ranulf turned slowly, studying the windows staring down at him like so many blind eyes.

No. It didn't feel right. Fire was no good unless you could feel its heat and smell the smoke. The arsonist would have needed to be close to ground zero to get the most bang for his buck. This time Ranulf studied the various possible vantage points at ground level. His eyes drifted past an alley, then were drawn right back to it.

He was on the move, heading straight for it almost before he realized that he'd made the decision. Once he reached the mouth of the alley, he stopped and looked back toward the club. Yes, this felt right.

Placing one hand on the brick wall and the other on his talisman, he once again closed his eyes, and slowly walked into the damp chill of the alley. Filth and lust and fury burned along his nerve endings, swamping his mind and sending him stumbling to his knees, queasy and sick to his soul. Oh, yeah, the firebug had been here all right.

And judging by the strength of the emotional stain he'd left behind, the bastard wasn't only Kyth, but a Talion. May the gods help them all, one of Dame Judith's personal warriors had started this fire to watch humans die.

Ranulf summoned the strength to lurch back up to his feet. Careful not to touch anything he didn't have to, he staggered back out into the parking lot, anxious to put some distance between himself and the horror of the alley.

He considered calling Sandor again with the news that they were both definitely hunting Kyth, but decided that could wait until he knew more.

Once again Kerry found herself riding in Coop's nondescript sedan. "Thanks for the ride, but I could've taken a cab."

"It's no bother. Besides, I needed to talk to you." He jerked his head toward the file laying on the seat between them. "Take a peek in there."

Slowly, she opened the file and found herself staring right into the face of the man from the alley. Next to the picture was the sketch she'd provided to Coop and the police. The likeness was uncanny.

"It's him."

Coop kept his eyes on the road, but she had the strangest feeling he could see her anyway. "You sure nailed his likeness with that sketch of yours, right down to that small scar on his chin."

She studied the picture. He'd been hovering on the outside of the crowd when the picture had been taken. Even in the grainy photo she could feel the intensity of his interest in the fire, as if the flames fed some need inside of him.

"Do all arsonists look like him?"

Coop laughed. "It would make my job a helluva lot easier if they did."

"Got any leads on who he is?" Not that she wanted to know any more about him than she already did. He'd played far too prominent a role in her dreams as it was.

Coop frowned as he slowed for a stoplight. "No, but we'll find him." He looked over at her. "Do you have someone you can stay with for a while? I feel like you'll be a sitting duck in that apartment."

"I can't spend my life hiding, Coop. Once you run his picture in the paper, everyone will know who he is. That will eliminate any need for him to come after me." She wished she was as sure of that as she sounded.

Coop hit the steering wheel with his fist. "Damn it, Kerry, we can't predict what a psycho like this guy will or won't do. Running his picture in the paper is a crapshoot. Someone might recognize him and come forward fast enough that we can net the bastard before he can run. But he's just as likely to be watching for any hint that we're onto him. At the first sign that we're closing in, he could go on the attack. If he was willing to murder a club full of people, there's no reason to think he would hesitate over killing one."

"Okay, Coop, you've succeeded in scaring me. But I